BLOOD KING

AMBER K. BRYANT

CITY OWL
PRESS

BLOOD KING
Spirit Seeker, Book 1

CITY OWL PRESS
www.cityowlpress.com

Cover Design by Mibl Art. All stock photos licensed appropriately.

Edited by Tee Tate.

For information on subsidiary rights, please contact the publisher at info@cityowlpress.com.

Print Edition ISBN: 978-1-949090-39-0

Digital Edition ISBN: 978-1-949090-40-6

Printed in the United States of America

For Drew and Silas,
who would follow me down a path into a
forest filled with invincible monsters if I asked them to.

CHAPTER ONE

UNLIKE MOST OF THE PEOPLE IN ATTENDANCE, SYBILLE ESMOND HADN'T COME to the county fair to watch a rodeo show or stroke the glossy fur of ribbon-winning show rabbits.

She came to be hypnotized.

Sybille stood among the selected volunteers as the would-be hypnotist, Elis Tanner, circled them, his scrutiny of his subjects aided by a flourish of his hands to the waiting crowd. Their environment presented a jarring mix, up-tempo techno music blaring like a nineties rave set against rainbow-themed carnival tents and food stands hawking deep-fried butter.

Elis raised his uplifted arms higher, mimicking a conductor about to direct an orchestra. As he closed his hands into fists, the music cut out. The crowd stopped their chatter, blueberry snow cones lowered, gazes raised as the man on the stage commanded their attention. A chill ran up Sybille's spine.

They were ready to be entertained and mesmerized, and though Elis Tanner had yet to do either, people were already leaning forward, hushing young children, silencing their phones.

The music came on again, another driving beat. Its vibrations tickled Sybille's toes.

She couldn't blame the crowd for wanting to be tricked in exchange for a bit of harmless fun. Only in this case, they weren't being tricked, not the way they imagined.

And Elis Tanner was far from harmless.

"How many of you have been hypnotized before?" He spoke with a vaguely British inflection, like someone who had lived stateside long enough that only scraps of their original accent remained. It reminded her of black and white movie actors. Cary Grant but a bit less Bristol.

A few people raised their hands, garnering a knowing smile from him. Sybille kept hers down. "The truth is, you've all been hypnotized multiple times. Every one of you."

The audience shifted. Sybille remained still. Elis was right: hypnotism was no magic. Not under normal circumstances. Today's show would present a different story, however. If he was nothing else, Elis Tanner offered the most abnormal of circumstances Sybille had ever come across.

"Hypnotism is simply another state of consciousness, no different than the ones we pass through on the way to and from sleep," he explained to them.

He searched the audience with clear grey eyes and then turned his gaze to the volunteers, stopping at her. It was a slight hesitation most would have missed, but Sybille was determined to miss nothing. In the briefest of pauses, perhaps there lay a hint of recognition.

Or perhaps not. Either way, Sybille must tread carefully. The enraptured audience had made themselves totally vulnerable. She glanced at her fellow stage-mates. They'd been naive enough to volunteer in handing their will over to him to play with for an hour. Sybille volunteered as well, but unlike the others, she did so with full knowledge of what she was getting herself into.

The music continued to blast. Intolerably loud, it forced its way into her, her head throbbing within a wall of sound.

Elis asked the volunteers to take seats in the metal folding chairs set out on the stage. "Are you ready?" He looked at her when he said this. Eleven volunteers nodded. Sybille smiled. She was ready. It was Elis who had no idea what was coming.

Elis spotted her as soon as she'd pushed through the crowd to take a seat midway from the stage. She wore sunglasses even though the day was never going to be anything other than dull and overcast. All day, he'd watched fair-goers glance towards the heavens, shaking their heads and cursing the weatherman. It could rain any moment and then their day would be ruined. For Elis, the clouds were welcome. This sort of sky kept the elements close, blanketing them low to the ground. A dark sky meant a world thrumming with electrical charge. He gathered this power on his tongue, like a child catching snowflakes, and then licked his lips.

Even with the weather in his favor, the woman in the sunglasses was an odd presence Elis was ill prepared for. She was as steady as a ticking clock where those around her, himself included if he was to be honest, registered as jumpy and nervous. Either she really was this calm or she hid anxiety well—he determined then to find out which was the case.

She would become one of his volunteers. She'd raise her hand, without a doubt. She was here for a purpose beyond entertainment—beyond a carnival sideshow act. She sought something. Something from *him*.

His heart strummed, fear of her unknown intentions making his palms sweat for the first time in ages. This was unacceptable. His act necessitated that he command the stage and here he was already having to work to maintain composure.

Elis shouldn't pick this woman. He already doubted his ability to control her, which made no sense—he had no reason to doubt himself.

He shook free of his mind's pointless meanderings, asked for volunteers, tried to select a diverse group—a girl wearing a state university sweatshirt, a man in his thirties with a goatee, a few middle-aged folks. Not wanting to seem too obvious, he picked the woman neither first nor last. He led his volunteers up onto the stage and instructed them to sit on rickety chairs.

The woman still had her sunglasses on, the audience visible in their reflection. Maybe she was one of *those* people—the skeptics who believed they could not be hypnotized, who assumed it was possible to hide their thoughts behind a layer of cheap plastic.

He didn't need her to remove the lenses, but he wanted her to. He wanted to see her without their interference. Maybe her eyes would tell him something her emotional restraint was able to hide.

"If you could take off your sunglasses, miss." He kept himself turned to the audience, his words, as always, spoken with a smile. "I bet there's more than a few men present who'd like to see what's behind them."

"Including you?"

His smile nearly broke at her words. There was a heat behind them, like an appetizer with a kick to it.

The audience laughed at her insinuation. She'd be great for his act. Her punchiness, conveyed in just two words, already made her a crowd favorite. He could use that.

"I'd be lying if I said no." Only now did he step in front of her, crouching near her chair. He breathed through his mouth, afraid her scent would be too distracting. Reaching forward, he lifted the glasses from her face. Now there was no breathing at all. Large hazel eyes looked right at him, olive green with a circle of warm brown framing her pupils. She was the strangest of strangers to him, yet her gaze was oddly familiar.

The steadiness he'd sensed in her earlier hadn't gone anywhere. If his touch affected her at all, she didn't show it. He could have studied her eyes for the rest of the afternoon, but he had a show to run. Besides, *he* was the one who did the mesmerizing, not the other way around. Elis placed the glasses in the woman's outstretched hand and stood again, twirling towards his audience.

"A beautiful woman has been revealed. We've gotten what we wanted." But he wasn't sure that he had.

⚷

It was foolish but necessary to let him come close. Could he truly not remember her? She had to be certain and now she was. A man capable of hiding such things from himself—who knew what else he was capable of?

The music no longer pounded in Sybille's ears. Instead, it cascaded into a repetitious and melodic raga. A flute quipped out note after note. It warbled gently, the underlying drone of a sitar making the piece quite mesmerizing, as was surely the intent.

Elis' voice was like the music—soft but intentional, magnetic, enticing. From her position at the end of the row of chairs, Sybille eyed the other volunteers. Their limbs were already relaxed. The girl next to her, dressed in her school's colors, nodded in rhythm with the music.

"…wants what's best for you." Sybille's attention returned to Elis' voice mid-sentence. "Your fear is floating away as you bob along the current, but you make no attempt to reach for it. You watch it go. Let it go...let everything go..."

She did her best to relax her limbs, allowing her shoulders to curl forward while loosening the tension in her neck, but no way in Hell was she going to let herself go.

"I'm going to take you deeper, farther away from your fears and closer to who you truly are. Each word I speak calms you, gives you back a piece of yourself you'd thought was gone forever."

That sounded nice. If only she could believe him. The girl next to her had no trouble. She sighed, her lips curled up into an easy grin. Sybille kept her mouth open slightly but made no attempt to smile. At this point, it would feel too strained. If she let anything break the pace of her mind, there was no telling what he would do to her.

Elis strode back and forth in front of his volunteers. He paused when he came to her chair. Her head tilted forward, it was impossible to see if her eyes were closed or not. She appeared like all the others, which of course meant little. If there was one thing he'd learned in life, it was that a surface often hid what lay beneath.

She was so steady, so unmoved. So unexpected.

"Many extremely intelligent people have said to me that they believe they cannot be hypnotized." He spoke to the audience, to the hazel-eyed woman slumped behind him. "There is a common misconception that only the weak-minded can be put under, but I assure you, the opposite is true." He turned so that he could see her reaction, if there was to be one.

"I have hypnotized doctors, lawyers, physicists, all at the top of their fields. It's the weak-minded who can't achieve this state of consciousness, not the reverse."

He imagined she raised an eyebrow at this, knowing his words were spoken for her benefit. One thing was certain: she was no feeble-minded townie. And even if she had been, it shouldn't have mattered. He played at being a mentalist; it's what everyone assumed he was. His act was a good one, but it was *his* show and he knew what lay behind the scene. Elis was no humbug on the other side of the green curtain. His abilities were fool-proof—that's what he had believed until today.

Elis led his subjects into a deep sleep. The hazel-eyed woman slumped to the side, resting her face on the back of her neighbor's chair, her breathing relaxed and even.

One by one, he tapped the sleeping volunteers' shoulders, giving them make-believe scenarios to play out for the amusement of the audience. At Elis' suggestion, a young boy believed himself to be a carrot about to be eaten by a rabbit. The college student transformed into a dental hygienist who cleaned people's teeth by singing Broadway show tunes.

The audience roared. Elis was a star, a marvel, a wonder.

He tapped the woman's shoulder last.

"You are at a fancy ball. When I ask you to dance, you're thrilled, but when you move to the dance floor, you realize you've forgotten how."

He tapped her shoulder again, a light and uncertain pat. There was no explanation for how this woman had avoided being mesmerized. Was she doing this to make him look the fool?

She raised her head, her eye blinking open. He offered his arm to her. "May I have this dance?"

The audience sat with rapt attention as she rose to her feet, a congenial smile on her face. She moved aside an imaginary princess skirt from her imaginary gown so that she could step forward. "I thought you'd never ask."

They took a few steps to the front of the stage. He calculated his reactions to his own movements, his hand placed on her lower back, the other clasped in her own. As he tamped down the thrill of it, he tried not to wonder what she tasted like, immediately finding he couldn't help himself.

Cinnamon…it would be cinnamon.

He stepped forward to begin the dance. She shuffled awkwardly to the side. The audience's laughter grew as she stumbled with every move until, while attempting to get her feet out of the clumsy position she'd found them in, she stumbled and collapsed against him. He caught her and for a moment, his lips were near enough to whisper something to her. If anyone caught him doing so, they'd assume it was part of the act.

The woman's hands crossed in front of her, pressing against his chest as though she was using him to regain her balance. She paused there, her hand to his heart—his unnaturally slow beating heart. She took a step back from him and he snapped his fingers.

"You may sit down now." He turned away from her, hoping he came across as aloof and unphased. "Wasn't she amazing, ladies and gentlemen?"

The audience broke into applause. She *was* amazing. They had no idea how much so. Elis twitched behind his calm façade as he swept his hand in the direction of the volunteers, giving them their due. They were awake but still mesmerized, still without memory of the events that had unfolded over the course of the show. He walked behind them, again tapping each on the shoulder, this time releasing them from his hold and giving them back the past hour of their lives. They laughed behind their hands and shook their heads in disbelief, all skepticism vanished. Eleven charmed people returned to their seats. The twelfth stepped away seemingly unchanged, the steadiness of her gate a stark contrast to the clumsiness she'd allowed people to see during their dance.

"You are an impossibility," he'd whispered to her. Now as he watched her sway towards the back of the benches lined up to face the stage, the urge to follow her came on him like a hunger. But he had enthralled this audience for a reason and now his ability to pursue her was hampered by a throng of admirers who couldn't help but want to purchase his CDs. He collected their money and steered several exceedingly eager people to the pricy hypnotherapy course on his webpage. He encouraged them all to make an appointment—first consultation is free! By the time his newfound fans dispersed, his impossible woman had disappeared into the crowd making their way to and from the midway.

The disappointment at her departure sparked an uncomfortable memory from a time he'd believed was well behind him.

CHAPTER TWO

It's often said that the undead cling to the life that has been taken from them. Juliana, however, could have let hers go easily had it not been for Elis. On the night they met, she handed him a peppermint stick to keep him pacified during Angel's Mass. She appeared like any other nun to him, though younger than most. Her starched wimple hid well the scabs dotting her neck. Taking the sweet, he hardly noticed the chill of her skin as it brushed against his hand.

Elis would see her again many times as he grew from boy to man. He changed, of course, but Sister Juliana stayed just as she had been that first Christmastide: youthful and cold, with a distant look of unsated need in her eyes. Now a young man, Elis squirmed in his church pew, sweat prickling the line around his neck where wool met skin, knowing without seeing that those ravenous eyes were upon him. Every time he dared look at her, her gaze would be demurely cast upon her folded hands. But he knew hunger when he saw it. She was lovely and frightening, like a feral cat that purred as it ate the heart of its kill.

A fortnight after Elis turned twenty-three, now working as a tanner alongside his uncle, word came that a tragedy had befallen the convent. A nun had been savaged, according to his uncle, her blood drunken by the beast responsible. Dread froze his hand, knife set to mid-scrape upon cowhide.

"Was it…" It couldn't be her. *Please, not Juliana.* "Who was it?"

"Sister Anne." Uncle crossed himself. "Best not to go out alone until the beast is captured."

Sister Anne. Which meant…*thank God.* Elis could have cried with relief and then cried from the shame of feeling such relief for the life of a woman he had no claim over and never would. Men were damned for far less than harboring the desire to steal a bride of Christ away from the Almighty.

Uncle clucked his tongue. "Who knows what the beast has done with the other one."

This time, Elis' hands left their work altogether, knife clattering to the ground. "The other one?"

"Aye." He nodded. "Sister Juliana is missing. We must pray that God, in His infinite mercy, sees fit to spare her."

Elis insisted on joining the search. Into the thickets the villagers tumbled, men with torches lit and bravado raised. Each was set upon finding the beast and destroying it and, if they would admit to it, each also fantasized about saving the fair Juliana. Every man prayed he would be the one to whom she would owe her everlasting gratitude. These thoughts carried them deep into the forest. Illusions of heroism and the curve of Juliana's backside as it swayed under her tunic spurred them on long into the night.

Elis had similar fantasies but, unbeknownst to him, he was different from the other would-be rescuers. Those men held to their desire, knowing its object was unattainable. For Elis, though, what should have been love unrequited was love returned ten-fold. Juliana had waited many years for this moment, for Elis to become a man, for him to come to her.

She hadn't expected it to take quite so long. In fact, she'd waited for him, believing the growing pull between them would bring him to her as soon as he reached manhood. If it had, she'd have been ready. Every night, she jammed the door to her cell with a bit of wood to ensure it would remain unlocked in case he came. Each morning she made a point to pass the tannery on her way to market, knowing he'd spy her through racks of salted pig hides. She endured the tedium of endless masses, kneeling and praying to a God whose favor she no longer sought, and she did it simply to be in the same room with him.

For years she stayed, playing out a role cast upon her by her father in the life before this one, this life of hunger and obsessed desire. All for him. All so that they could be together.

Weeks and months and years passed, and still he didn't come. Juliana grew tired of waiting. Still, never would she lower herself by going to him. No.

She would make him come to her.

Normally, Juliana survived on the blood of sheep and cows and wild creatures—prey whose deaths were likely never to lead back to her. She had a great thirst for blood of any kind, of course, and Sister Anne had made a hearty meal. Vanquishing hunger was one thing, however; vanquishing need was quite another. And that need could only be met by the strapping young Elis. There would never be anyone else who could give either of them what they soon would give to each other.

Elis was coming for her. Just as she'd planned, Anne's messy death and her own unexplained disappearance had led men on a hunt. But only Elis would find her, she had made sure of it. And when he did, he would know everything she knew.

They would spend the rest of eternity sating each other's thirst.

The search party, along with their dogs, turned south, convinced that her trail led in that direction. Something—an inkling, intuition perhaps—told Elis to continue west, though he was advised against it.

"There's nothing but a deep ravine in that direction," the smith warned him. "In this dark, the only thing you'll find to the west is your own death."

Smith was right, though not in the way he'd been thinking. Death did pay Elis a visit that night. It had come and then departed, not even staying long enough to drink a cup of tea.

He found her asleep, her back pressed against the wall of a shallow cave, dank and cheerless, eight miles directly west of the convent.

"Juliana!" He rushed to her side, hoping she was asleep and fearing she was dead. In truth, she was both, but neither. She had died long ago when, as a novice, she'd been bitten by a visiting priest with a penchant for nubile penitents. Although she rested at times, closed her eyes and dreamed of dreaming, she hadn't properly slept since before she was turned.

Elis grabbed her arm, shaking it gently, repeating her name. Her touch made his nostrils flair, a trace of mint splashing up from a tide of fetid rot.

"Juliana." His voice echoed the tremor of her heart. She lifted her head as he brushed her hair back from her face. Finally, she allowed his gaze to meet her own.

His breath caught. Her face was as cold as midwinter. "Are you hurt?"

She smiled. "Not with you here."

She took him then. Or rather, she gave to him, gave him a death that yielded more life than his existence as Elis, assistant tanner, ever could.

Her lips made his tingle. Her kiss pacified his fears the way her peppermint candy had once pacified his tongue. He barely noticed when her mouth trailed along the pink flesh of his neck, leading to the throbbing artery bringing blood from heart to head. His struggle was short and without commitment.

He wanted this. He'd come to her, just as she'd always known he would.

They left the area as soon as he'd regained the strength needed to travel. First, they sailed to Ireland, and eventually, they followed the surge of the persecuted and brave on to the New World.

They subsisted on pigs and strays and each other. For many years, there was no one but them, no one to break the trance that held them together. Her blood tasted of fresh mint and honey, his of leather and lime. The world pressed on but for them it never changed.

When it suited their purpose, they would kill a human. There was no shame for them in doing so, but also no immense pleasure beyond the thrill blood always gave. Should a farmer catch them feasting on his flock, they would simply do what they had to do and then move on. They moved on and moved on. This is what they would always do. There was no question of them ever stopping.

Juliana had never been a nun—not in her heart. She'd been turned while still a novice and her years with the Sisters had been endured to pass time while waiting for Elis rather than because she clung to any religious conviction. Still, as the Protestant Reformation fueled the emergence of countless sects, she found herself drawn to observation, reading revivalist brochures and religious dogma. So it was, she found herself under the shelter of a canvas tent one rainy autumn evening on the plains of North Dakota.

Browned corn stalks lay trampled around the tent and, inside, a small group of believers swayed in a circle. An old woman with free-flowing silver locks stood at its center, arms raised to the heavens.

The woman crooned, a muffled sound that struck Juliana as halfway between language and madness. She took a step towards the circle, hoping to be able to ascribe meaning to seemingly random utterances. One step forward, two steps, three, and the woman fell silent. Her audience ceased their swaying. All eyes turned to her in a unison that made even one as preternaturally cold as Juliana shiver.

"What is this?" The woman moved in Juliana's direction. Breaking the circle, she was released from its protection. The adherents formed a wall at the woman's back.

Juliana suppressed the urge to turn and run. Never had she felt such fear, not when Father Maurus had turned her, not when she'd made her first kill, not even when a mob had formed one autumn night in colonial Virginia, determined to take out the monsters they'd rightly believed her and Elis to be.

The woman approached, laid hands upon her shoulders and still, Juliana refused to move, refused to flee. She considered the strange woman's eyes, puzzled by the recognition she saw there.

"It's you!" the old hag laughed—*laughed* at Juliana. "You've come. She has waited so long for you."

Had Elis been there, he'd have made her leave with him, packed their newly unpacked home and left for yet another fresh start somewhere. But Elis wasn't there. He loathed religion in general and religion as entertainment especially. *A sacred circus*, he would have called this. Without Elis, Juliana had only her own judgment to guide her and it led her right into the center of the newly rejoined circle. Her hands clasped with the woman's, she closed her eyes and listened as rain pelted against the tent.

"I knew because you smelled like her."

Juliana's eyes opened wide as the woman breathed these words against her neck.

"Like peppermint."

She tried to pull her hands from the woman's, but the woman held on fast. "You don't really want to leave, do you?"

Juliana shook her head. She didn't. She hadn't felt this sort of pull since meeting Elis, but it wasn't the woman herself she was drawn to, it was something around her. Juliana scanned the faces of the revelers; each was as meaningless to her as the next.

"She is here, Juliana."

Juliana. A name she was sure she hadn't given the woman. "Have we met?"

The woman laughed again. "The spirits are in their glory this All Hallows' Eve. But such things pass. She is here, on the cusp. We must act before it's too late."

Elis would hate this woman's overly dramatic speech. Cusps and glory. His eyes would roll, and he would miss entirely that there was something deeper behind her rhetoric.

"I... I don't understand." It had been so many years since she'd panicked, she was slow to understand that that was what she was experiencing. She longed to claw at her arm where her skin had begun to crawl. Something was gravely wrong here.

A howl arose from the woman's throat. On cue, her followers cried out as well, matching the otherworldly pitch. The circle tightened. Juliana imagined a pack of starving wolves surrounding her, ready to make their kill.

Still clutching her hands, a warmth spread from the woman's fingertips to her palms, her wrists, her arms. Juliana couldn't have pulled away if she'd wanted to. Her touch might as well have been the sun for all it bleached out Juliana's other senses.

The woman continued to moan. Her weight shifted from leg to leg. The crowd shifted with her. With each unruly gust of air, swaying oil lamps threw fragmented shadows across their faces.

The woman's grip tightened. Her eyes flew open and it was all Juliana could do to stay upright. They were worlds made of glass, swirls of green and blue without a pupil to be seen. She opened her mouth again, but instead of an unearthly howl, a voice as sweet as a peppermint stick sounded.

"Juliana, Juliana."

She recalled the night she'd turned Elis, how he'd repeated her name again and again when he'd found her. But this wasn't Elis' voice and it wasn't the old woman's either.

It was her own.

"It's not your fault we were separated, Juliana." The woman's globe eyes lit upon her. "You are a monster, but not of your own making."

"Who are you?" In her shock, she had to ask, even though she already knew what the answer would be.

"I am you. Your soul. I watched three brothers die and an older sister marry a man she loathed. My parents gave me to the church, where I was meant to stay until I died. And so I did."

Juliana shook her head as the spirit continued. "You are dead without me, Juliana. You know it. Even Elis cannot give you what you truly need. You are a beast, separated from your conscience in a way that never should have been."

"No. No, no!" Juliana tried again to break the connection to the old woman, but the warmth had spread from her shoulders down to her chest, to her thighs. She couldn't stop it. "What do you want from me?"

"No, tell me what *you* want from *me*." The spirit's command, like the warmth spreading through Juliana, could not be ignored. A thirst as overpowering as bloodlust came upon her, but instead of supple flesh, all she wanted was more of what this spirit was already giving her.

"I want more. *Everything*."

The woman continued to sway. "I can give you that, but only for a while. I was meant to pass beyond this world long ago. You've kept me here, a spirit in the ether. I will have to move on before much longer."

Juliana nodded. She wanted this more than anything, no matter how impermanent it may be. Her will was all the spirit needed. She was filled with it, as suddenly as the sky is filled with light as the sun crests a hill.

The howling resumed its maddening lament, yet none of the believers nor the silver-haired woman made a sound. All were silent save for Juliana, the burden of her newly returned soul lifted only by her screams echoing into the slate grey dawn.

CHAPTER THREE

She would eventually return to him. Elis knew this, knew Juliana often left on one of her futile spiritual expeditions and stayed away for a week or more. Yet when she had been gone only two days, he found himself worrying, his mind straying from his own studies, books on astronomy and electrical transmitters sitting unread under porcelain cups of fermenting sheep's blood.

By the fourth day, unwilling to pace the floors any longer, he left in search of her. It had been some silly traveling evangelist she'd expressed curiosity about—Presbyterian or Methodist or some such thing. He inquired about it in town. The miller mentioned with a sneer that there'd been a meeting. "Spiritualists." He shook his head disdainfully. "A bunch of damned souls, if you ask me, seeking to talk with the other side. Pure evil."

Spiritualists...of course. That was the sort of extravagant dog and pony show Juliana would be drawn to. He followed the miller's directions out of town, passing several farms until he came to a tent in the middle of an abandoned corn field. Under his boots, dried husks crunched into hardened mud as he stepped towards the tilting structure. He'd never had Juliana's calmness of mind, though the chill in his veins did temper his anxiety somewhat. Had it not, the scene that awaited him would have done him in altogether.

Putrefying bodies, at least a dozen or more, lay strewn around the tent, Sunday-best clothes stained red, vacant eyes staring upwards as though their last thoughts had been of their salvation.

Elis stepped over the carnage, that horror barely registering in his concern for his beloved. "Juliana!"

Bodies formed a halo around her. She sat perfectly upright, unmoving, her eyes glistening. He couldn't tell if she'd heard him or if she even knew he was there at all.

"Juliana!" He went down on his knees in front of her, a supplication to the only deity he could ever believe in. "What has happened?"

Finally, her gaze lifted to his. He rubbed dried blood from her lips. "She resisted me when I returned to her." She gestured to the dead at their feet. "She did this before I could stop her."

Elis' body tensed. If there was another undead creature here, they could both be in danger. "*She*?"

"Juliana. *Your* Juliana." She brought her hands to his and stilled them as they rested upon her cheeks. "She thought she wanted me back, but when I came, she saw our death. And she was afraid."

"What madness is this, Juliana? There is no death for you."

A gurgling sound escaped her throat, a strangled laugh. "Death is all we have, Elis. Death is what we live. Now that I'm here, spirit and beast together, there is no escaping its finality."

"You make no sense, love."

"The one you knew is a beast inside of me. I can hold her at bay for only so long." She let go of his hands and ran her own up his arms to his face, cupping it gently. "Your Juliana cared for you and so I do too. That's why I've waited for you. I knew you'd come for me, just as you did all those years ago. We can leave together, Elis. I think it must be that way. We must both go."

"You know I'd go with you. Always. But to where?"

She patted his cheeks. Her blood-dried lips curled into a smile. "To Hell. Where we can pay for our sins."

Letting her hands fall, it took only a moment for her to secure the wooden stake she'd hidden in the folds of her skirt. Hands raised again, she thrust it towards his chest. Elis veered to the side. The stake scraped along his shoulder, tearing his shirt.

"What are you doing?" He grabbed the wrist that held the stake, but she twisted out of his hold easily, the blood of a tent full of humans fueling her strength.

"I'm sorry, Elis. I am!" Both were on their feet now, dancing around each other like boxers in their corpse-lined fighting ring. "It's because I love you that I'm doing this. Your spirit is somewhere in the ether as well, hovering, held hostage by you so long as you walk this world. But I can free it. I can free *you*!"

She lunged at him again, and again he barely evaded her. "I care nothing for this spirit you speak of, Juliana. The only thing I want is you. Please, stop this."

She wouldn't stop. She never would. It had been a mistake, searching for her beastly self, rejoining with her. Now the deaths of these humans blighted her once unmarred spirit. Although she had a mighty strength, Juliana could barely breathe under the weight of her guilt. And now Elis refused to come with her, refused to free his own severed soul.

Perhaps there was another way…

She plunged the stake, not towards him this time, but in the direction of her own heart. He had her in his arms before she hit the floor, the fact that she'd wished him dead made irrelevant by her sacrifice.

"Juliana! Why? Why have you done this?" He bent over her, trembling fingers brushing the hair from her face.

"There's an end to everything, Elis."

She gasped as her back arched, then jerked with spasms so violent, Elis struggled to keep hold of her. As blood escaped her beast's ruined body, so too did Julianne's spirit. One final spasm, and she was free, weightless and unbound. Had Elis not been focused on the corpse sheltered in his arms, he might have spotted her hovering above before the pull of her newly found mission carried her away.

She would search for Elis, the *true* Elis—the little boy with sticky candy fingers who grew into a man guilty of making only one mistake: loving the unlovable. She would find his spirit and bring him back to himself.

When that happened, it would truly be the end of everything. The world would be freed of them both, two less monsters to fear in the night.

Juliana was gone but not truly gone. Her memory became a torment that refused to ebb over time. Had she left Elis alone, fully alone, perhaps he could have gotten past what had happened. But her spirit still wandered the world, dipping in and out of his life at her leisure. This was not really Juliana, this was her disembodied spirit, the soul of the girl who had departed her physical form when she'd been turned. And yet, it was her. It looked like her, spoke like her. It had picked up hundreds of years of her memories. It knew him the way she had.

The smell of peppermint came first, and then she would appear to him, the spirit who was Juliana but not Juliana. Whether she was the same or not, he savored the torment her presence brought. Torturous though it may be, it was still better than the time spent without her altogether.

She came to him whenever she pleased, but always, without fail, she appeared on two particular eves: Christmas and All Hallows'. Christmas was, of course, the anniversary of their meeting and Halloween was the night in which she danced most freely upon the earth.

For years she'd been giving him updates he didn't care to receive on his supposed spirit self. Each update was the same: "I haven't found you yet, Elis, but I will. Don't worry."

"I won't." He'd turn to his newspaper, or later, to his computer and then to his phone, and pretend her appearance didn't affect him. He wanted her to go away and also to never leave.

"You're out there somewhere, Elis. You'll be reunited. You'll be freed."

"Great."

She'd say something more and he'd ignore her. When she left, he'd put down his newspaper, or his laptop, or his phone, and he'd weep.

It was no surprise when upon opening his door that October evening, she appeared on his porch alongside a group of superheroes and zombies. After tossing candy into the children's sacks, he retreated inside, Juliana's spirit at his heels.

"You're still passing out breath mints, Elis? I'm surprised your house hasn't been egged."

Elis bit his lip. How would she know anything about such things? His house *had* been egged last fall, in fact. He'd never connected his choice of trick-or-treat candy with the petty vandalism.

"They remind me of…of…"

"Of me?" The spirit moved towards him, glowing bright. "Oh, Elis, you've a sentimental side to your beast, haven't you?"

Elis' eyes darkened. He hated when she referred to him as a beast. If anyone was a monster, it was her, ravaging him with memories of his beloved for the past century. Sanctimonious fool. She couldn't see how hateful she truly was.

Juliana, or what was left of her at any rate, scanned his living room, taking in the clothes strewn here and there, crusty blood-stained cups left scattered across the coffee table. "Nothing changes with you, does it?"

Elis sighed. "Can we just get on with it, Juliana? You haven't found him. You'll keep looking. It's for the best. Get the lads and lasses better candy next year. So long, see you at Christmas."

"Elis!" She clasped her ghostly hands together, shaking them in front of her. "There won't be a Christmas for you this year, because…I've found him!"

Dropping his bowl, Elis staggered backwards. Cellophane-wrapped pink and white pinwheels scattered over the tile floor. "What?"

She held out a hand, forgetting in her exuberance that he had no way to grasp onto it. "Come with me. We must do this now, before the night passes."

For better or for worse, curiosity made him follow her out into the street, past groups of Halloween revelers, ghosts and witches, and vampires with fake fangs protruding from their silvery faces. Elis watched them with more than a little envy. They would remove their fangs and makeup at the end of the festivities. Their lives would be short and in that brevity, there would be meaning. Any suffering they felt would be as impermanent as they themselves were.

Juliana glided through the night, turning down one street and then another until they came to a neighborhood unfamiliar to him. She stopped at a nondescript yard, and he pushed open the rusted gate leading to a ranch-style house in need of a fresh coat of paint. They both paused at the front door.

"Knock," she told him.

A balding man answered and let Elis in without question.

"Do you have any idea how dangerous it is to invite someone like me into your home?"

The man nodded. "I do. Let's begin, Juliana."

Elis nearly fell over. In all the years that had followed that day in the tent, no one but he had been able to see her.

His unease grew as the man offered him a seat at a tiny lace-covered table. Still, Elis let him grab his hands. He didn't pull away when a warmth he'd forgotten was possible passed slowly from the man's hands to his own.

"He's here, Laurence, isn't he?" Juliana stood behind the man, Laurence. Laurence rocked back and forth. She looked up at Elis. "Laurence calls spirits from the ether. He's quite powerful for a human."

Elis focused on the sound of her voice. He loved and loathed the sensation spreading through him, and he feared what would become of him if it continued. "Did he call *you*...from the ether?"

She gawked at him as though he'd gone mad. "I was called one hundred years ago. I'm here now, on this plane, and here I'll stay until your soul is released and you are destroyed."

For the first time, Elis began to struggle. He pulled his hands away from Laurence's grip, but the man refused to let him go. Warmth washed over him. He hated that he loved it.

"Let it happen, Elis. He will come to you if you give your consent." She flitted over to him, mint in his nose, honey on his tongue. "You want this, just as Juliana did."

He closed his eyes. Juliana's perfect midwinter face appeared in the darkness. "This is the way it has to be, Elis. Eternity has an end after all."

The spirit came to him then. His shrieks filled the house, the block, the town, the world.

He resisted just as Juliana had, but unlike the spiritualists, Laurence knew what to expect. Elis was handcuffed to his chair before he had the wherewithal to lash out at those around him. The pain was excruciating.

"Why don't you kill me now?" He could barely stop himself from begging for the stake.

"Your spirit must defeat you first, beast." Juliana cocked her phantom head. "It won't be long."

It *was* long. Longer than the entirety of his life, longer than the future with Juliana he'd once believed stretched out endlessly before them. It felt like he was stuck in a nightmare loop. In his delirium, he imagined his fingernails being pried up one by one. Even though he screamed and begged to have his entire hand chopped off just get the torture over with, the pain continued.

When morning broke, he broke with it, beast and spirit shattering into countless pieces within one timeless body.

It was later in the day when darkness threatened to fall again that the pieces began to fuse back together. The boy who craved peppermint, the turned creature who thirsted for blood, their desires merged in the most unexpected of ways.

The night was thick and dark when he said, "Uncuff me. I'm ready to meet my fate."

Juliana cried with joy. His release would be her own, she claimed. They would depart this world, finally, together. Laurence unbound his wrists and stepped away quickly.

"The stake?" He held his hand out to Laurence who, with trepidation, gave it to him.

Elis clutched it to himself. It would be so easy to do what Juliana wished of him. If he went to Hell, the torment could be no worse than what he'd already suffered these past hundred years. Forced to endure without his goddess Juliana, separated from himself, driven into a fractured existence.

Juliana may never have accepted that the spirit and the beast could co-exist, but he knew it to be true. He was a monster and an innocent all at once. The joy and guilt and sorrow and happiness were his to bear for as long as he could. If there was to be justice for whatever crimes he'd committed, it would be for him to *live* rather than to die.

"Forgive me, Juliana." He dropped the stake and left, running until he reached the edge of town and then on into the wheat fields beyond, hoping she would not follow.

He ran until he didn't recognize where he was, until his feet ached and the soles of his shoes wore through. He ran and his spirit soared, and he with it, two halves of one imperfect, immortal being.

He ran until the thirst called to him, stopping him in his tracks.

Spirit and beast crashed back down to earth. Both would have to be fed. Both would have to live with the other, make amends for whatever Elis did. Both would endure together without their beloved Juliana.

Elis headed towards the horizon, a hazy skyline rising from it like a mirage, his mind—both minds—made up.

If Juliana could no longer satiate him, he'd find someone else who would.

CHAPTER FOUR

For all the confusion Elis Tanner displayed at the county fair, *he* was the one who had first contacted Sybille. She'd been on spirit seeker duty in place of her cousin Zareen that night. It was hard not to wonder if Zareen would have handled the situation better. Zareen had five more years of experience but having been trained in the family business since birth, Sybille was no novice. Besides, her great-gran had told Sybille that her gift, amongst a family of gifted, was extremely potent.

"Like a poison or a fine wine?" Zareen often asked in jest whenever Sybille brought up Gran's declaration. No one was sure what the answer was to that. To her dying day, Gran refused to say.

Maybe he had come to her because of who Sybille was. Perhaps that made no difference and it had just been a matter of timing. Whatever the case, Zareen's youngest was sick and Sybille agreed to cover for her. And so it was Sybille who opened the channel; it was Sybille who received him, though she hadn't realized it at the time.

She should have known there was something awry right from the get-go. In the moment, though, she'd thought him strange, which in and of itself was normal. Each spirit had its own peculiar way of making contact. Aside from the occasional zombie or wayward shifter, it was bloodthirsters her family dealt with, and spirits of bloodthirsters, often disembodied for generations and grown eccentric in their isolation, were the most unpredictable of all.

The evening was stiller than most; no prospective clients pushed their way into her consciousness. She sat in a tiny office nook adjacent to the kitchen, phone turned off to avoid distractions, hands folded in her lap as her mind wandered in the ether. She didn't move except to take an occasional sip from the mug of coffee she'd placed on the desk in front of her.

She stretched herself out and brought herself back. Ideally, she wanted the spirits to come to her, not the other way around. A prolonged out-of-body experience for a hierophant like Sybille was risky; confused, disembodied souls would keep her with them if they could, hounding her with questions, begging her to fulfill requests or do their bidding. They never seemed to realize that she couldn't help them while detached from her body.

Sybille kept herself close, dipping in and out, never staying in the ether for longer than a moment before coming back to herself. With each new return, she hoped to bring a spirit with her, one that required her family's services.

Last time she channeled, she'd been approached by the spirit of an elderly doctor. George Brownstein had been trapped for several decades—not a long stretch at all compared to some of her clients. Having been dead for so little time meant that the doctor was coherent enough to give Sybille a detailed description of the moments leading to his death.

Doctor Brownstein's fatal mistake was to walk in on a fellow pathologist drinking the blood of a woman with stage four cancer. The pathologist saw nothing wrong with his actions—the woman was dying anyways—but Dr. Brownstein had been mortified. Knowing he was about to be exposed as a bloodthirster, the pathologist set to biting and turning his defenseless colleague. As the life drained from Brownstein, so had his spirit.

Two decades spent wandering in the ether passed. Brownstein's spirit gradually came to realize he was trapped, unable to move on because of the creature walking the earth wearing his body. Like all bloodthirster spirits, he wanted this torment of existing neither here nor there to end.

"What do we do now?" he asked Sybille. "Can you help me?"

Of course she could. She circled her mind around him, wrapping him in a celestial embrace. "I can help you find the freedom you seek. For a price."

"How can I pay you?" the doctor asked. "I'm a spirit. I left materialism behind with, well, with my material self. I have no money."

It wasn't money she was looking for. Not from him. "I need you to pay me in service, not cash. And I'm warning you now, it won't be pleasant."

"Anything is better than this ceaseless wandering."

"Not anything. But in this case, what I'm proposing most likely is and it's a means to an end. Your end. Tell me, doctor, what do you know about spirit possession?"

During that tenuous moment of contact, Sybille kept her explanations to a minimum. Spirits often flitted in and out of the Now World, otherwise known as the realm of the living, if they were inundated with too many alarming facts. She couldn't afford to lose this client.

"You'll be given instructions when the time comes and then you'll possess me. Only for a little while. Then you'll be freed."

"Is that what it takes? Freeing me from my beast, I mean. Why?"

"That's all you need to know right now. I have no reason to deceive you, but you must trust me, or this won't work. Do we have a deal?"

The doctor spun himself around in circles, babbling to no one in particular. Sybille thought she might be losing him, but eventually he stabilized and, nodding slowly, agreed to her stipulations. She passed on the particulars of his case to Devin, the field agent working for her family, and that had been that.

This night was different. There was only so much time Sybille could stretch herself out into the ether before risking harm. When no clients had presented themselves in over two hours, she'd had enough. Head aching, she closed the channel and gulped down the rest of her coffee, grimacing as the bitter sludge hit the back of her throat. She put the kettle on and sifted through mason jars filled with her mom's herbs until she found what she was looking for. Scooping a teaspoon of mugwort leaves into a metal tea ball, Sybille leaned against the counter waiting for the water to boil. It was a rare treat to find herself alone. With Zareen at her own house two doors down and her mother and uncle attending a conference up north, Sybille had the house to herself, not even a spirit present to destroy her solace.

She should have moved out years ago, but her mother and uncle weren't the most self-reliant people. The state the house had fallen into during the semester she'd spent away at college had been alarming enough to make her return home and stay there, finishing out her undergrad studies at the local university.

They needed her and, in a way, she needed them too. A family of hierophants was a powerful thing, able to channel spirits as well as glimpse possibilities within timelines that had yet to occur. But what made them powerful also made them vulnerable. Many had trouble functioning in the world—Sybille wasn't totally immune from this struggle herself. Beyond that, there were always the classic power-seeking asshats wishing to use a hierophant's gifts for their own purposes. It helped to have a band of hierophants living in close proximity. Safety in numbers, as the expression went.

Tea steeped, Sybille headed upstairs to settle in for the evening. This was her idea of a perfect night: snuggled in bed with a cup of tea and a romance novel. Two chapters into the story of a dashing young pirate and his lady love, it happened. Or rather, *he* happened.

"That cover promotes unrealistic expectations of men's abs. Also, clearly, whoever designed it wasn't thinking about historical accuracy. Is that a zipper?"

Sybille threw her book to her lap. A man with raven-black hair and cheekbones carved by Rodin stood at the base of her bed. The tight shirt he wore led her to think that the cover of her book wasn't entirely unrealistic in its portrayal of the male physique. Not that the person in front of her was normal, or even a real person for that matter. The pale yellow aura silhouetting him and the fact that his feet didn't quite touch the carpet were a bit of a giveaway. "What the hell are you doing here, spirit? I closed the channel almost an hour ago."

"Did you? I don't know anything about a channel, love." He shrugged and circled around to her side of the bed. "Nor do I know why I'm here. I must be dreaming."

"Spirits don't dream."

He laughed. "They do if they're bound to a living body."

Sybille resisted the urge to reach out and run her fingers through his spectral arm. "I don't deal with the living, I deal with the disembodied spirits of unhumans."

"Unhumans?"

"People who were once human and have since been turned into…"

His eyes danced. "You can say it."

Sybille sighed. Poor guy. He was too confused to realize he was confused.

When spirits came to her, they came devastated, vengeful, or both. Most were desperate. They were kept in the ether because their bodies still walked Earth in one form or another. They wanted only an end to their suffering. This must be what he wanted as well, only he was too far gone to be able to articulate it. She'd have to lay it out clearly for him.

"If you want us to find your body and destroy it, there will be a price."

He laughed again. "I already found my body, and I'm quite happy with it as is. I'd be grateful if you kept it in one piece."

"What're you talking about?" He must have been an old one. Ancient, maybe. The eldest bloodthirster spirits were easily confused, having been untethered for so long. "If you'd already found your body, you wouldn't be here. You wouldn't need my services. And while we're on the subject of me, I still want to know what you're doing in my head. You weren't here when I closed the channel, but now you are. I don't like it."

He pursed his lips and turned to pace the narrow strip of floor between her bed and the wall. "I still think I'm dreaming."

Sybille swung her legs out from under the covers and stood. "Do you know why spirits summon me?"

He turned back to her and took in her bedroom attire, a tight black chemise with matching lace panties. "I can imagine. In my youth, such an outfit would have branded you a witch."

"I'm guessing that in whatever century you were a youth, I could be clothed head to toe and still be tossed off a ship to see if I floated.

The spirit flinched. "That is undoubtedly true."

Sybille raised an eyebrow. She'd struck a nerve without intending to. Perhaps she'd been wrong to think this one an average bewildered spirit. "I'm a hierophant. It's a kind of medium-slash-oracle-slash-psychic. My family specializes in assisting your kind."

"My kind?"

"Bloodthirsters." That word got his attention. He took a step closer to her, made as if to breathe in her scent, which of course was impossible given the fact that he wasn't physically present. She repressed a shiver.

"How do you know that word 'hierophant'?"

She shrugged. "I've always known it, just as I've always known spirits like you. I called my first spirit when I was five."

He sniffed again. "But why? What do you want from us?"

"It's not what I want from you, it's what *you* want from *me*. You want me to free you."

"I already told you that's not the case. I'm quite content."

That was unlikely. "Well, fine, not *you*. But I mean, your *kind*. Spirits don't like feeling trapped." She steadied her breathing again. Having him so near, non-corporeal or not, was highly distracting. His lips were temptingly close to her exposed neck. If he were to…

Why was she even thinking like this? She wasn't one to become attracted to her clients, especially given what they were. She wanted to help them, sure, but only in a professional capacity. Sybille didn't like things to become personal.

"You can reconnect the soul of a bloodthirster."

"What?" Her mouth gaped open in shock. "Absolutely not. Are you nuts? We don't reconnect *anything*. That would be dangerous, possibly catastrophic. Honestly, the thought of giving a bloodthirster back its spirit, it's…it's…"

He stood behind her now. "It's intriguing?"

Maybe a little, but she wasn't going to let him know she thought so. "You're surprisingly coherent given that you must be, what…four hundred, five hundred years old?" He took a step away from her, eyes darkened, forehead furled. "Not that you look a day over three hundred… or thirty, for that matter."

"Well, it's been good to be back with my body."

"Yeah, see, that's what I'm struggling with. You seem like you know what's what until you say stuff like that, so let me fill you in. You died. Your spirit floated in the ether for all these years while your body went around pretending to still be you, feeding off the blood of animals and also humans, when possible. You had no choice in the matter, no control over what unforgivable things your corporeal self did. Now you've come to me because you want me to find your body—your bloodthirster—so we can kill it for you, and you can be released…move on. Whatever you think has happened, that you've been brought back to your body, that you *cohabitate* with the monster your body became in your absence—that misguided belief is just a byproduct of too many years in the ether."

His face remained impassive. She assumed he must be processing. Given what she knew of him so far, that could take some time. "What I mean to say is, you're a little nuts. Don't worry, though, I'm here to help you."

"Where's *here?* Where am I?"

"What? You're in my bedroom, obviously."

"No, I mean, where do you live?"

Sybille hesitated. Spirits never cared where she lived, only that she was somewhat near wherever their bloodthirsters were, so it wouldn't be too impractical or complicated to track them down.

"Why do you want to know?"

"I live in Port Everan." He circled nearer to her, eyes tracing the line of flesh where silk met breast before raising his gaze to meet her own. "And I'm betting that's where you live as well."

"You don't *live* anywhere. Your bloodthirster might, but you…"

"I'm waking up." His body tensed, but his eyes softened. "I'm going to find you."

"You already have."

Her words echoed off the walls of the empty room.

CHAPTER FIVE

ELIS COULDN'T GET USED TO SLEEPING. BLOODTHIRSTERS, THE KIND OF creature he'd been for centuries, had no need for it. They rested, lounged about, closed their eyes, meditated. But they had no mental or physiological need for sleep.

The situation changed for Elis when that crazy spiritualist, Laurence, managed to reunite him with his soul. It was tiring work to have a conscience.

Nearly two years had passed since Laurence had worked his magic, and still sleep seemed like something Elis had shrugged off as a child, a hobby he'd lost interest in. Yet he needed it now. He'd tried in the beginning to stay awake. Falling asleep felt like he was giving up his spot in the driver's seat, so he'd resisted it with every bit of his control-freak mind.

It was a battle in which he was soon defeated.

At first, he dreamed of Juliana. In his dreams, she was not the spirit who had tormented him for the past hundred years. She wasn't the beast, the bloodthirster with whom he had shared his life for so long. She was as he'd never known her to be: human. They lived together in a split-level house with a two-car garage and a picket fence. She baked cookies for him.

Endless batches of cookies.

These should have been happy dreams, but nothing associated with

Juliana was ever truly happy. He hadn't seen her since he'd gotten his soul back. She'd failed to show up at their usual meeting times—Christmas Eve, Halloween, a second Christmas Eve. Even battling with his newfound soul —a soul which was now a part of him as well as a fierce opponent of all things Juliana—he still missed her.

Human Juliana, complete with apron and a fifties housewife vibe, was pure fantasy; even in his sleep, Elis knew it. He'd wake from a Juliana dream full of frustration, his brain throbbing. In wakefulness and in slumber, he couldn't escape her hold.

These dreams, these futile *American Dream* dreams, were remembered with a clarity Elis fought hard to muddy with copious amounts of whiskey-laced blood. In the dazed state the spiked blood imposed on him, her empty eyes still glared at his from behind a tray of warm peanut butter cookies.

Then there were the dreams he could scarcely hang on to. These dreams, so intricate and vivid while he was experiencing them, became a chalk outline as soon as he began to stir. By the time he was wakeful enough to be able to make sense of them, the outline had been obscured, the chalk wiped away almost entirely.

Elis was left with the sense that he had journeyed someplace else for a while, someplace realer than the black and white linoleum kitchen of his Juliana dreams. The aftermath was almost worse, however. For the first time since he was a young man, he'd had dreams that were pleasurable, only to have their contents lost to him, the torturous parts of his slumber remembered instead. This was so typical of Elis' lot in life, he could only shrug and go about his day in a half-miserable, half-apathetic stupor.

Spirit and beast—Elis had accepted that he was each of these things. He resented and cherished both and he most certainly hated Juliana for finding his spirit, for letting Laurence call him from the ether and return him to himself. Having a conscience was no way for a bloodthirster to live. The mere suggestion that he might have to kill a human to feed, something that would have raised no alarms in the past, now sent his own blood racing, making his wrists tingle and his chest tighten. Even slaughtering an animal brought about a certain amount of unease. Having become so unpracticed in feelings of personal accountability, it was no wonder he resented the fact that he was forced to feel them now.

All the same, there was something to having a moral code again. A conscience. At one time, it had been Juliana and only Juliana who could make him feel anything resembling remorse. Now, his life was an artist's palette of regrets—blue for his inability to connect with anyone else and yellow for every memory he had of every wrong he'd committed in his hundreds of years of existence. And always, deep, rich red for the fact this his sustenance so often meant someone else's demise.

As depressing as this palette might be, he had come to realize that his former life had been without color for so long, he'd accepted unquestioningly his monochrome, guiltless existence.

He couldn't go back to that. He *wouldn't* go back.

The thought that his forgotten dreams were the most colorful and happiest parts of his life haunted him. Given his luck, it figured that this happiness wouldn't even be left to him as a memory.

⚷

He came to Sybille every night for nearly a week. It was always after her channeling sessions, sessions that ended fruitlessly, not a single spirit making contact. Then, when she'd closed the channel and assumed she was by herself for the night, there he was, hovering over her kitchen stove as she stirred the pasta sauce, or in her bedroom, asking to be read a passage from her paperback.

"You're a closet romance lover," she'd said to him on his third visit. "It's okay, a lot of men are."

He'd scoffed but hadn't outright denied it either.

Slowly, Sybille became used to his presence. On the sixth day, her mother and uncle returned from their trip.

"Darling!" Margot gave her daughter a kiss on the cheek. "Any clients come in while we've been gone?"

"An older man, George Brownstein. Devin's already taken care of his bloodthirster."

"Oh good…and the show?" The "show" as she referred to it, was the payment the spirits agreed to make in exchange for their eternal freedom upon the death of their bloodthirsters, the one she'd warned Dr. Brownstein would be unpleasant but necessary. Her family may deal in the supernatural, but their needs were very mundane—food, shelter, warmth.

In other words, if they were going to do this sort of work, they needed to get paid.

Luckily, there were people willing to compensate them, but only if they were given a proper shaking table, eyes rolled into the back of the head, speaking in tongues show. And so, that's what they did. If the spirit wanted Sybille and her family to track down its body, to do the dangerous work of making their undead body dead-dead, then it had to agree to something it might find disagreeable: possession.

It wasn't exactly a walk in the park for Sybille either. It was one thing to open the channel, to let a spirit converse with her. It was quite another to let that spirit take over outright, use her voice to speak, use her hands, her legs to move. Lack of control during a possession was something she could never get used to. It left her exhausted, weak, and with a hangover that could battle a night at the bars.

"Don't worry, we got paid. He didn't want to leave though. Talked on and on about his wife, who's dead too, by the way. But, whatever, it's done now. Devin says it was a straightforward kill."

Her uncle Peter swept into the room and Margot filled him in. "Zareen's kids are sick for the millionth time and Sybille had one client while we were gone."

"Well, two actually. Sort of. I'm not sure."

They both turned to her in unison.

"Go on." Uncle Pete motioned for her to continue. Neither of them seemed too concerned by her confusion. The work hierophants engaged in was often puzzling, after all. "Do you expect it's a vision?"

There it was…the same question Sybille had been asking herself. This spirit was peculiar, both more remote and more personable than a spirit normally was. Yet he didn't act like he was trying to forewarn her of some future event. If anything, he seemed mired in the past. Nothing about him made sense, and while filled with hidden meanings, a clairvoyant experience was just as its name would suggest it to be: clear. Sybille's visions, like those of all hierophants, were rare. But when she did have them, it was always perfectly apparent to her that that's what they were.

She had no idea what the man who had been visiting her every day was.

"I don't think so. He's strange. Not a normal spirit, but a spirit nonetheless. He's been coming every evening and…"

"*Every* evening?" Her mother held her hand up to her chest, her painted-on eyebrows situated in their perpetual state of mock surprise. "For how many evenings?"

"Tonight will make six if he shows."

"Be careful, my dear." Uncle Peter looped his flannel scarf onto a hook and headed for the stairs. "It sounds like it could be a *preta* rather than a bloodthirster spirit. *Preta* are such hateful little shits." He paused, hands pressed to his lower back. "I tell you, my sciatica's killing me tonight. I'm getting far too old for these long car trips. Margot, I'm heading up to bed. Say an extra charm or two for our girl, okay? See you both in the morning."

The women muttered their goodnights to him as he disappeared into the shadows of the house's second floor. Margot turned her attention to Sybille, patting her shoulder. "He's probably just an old spirit, but Peter is right. It's possible that he's a *preta*. Do use caution, okay, sweetie?" She poured each of them a cup of chamomile tea and handed a steaming mug to her daughter. "Drink up. You need it. What with all the coffee you insist on consuming every day, you're going to make that extraordinary brain of yours short circuit."

"Please, Mom." If Sybille's brain *were* to implode, her mother would most likely be the cause of it.

"Oh, I really must tell you about the conference. You'd be sickened at how wonderfully those charlatans, who shall remain unnamed, made out at this one. Truly awful, the level of gullibility some of these New Agers display. We could make a fortune off them if we were that sort." She glanced at Sybille, who kept as impassive an expression as possible. No good could come from feeding her mother's current line of thought. "But of course, we aren't that sort. We would never stoop to unethical behavior just for money."

She droned on about the various manipulative practices deployed by some of the family's chief competitors—the Thorstens, the Rometty family, amongst others—forgetting she'd promised not to name names. It was nothing new. Sybille had been listening to Margot's complaints as long as she'd been able to understand these sorts of things. It would be futile to point out to her that they themselves had been engaging for years in their own form of psychic showmanship, all for the sake of a paycheck. Margot wouldn't see it in that light. What they did was beyond reproach as far as she was concerned. They were ridding the world of monsters, after all. Even Sybille had to admit that this made a compelling argument in her family's favor, morally speaking.

Margot kept on with her overblown accusations while Sybille obediently drank her tea, doing her best to tune out the older woman. Soon, thoughts slipped from overpriced, careless tarot readings to raven hair and cheekbones carved from marble.

It wasn't long before her mother headed off to bed, spells uttered and a bowl of rice and sliced peaches meant to feed the supposed *preta* shoved in Sybille's hands "just in case." Sybille began her preparations for opening the channel again. Halfway in, she realized she no longer expected a normal spirit contact, but instead assumed Elis would come to her later.

Annoyed with her lack of focus, she made her mind reach further into the ether. She brought it back, then stretched it out again.

She shouldn't have let him interfere with her work in such a short amount of time. Perhaps she hadn't even been trying to contact a spirit, an honest-to-goodness in-need money-making spirit, but instead had been lazy in her attempts, hoping that instead of them, she'd find Elis working his suave way into her mind.

Just the suggestion that this was a possibility was enough to make her livid.

She dipped into the ether a fourth time, a fifth, each attempt more impatient than the last. Finally, on her sixth trip, something caught.

When she returned to herself, she did not return alone.

Her prospective client had been trapped in the ether for over one hundred years. He'd been in his early thirties when he was turned. In his human life, he'd made his way in the world as a logger. Tall and brawny, his legs were as sturdy as the tree trunks he'd spent his days chopping down.

"Your bloodthirster must be terrifying." She could only imagine the horror a beast his size could inflict on the world.

"I need you to find him." Much to Sybille's surprise, her big, strong bear of a spirit chose that moment to fall to the ground, weeping until his unkempt beard was drenched with tears. "I need you to stop him. I've been waiting for someone to stop him for so long."

She made the call to Devin, who was there within twenty minutes. The spirit hovered in the corner while Devin took down the details Sybille related to him. "His name's Nathanial Atkins. About six-two–wait…he's correcting me. Fine, fine, whatever… He's six-three." She smiled slyly. "You know how you men are, right? Totally pissed if we underestimate your size, even if it's by just an inch." She rolled her eyes and Devin chuckled. He might not be able to see spirits, but he was familiar with their peculiarities and a good sport about Sybille's not-so-subtle, lighthearted jabs at the male species.

"You're going to love this, Devin. Guess where the spirit believes his bloodthirster lives?"

Devin let out a long groan. "Don't tell me it's Low Hollow again. Is he sure? I mean, how reliable is this one? He seems kind of off…and by a lot more than one inch."

Sybille ignored the string of obscenities the spirit flung in Devin's direction. "Don't fool yourself, Devin. If he says his bloodthirster is in a forest northwest of here, then northwest it is. And that means the Low."

Devin nodded as he finished jotting down some notes. "All right. I'll see what I can find out and then I'll head up that way in the morning. God, I fucking hate Low Hollow, though. Why does it always have to be there?"

"Not *always*. Seventy-three percent, last I checked my records." Sybille sighed. "You know how it is. His kind are there and there are lots of trees. This one likes trees."

Devin stood to leave. "I'll let you know when I'm close so you can plan the show. You inform the Patron yet?"

She batted her lashes at him. "You're always my first call, Devin."

"Don't I wish that were the case." He took a step towards her, then hesitated, fumbling with the zipper on his leather jacket like it was suddenly of vital importance that it receive his full attention. "You wanna… I don't know, get drinks, maybe? After this one's been dealt with?"

She slapped his arm playfully. "You know I can't drink."

"Right. Coffee then?"

She shrugged her shoulders. "Sure." Hopefully he wouldn't read too much into her noncommittal response. It had been apparent from Devin's first day on the job that he'd wanted to have more than just a professional relationship with her. She had to admit, he had a certain Wild West lawman swagger to him that she didn't particularly dislike. Still, he was their field agent and a good one at that. Competent field agents willing to get their hands dirty weren't exactly crawling out of the woodwork. Her family needed him to stick around, and Sybille wasn't about to ruin the good thing they had going with him by complicating their relationship. Whether she liked to think of herself in that light or not, she was a bridge burner.

"Okay, I've got a long night ahead of me." He shifted back towards the door. Instead of following to see him out, Sybille plopped herself down on the couch and put her feet up. No point in her observing whatever look of longing he may be casting her way right now.

"Night, Devin. Call me when you have something."

With a sigh, he opened the door and slid through it. "Yes, boss."

CHAPTER SIX

THE TV SHOWERED SYBILLE'S LIVING ROOM IN A SEA OF MINDLESSNESS. SHE kept it on, switching channels every few seconds, unable to find anything to her liking but unwilling to turn it off altogether. Without it, she'd be alone in her silent house with nothing to compete for her attention but her own brain ticking away a mile a minute. She didn't want that. Not tonight. She held her thumb over the remote, a brief pause as she came to a channel airing a paranormal reality show. On it, two investigators explored an old hotel purportedly haunted by the ghost of a woman who'd been strangled by her jealous lover. One of the investigators held up an EMF meter, which he claimed was "spiking like crazy." He turned to the side abruptly, then motioned to his partner.

"Did you feel that, dude?"

His partner backed away, breathing hard. "Oh my God, dude! It was like…like a cold hand scraping against my skin!"

Sybille snorted at the screen. "You don't know shit about ghosts, do you, *dudes*?"

"What are we watching?"

Her heart did a somersault. Next to her sat Elis, staring at the TV with his head cocked to the side.

"Is this supposed to be real?"

"'Supposed' being the operative word." She clicked off the television and turned to him. "I thought you weren't coming this time."

"Why would you think that?"

"Well, you're late for one thing, and besides that, I already have a visitor tonight. I never get two spirits at the same time. Never."

"Two?"

Sybille motioned towards the archway that led to her dining room. There the spirit of Nathanial Atkins sat hunched over the table tracing its lace covering as though he was a forensic scientist searching for clues in blood splatter.

"Say hi, Nate."

Nate stirred, glanced over his shoulder at them and raised a hand in greeting before turning back to the tablecloth.

"You'll have to excuse him. He's just a little unused to company after all that time he spent floating around in the ether. You know how it is."

"I do, unfortunately." Elis got off the couch and circled towards the other spirit. "What's he doing here? What does he want from you?"

"Haven't we gone over this before, Elis?" She followed him into the dining room. "I've got my field agent searching for his bloodthirster now. If we're lucky, that bloodthirster will be found and destroyed and Nate here will be moving on in a day or two."

Nate smiled, head still lowered. "That would be nice. Thank you, Sybille."

Elis stiffened. "You know, hierophant, your callous attitude towards killing is incredibly disturbing and that's coming from a heartless monster who drains people in order to feed."

Sybille crossed her arms, pressing the tips of her fingers into the flesh around her elbows. "I don't kill anyone, Devin does. And besides that, he's totally justified. We're putting your kind down in order to save you from future bad karma."

"That's a lot of guff you're pedaling. I may not know much about karma, but I was raised in the church and I'm more than familiar with penance. I'm doing that bit right now all on my own, no need for your assistance, love."

Sybille leaned against the table. Nate glanced nervously back and forth between them like a little kid watching his parents fight. She gave him a reassuring smile and turned her attention back to Elis. "What would you call what I do then?"

"You're more like a supernatural bounty hunter."

"How do you even know what a bounty hunter is? You've been out of the loop for hundreds of years."

"My bloodthirster hasn't been. I told you, we've been reconnected. I'm him and he's me, and I was bored enough in the 1990s to watch every episode of a show called 'Renegades.'"

"Not familiar with it, but I do like the sound of spiritual bounty hunter. Do go on."

Arms crossed to mimic Sybille's, he stepped in front of her. "You don't give a damn about the sake of the world—that's not why you do what you do. Otherwise, you'd pursue us like proper hunters and attempt to eradicate us entirely. No. What you do is...you collect us like wanted criminals and then kill us for money. It doesn't matter to you whether we're saints on earth or unrepentant devils. You want to get paid and you justify what you do with the belief that your actions are honorable, maybe even righteous. You make the world a safer place, right? Hell, you've even convinced yourself that you're on *our* side, sparing *us* bad karma, saving my kind from further damnation by showing us the sharp end of a pointy stick. As long as you get paid, that is. Otherwise, screw karma; you're not doing shit." He nodded like he'd just convinced himself of something. "You know, maybe I should call you a paranormal assassin rather than a bounty hunter."

"I know that's supposed to be an insult, but actually, it sounds pretty awesome."

He held his hands up, giving Sybille one of his charming smiles to show that perhaps he wasn't as put off by her profession as his tirade implied. "There was a time when I would have agreed whole-heartedly with everything that you do. I myself once worked with a man similar to you in order to find my bloodthirster. I believed in, as I called it back then, 'bringing him to justice.' Death was more than he deserved, in my mind. That was before."

"Before what?"

Elis paused. Clearly, he was contemplating what he should or shouldn't say to her. She tapped her fingers on the table as she waited for him to continue, then finally cleared her throat. "Well, Elis?"

"It's hard to explain. I've already told you what happened, just not how."

"Spit it out."

"Well, this man, Laurence…he could do what you do and then some."

"And *then some*?" Who the hell was this Laurence guy? Was he one of the Rometty cousins? There were too many to keep track of properly, and she'd never paid much attention to their names. Not that it mattered, but if he was more powerful than she was (doubtful, but still…), that was something to pay attention to.

"He could call a spirit from the ether, which is the first thing he did for me. Then he had a helper locate my beast—that's what he called the bloodthirster half of me. The bloodthirster was lured to Laurence and then I was brought back to him. Rejoined. Re-souled. Whatever you want to call it."

How many times would she have to shake her head at him? "That's nonsense. You've got to be remembering wrong."

"I'm not!" He slammed his fists down on the table, which of course had no effect whatsoever. Ghostly hands slid through lace and wood. He sighed in frustration.

After letting Elis collect himself for a moment, Sybille waved her fingers in front of his face to bring his attention back to her. "Do you know what a *preta* is, Elis?"

He shrugged his shoulders. "Some sort of hipster pizza?"

She laughed. "Seriously? I can't get used to the fact that you know what a pizza is much less a hipster. Anyways, it's a ghost, a ghost that walks the world desperately hungry; it's never satiated no matter how much hipster pizza you feed it. It will keep taking more and more from you until it consumes you entirely."

"What are you saying? That I am one? It doesn't sound anything like me."

"No, *of course it doesn't*…not one little bit. Look, the point is, my family warned me you might be a *preta*. Please don't prove them right. I hate it when that happens."

There it was again, that smile. But only half of one this time. "I want you to believe me, Sybille."

"Why? If what you're saying is true, you don't need me."

"If I don't, why am I here? Why do I dream of you every night?" He stepped away and began pacing as he had in her bedroom the first evening he'd appeared to her. "I need you, I just haven't figured out for what yet."

A chill ran down her spine. She couldn't begin to say if his words thrilled or terrified her. Probably more than a little of both.

"Look, Elis, what you're talking about—being back together with your beast—it's a lot to take in. You probably don't want to hear this, but if you really are a bloodthirster with a restored spirit, you're something the world has never seen before. Although there have been stories…"

He perked up at this. "Stories?"

"More like cautionary tales, like the grimmest of the Grimm's' fairytales."

"Are you saying I'm dangerous?"

"Can you possibly claim you aren't?"

"I don't think I'm so terrible. I was much worse before, trust me."

"Yeah, that last bit isn't going to happen." She thought back to when Elis had promised he would locate her while in his physical form. Evidently, this hadn't happened yet, because he was confused or a liar…or possibly a confused liar. Or like he claimed, he legitimately couldn't remember her during his waking hours.

Perhaps it was time to find out the truth of this matter for herself.

"Look, as much as I enjoy these nightly visitations, I think it's time we meet. In person. I need to know what I'm dealing with here. So, tell me Elis, where can I find this beast with a soul of yours?"

Locating her client's hundred-year-old lumberjack bloodthirster was proving more difficult than Sybille had anticipated. Devin called her in the morning with the news that he'd spent most of the night combing the Hierophant Network's deep web databases, turning up nothing but a few clues that failed to pan out. His plan now was to head up to the Low and meet with a contact, see if she knew something the hierophants didn't. Convinced she wouldn't be called upon to perform a spirit possession for the time being, Sybille spent the day at the county fair. That adventure consisted of her eating way too many foods-on-a-stick following a stint as a volunteer for a certain hypnotist's stage show.

The whole experience had been illuminating. First, she'd come to determine that deep-fried avocados were an affront to all that is good in the world. At least deep-fried butter was what you expected it to be— unpretentious in its sickening awesomeness. Avocados, on the other hand, were being reduced to an artery-clogging mess to tempt foodies ashamed about their GMO-laden hydrogenated food cravings. It was just wrong.

And then there was Elis.

Daytime bloodthirster hypnotist Elis may not have remembered her, but the Elis who invaded her neural pathways each night knew exactly what she'd done at that fair. He made it clear that he was none too happy about it as soon as he showed up that night.

"You came to see me!"

"Why the angry face? I came to see you. So what? You told me you'd be there."

"Yes, but you *toyed* with me!" He shook so much she feared he'd give her an aneurism.

Her stomach growled as it protested the fact that it was being forced to digest her fair fare.

Had she really done something that Elis could find that offensive? She leaned back in her uncle's easy chair, finger tapping against her lips as she searched her memories of the day.

No. This was a case of Elis' overly sensitive ego running amuck. If he was going to pick a fight with her about this, it was an argument her other spirit houseguest didn't need to witness. She pushed the foot rest down and extracted herself from the chair's cushy warmth. "Nate, hang out down here for a bit okay? Watch your stories."

Nate's eyes never left the television and the primetime soap opera that played upon it. He leaned forward, entranced by a blond actress with comically smeared mascara. His eyes grew wide as she confronted her emotionally unavailable husband about his affair with their nanny. "I can't believe he would cheat on Stacey!"

She left Nate to contemplate Stacey's predicament, leading Elis up the stairs, down the hall, and into her room. Shutting the door, she turned to him. "I told you yesterday I was going to go find you and so I did."

"You found me, sure, but you didn't *tell* me anything about who you are, or what your family does to my kind. You left me confused."

She clasped her hands together in glee. "Did I?"

Elis curled his upper lip and glowered at her from where he hovered in the corner.

"Look, Elis, I needed to see how much you knew. Which was nothing, by the way. Still, you did realize there was something different about me. So, props to you for that."

"Obviously. I grasped the fact that I couldn't hypnotize you."

"Because I'm a moron, as you implied."

"You knew I knew you weren't a moron. You understood you had me stumped. That shouldn't happen. That *never* happens. How in the hell were you able to resist me?"

"I need to start recording the things you say."

All joking aside, his question was understandable. Mind control wasn't a skill the majority of bloodthirsters had at their disposal. It was an ability gained over hundreds of years. Elis had probably only been capable of it for a century or so and only adept at it for the last few decades. Once thirsters perfected this ability, it tended to be pretty effing absolute.

"Speaking of your *irresistibility*, when exactly did you decide to scam people for a living?"

"Scam them? I take offense to that. If you knew me better, you'd know how much I despise charlatans. They prey on people's vulnerabilities."

Sybille couldn't resist grinning. "You should have a conversation with my mother. The two of you could talk for hours about conmen and swindlers and never realize you were drowning in your own irony."

"I run a legitimate show. There's no swindle. People get what they pay for."

"I doubt they're paying to be mesmerized by a bloodthirsty hell beast, but whatever." She sat on her bed, tucking her knees under her chin.

"They pay to be hypnotized, or to sit in the audience and be entertained and that's what they get, on both counts."

"You didn't just hypnotize your willing volunteers today, though, did you? The whole audience was under your control and they never knew it. How many self-hypnosis CDs did you sell, by the way?"

"A thirster's still got to eat…or *drink*, at least." A sly smile crept onto his face. "I didn't do too badly, though. Thanks for asking. I have a limited window to make this sort of impact on people. The fair only stays in town for ten days. I spent a few months traveling around with it last year, but the carnie life is not the life for me. Now, once it leaves town, I stay put.

Then it's up to my private practice to keep me in organic grass-fed cow's blood. That stuff's not exactly cheap, you know."

"You have a source for grass-fed blood?"

"Local, of course."

"No wonder you brought up hipster pizza yesterday. You're one well-groomed mustache away from serving your clients mason jars filled with homebrewed kombucha. Which reminds me: Elis Tanner, Hypnotherapist. 1023 West Crawling Avenue. That's a pretty swank neighborhood."

"You looked me up?" He raised an eyebrow.

"Google is my friend." Of course, she'd looked him up. It was what her family did. Bounty hunters. Assassins. Psychic monster hunters. Whatever he wanted to call them. They found bloodthirsters, whether those bloodthirsters wanted to be found or not.

"Come by tomorrow. I'll be there."

She picked up a nail file from the bedside table and began to inspect the tips of her fingers. "Oh, I don't know…your website says, 'by appointment only.'"

"Consider yourself to have a standing appointment."

Setting down the file, she cocked her head as she leveled her gaze at him. "This is dreaming Elis talking, not daytime, bloodthirster, incarnated soul Elis. He might not want to see me after what I pulled at his show. At *your* show. I mean, *you* seem pissed about it, and you're not even the bloodthirster half of the Elis equation."

"Trust me, he wants to see you just as much as I do. *I am him*, remember. The spirit and the beast—we're intertwined, inseparable."

Squinting, she lifted her hand up to his face, sliding it along what would be his cheek, if he'd been flesh and blood. "Are you sure about that? I'm just going to throw this out there, but if the two of you are so inseparable, how is it that you're capable of checking out of *casa de la beast* so you can meet up with me?"

He answered with a low groan followed by a question of his own. "Why is it that I can imagine I'm feeling you touch me?"

"I guess we both have questions that can't be easily answered." She stroked his spectral cheek one more time, then brought her hand back and picked up her nail file again. "I need you out of my head now. Gotta be well rested for my hypnotherapy session tomorrow morning."

He nodded, but his forehead scrunched up in confusion. "I don't know how to leave on command. It's like I'm not ready for the dream to end yet and so I can't go."

She threw a pillow at him, watching as it passed through his head and collapsed against the wall. "Make yourself useful then and go keep Nate company."

Elis grumbled. "He's going to make me explain every single thing that's happening on that imbecilic show. And, by the way, he's still convinced the actors magically live inside your television. A bit of a clod, that one."

"That's why I like him. He's simple. What you see is what you get, nothing hidden."

"Everyone is hiding something. You just haven't uncovered it with Nate yet because he's wearing such a heavy layer of stupid."

Sybille laughed. "Get out of here." She motioned towards the door. "Shoo."

"As you wish." He bowed low to her, then, ignoring the open door, he floated through the wall.

"Showoff!"

"Make sure to give me a kiss when you see me. Maybe add a little nibble to my lower lip. I've always loved that…" His voice trailed off as he floated down the hallway.

Damn him. Sybille hopped out of bed and closed the door, hoping that act would create enough of a psychological barrier to keep her from thinking about him. Behind closed lids, though, thoughts of that lower lip and what he wanted her to do to it—to the real flesh and bone Elis—kept her awake long into the night.

CHAPTER SEVEN

Low Hollow was Devin's least favorite place on the planet. It figured that his job would take him there often and figured even more that he'd have to play the pretender while he was there, acting as though the Low was his go-to vacation destination spot. Sybille's family kept a log cabin on a small lake along the edge of the Low's southern forest. After researching Nathanial Atkins and his supposed whereabouts, he got an early start, reaching the lake by late morning.

The cabin wasn't much more welcoming than a musty cave would have been. He hadn't visited it for several months and it showed. The Esmonds avoided the entire Hollow if they could, so it stood silent and empty unless Devin was there, curtains drawn, the inside like a cold, neglected tomb.

Devin threw open the drapes and started a fire in the wood burner. Winter's chill hadn't yet set in, but the heat would help rid the space of dank air. He hoped he wouldn't have to spend more than a night there, though something told him he couldn't count on things with Nathanial Atkins to end quickly or neatly.

Sybille had described his spirit as a bit on the dull side, but it seemed his bloodthirster half had taken whatever brains he'd had in his life and run off with them. Old accounts of his undead life existed in the hierophants' databases. He had successfully eluded field agents half a dozen times over the past fifty years. All while never leaving this damned Low. Then, about a decade or so ago, he dropped off their radar.

Devin was sick of working in the dark, but as disconcerting as it was for him, he could only imagine how much murkier Sybille's job could be. Though the ether was not a place he'd ever been, Sybille had described it to him, along with the process in which she sought out spirits. A formless realm where nothing was tangible and yet everything was felt. Where spirits like Nate dwelled, slivers of consciousness held together in a tenuous arrangement between fate and sheer will. Where a spirit with little awareness outside their own thoughts would exist in limbo until their consciousness happened to intersect with Sybille's. And if she was able to break through the fog, where they would be faced with a choice of remaining as they were or leaving the ether for the more confusing Now World in a bid for final release to the World Beyond.

After listening to Sybille, Devin felt little need to complain about his own work. At least it took place on Earth and the objective was always the same: kill.

Shifting the logs with his poker, Devin tried to shrug off the weariness threatening to stop him before he'd even begun the hunt. The Low had a way of keeping people like him from doing their jobs. He wasn't a mystical kind of guy, but he had to admit this place had its own feel to it, like it was a living organism with a mind of its own. And that mind had been made up long ago to side with the monsters Devin tried to take out. It's like they knew when he was coming and then did their best to fuck with him.

Things went missing here: weapons, his phone, his sanity, not to mention people. Normally a steady guy with years of training under his belt, Devin became unhinged as soon as he entered the Low. Whenever he came here, he seemed to trip over the smallest twig or stone. After the third flat tire he'd gotten while driving through the Low's dark stretches, he started keeping multiple spares in the back of his truck. On top of that weirdness, it was always foggy, no matter how cloudless the skies were elsewhere. The path in front of him was never clear.

The Low hated him and the feeling was mutual.

Unfortunately for him, bloodthirsters gravitated to the Low and nine times out of ten, it was a bloodthirster he was challenged to find. Why he'd given up his job as a cop to track down unrepentant, amoral monsters, to be dragged to the Low and forced to remember things he'd rather forget, was beyond him. Some days, he could almost believe that. He could convince himself that he didn't know why he was doing what he was doing.

Today wasn't one of those days.

It was Sybille—smart, sarcastic, infuriating Sybille. She wasn't interested in him and he knew it. But interests could be cultivated. They could change. They could grow. If he had to keep tracking and destroying nightmare creatures in the one place on the planet that was his own personal nightmare so he could see her on a regular basis, he would do it.

The cabin went from cold to stifling in less than two hours. He scarfed down a sub sandwich he'd brought with him, then resigned himself to settling in for the evening. He'd tied an old rag to a tree at the end of his driveway, letting his contact know he was there, but the chances of her seeing it today were slim. The day's light slowly dying, Devin used the quiet time to examine a stack of printouts pertaining to the case.

The spirit had been adamant that Nathanial would stay near the forest.

"Once a lumberjack, always a lumberjack." According to Sybille, those words had actually come out of his dumb-as-bolts spectral little mouth. Spirits were bound to become out-of-touch over time. The world sped on without them, after all. A spirit in the ether had no way of knowing what its bloodthirster was up to, but it could sense their general location. As much as Devin may wish he was, he doubted the spirit was wrong about Nathanial's whereabouts.

Before his first official trip to the Low as the Esmond's field agent, Peter Esmond had given Devin fair warning. "The whole place is one big hierophany. The undead are attracted to it because the veil is always thin there. They sense the other side and the other side senses them. But the hierophany has chosen to protect them. We don't understand why. They're given safe harbor, while we who are hierophants, we who share a name and an understanding of the world beyond what we see, we aren't welcome."

Peter and his sister Margot hadn't been to Low Hollow in years. They'd refused to bring their children there while they were growing up. Sybille had yet to set foot inside its boundaries. After hearing Peter speak about the Low's dangers, Devin couldn't help but be glad that was the case. As for himself, he already knew more about it than he wanted to. That's why Peter hired him in the first place.

"The ether and what's beyond—it knows what we are when we enter the hollow," Peter told him. "And it wants us. It wants us for its own purposes. The biggest temptation in a hierophant's life is to give the Low what it wants."

After he spoke, Peter watched Devin's eyes grow wide. Devin had only been working for them for two days and was already starting to have serious regrets about it. "It doesn't affect you, Devin, you know that. No worries there. I've never met anyone so entirely void of psychic powers. That's why we need you. If you don't spend too much time there, you'll be perfectly safe."

That was an out-and-out lie. Psychic or not, Devin was anything but safe in the Low. It knew he wasn't a magical portal-to-the-other-side-opener like Sybille, but it knew he sided with them, knew he'd always been inclined to align himself with the do-gooder-rid-the-world-of-evil types, even if he wasn't exactly a saint himself. It knew he was against the bloodthirsters—he had his own reasons for that and it knew those too. It felt his hatred, a hatred he'd spent all his adult years trying to contain within a little box stored safely in the back of his mind. The Low picked it out of him, opened it, rifled around inside, and laughed at it. It knew his hatred, knew why he hated. The Low found this all to be amusing.

And so it went. When Devin entered the Low, he was entering enemy territory.

At some point, Devin fell asleep. By the time he woke, face pressed against the papers he'd been examining late into the evening, it was already nearing midday.

He got up and stretched, ate a couple of power bars from his stash, then headed out. If his informant wasn't here yet, she would be soon.

The living inhabitants of the Low were only human in that they shared their DNA with the rest of the world's population. Their minds, however, had been slowly drained of their humanity over the years spent living with the push and pull of the supernatural world. Some seemed normal enough, but Devin had learned never to trust them. Only young children, born too recently to be entirely altered by their environment, could be counted upon to give Devin any straight answers. Fortunately for him, most of the parents in the Low weren't the helicopter variety. If Devin needed information on one of the Low's undead citizens, it was one of the free-range children whose help he sought.

Knowing he'd bring her candy and soda pop, Devin normally didn't have to search far to find one of the Low's youngest and brightest. Sure enough, after tripping over a loose rock, it was his most reliable spy, an eight-year-old girl with stringy blond hair and a missing front tooth who caught him and helped him to his car.

"It's good to see you again, Charlie." He handed her a Snickers bar. "You been doing all right?"

The girl shrugged as she peeled back the candy wrapper. He couldn't help but be happy to see her. Not only was Charlie whip smart, she had a good read on people. She knew there was something wrong with the adults around her and had enough sense to know Devin was different.

"Seriously?" She spoke through bites of chocolate and caramel. "When have I ever been 'doing all right?'"

"Hey, I had to ask."

She rolled her eyes. "I hope you have more where this came from." She flicked the wrapper at him. "You here tracking another monster?"

Devin pursed his lips. He hated that a child barely old enough to read had to know so much about bloodthirsters. Monsters weren't an imaginary being to children like Charlie. They didn't hide in her closet or under her bed. They didn't hide at all. Her life was full of them—bloodthirsters, shifters, even her parents, who paid less attention to her than they did the dog she said they kept tied up under their porch.

"I'm looking for a man named Nathanial Atkins. Big white guy. Brownish-red hair, lots of muscles. Probably prone to wearing plaid and suspenders. You know of a thirster like that?" She scrunched up her nose and held out her hand. "I may have heard the name…but it'll cost you."

"You know I'm good for it." He reached into his bag and tossed over half a dozen full-sized candy bars. "Where can I find him?"

"You don't even know who he is, do you?" She shoved the bars into the pockets of her coat. "He runs Hocus, for one. And he's super mean!"

Hocus? Of all the places it could have been. Which meant…

Devin slapped the door of his truck. *Damn it to hell.* That information hadn't been in the hierophant database. They'd dropped the ball on this one. "Does your dad do business with him?"

She rolled her eyes again. "Everyone does business with the Blood King." She turned on her heals, collected her bicycle and headed down the driveway leading away from the cabin to the strip of country road circling the lake. "Be careful with him, Devin. If he kills you, where am I gonna get my sugar fix?"

"Thanks for your concern!" He watched her speed away until she turned the bend and disappeared.

It was Charlie who really needed that concern—hers, his and anyone else who would listen. Helping him was a dangerous act and they both knew it. He kicked at the loose stone that he'd tripped over earlier.

How many years of sane living did she have left, anyways? Five, six tops. Either her parents or Nathanial or the Low itself would do her in at some point. He'd thought on more than one occasion about taking her away from here, bringing her back to Margot and Sybille and letting them care for her away from the Low's reach. He'd mentioned this to Sybille, who had looked both horrified and devastated.

"There's no such thing as 'away from the Low's reach,' Devin. Even if we got her out of the Low in a physical sense, she's still spent her whole life there. It's a part of her. More importantly, *she's* a part of *it*, and it's not bound to give her up easily. You'd only be putting all of us at risk." She'd sat down next to Devin, placing her hand on his knee. If it had been any other time, he'd have reveled in this moment, in her freely given touch. But it hadn't been any other time, and now he found himself teetering midway between anger and dejection. "It's too late for her, Devin. I'm sorry."

Devin leaned against his truck, remembering this exchange, thoughts of the home Charlie was pedaling back to interfering with the thoughts he should be having as to his next course of action. Maybe he'd take her away from the Low anyways. Maybe Sybille was wrong.

Not that Sybille had ever been wrong before.

Sybille...time to give her an update.

Taking out his phone, he sent her a text.

Have a lead on our guy. Bad MF. Database needs serious updating and a good slap. Going to get him now. Call the Patron. Expect this one to get messy.

He hovered for a second over Sybille's contact image. In it she held one hand up, trying to stop him from taking her picture. She may have objected to having her picture snapped, but her face betrayed a playful smile. He pressed send, threw the phone on the passenger's seat and started up his truck.

Nathanial Atkins was the Blood King. That was an unpleasant development. He'd heard rumors of him over the years, but no one ever mentioned him by any name other than Blood King. Most people likely didn't know his long abandoned human moniker. He was surprised that Charlie knew it, to be honest. Whatever his name, the guy was a bad dude, even by bloodthirster standards. Devin had tried to steer clear of him, fly under his radar every time he came to the Low.

Guess that wasn't going to happen this time around.

CHAPTER EIGHT

THE SOUND OF A WOMAN LAUGHING BROUGHT ELIS TO THE ENTRYWAY OF HIS office, situated on the ground floor of a turn of the century brownstone walkup. As he cracked open the door, the laughing stopped, replaced by the cheerful squeals of young children playing in the schoolyard across the street. Normally the playground's steady, boisterous noise had a mellowing effect on him, but at this moment, it did nothing to soften his shock.

"You!" He opened the door wide.

"Me!" Smiling, the hazel-eyed woman from the fair tapped a sign framed in iron hanging from the building's brick wall. "'*Elis Tanner, Hypnotherapist with a Heart.*' Awww! You are one cheesy guy."

Amazing! This woman believed she could insult him again and again even though she barely knew him. "I didn't expect to see you here. You didn't seem like you believed anything I had to say at my show."

"I believed everything you said. It's not that. I just wasn't there for the same reasons everyone else was." She took a step forward, only to have him place his hand against the doorframe, blocking her entrance. She clucked her tongue in mock outrage. "You're not going to let me in?"

His hand shook. With his nerves rattled and her standing so close, there was no way he could avoid taking in her scent. Warm, spicy, dangerous.

Had she worn her hair pulled away from her neck on purpose to tempt him?

Impossible. She couldn't know what he was.

"I know what you are."

She pushed on his arm, which had become nonoperational with her last words, and walked inside.

"Of course you do. You read the sign, didn't you?"

"That's not what I mean, and you know it." She glanced around his office, examining the simple lines of mid-century modern décor. His fastidiously selected yellow upholstery and lighter-toned wood grains offset the dark, rich accents of the room's interior—a plush green carpet, mahogany wainscoting and built-in cabinetry featuring arts and crafts-styled stained glass. He wondered if she noted how uncluttered and organized he'd learned to keep his space and then, with dismay, wondered why he should care what she thought at all.

Her gaze paused on a bookshelf where the painting of a woman with dark hair and heavily-lidded, morose eyes sat staring out at the room. "She's beautiful."

Elis couldn't have told her what had possessed him to paint Juliana's portrait and hang it somewhere where he'd have to see it every day. Perhaps after years of torture, he was uncertain how to live without that keening pain her image brought to him. He missed her less than he used to, it was true, but he didn't *not* miss her at all either.

"The only reason I'm allowing you to stand here in my office is because you are a mystery that needs to be solved. If you can't provide me with any clues, then I would ask you to leave. Please."

In response to his polite request, she sat on the edge of his desk and crossed her legs, brown riding boots tapping against the desk's front panel, black skirt pushed up to mid-thigh. Tempting…so tempting.

As if she was reading his mind, she uncrossed her legs and then crossed them again. "All right, what would you have me tell you?"

"For one thing, how you avoided being hypnotized. And for another, why you've put yourself in danger by coming here today."

"I can't be mesmerized. Not by your means, at least. As for today, I came because we agreed I would. And I'm not in any danger because you won't hurt me."

In a flash he was on her, pressing himself to her bare knees. "I agreed to nothing. And I *can* hurt you! I can *kill* you."

"Stand down, dear. We're not in Twilight. There's no need to be so dramatic."

The steadiness he'd noted in her at the fair permeated the limited space between their faces. She wasn't just acting unafraid; she was genuinely calm. He pulled back an inch. "I'm not being dramatic. I can kill you. I really can!"

"Oh sure, you *can* kill me. You *could* throw me on the ground and drain me dry. But you won't. You couldn't live with yourself if you did. Plus, you want something from me, and you haven't quite figured out what that something is yet."

Elis placed his hands over hers and leaned in towards her again. He was close now, close enough to feel how invitingly warm she was. And that scent... What was it about this woman? He couldn't let her think she'd figured him all out. He hadn't even figured himself out yet, and he'd had a lot longer than her to do so. "I know exactly what I want from you. That's what should scare you."

"Oh, God, spare me, please." She took a deep breath, not to steady her nerves, but to display her disappointment. "Your spirit was wrong after all. Here I'd thought that maybe..."

He backed away. "My spirit?"

"Yeah, your spirit. Dream time Elis has been busy while you've been catching your beauty rest. He's become my number one fan. I've got to tell you, though, it appears he's completely cracked. Keeps telling me he's *rejoined* with you. But here you are, clearly still a soulless asshole."

He leaned in again.

"Can you make up your mind, please? You keep invading my personal space and then pull back like you're allergic to peanuts and I just ate a PB & J. You're making me nauseous. I mean, what...what is this, what's going on here?" She pointed at his face like there was something wrong with it. "What are you trying to accomplish with your eyes going all glary on me like that? I've gotta warn you, Elis, I used to have staring contests with my cousin when we were kids, and I always won."

To make her point, she opened her eyes wide and locked them with his own.

Damn her! He blinked, looking down to his side for a moment before resuming what he hoped was non-predatory, normal, humanlike eye contact. "My spirit wasn't lying to you. There are people who have the power to reconnect us. This happened to me—to us—two years ago. It happened to someone else I knew long before that as well."

Did she raise her eyebrows a fraction of an inch at these words? Perhaps her seemingly immoveable calm was capable of escaping her after all.

Her expression remained impassive. "This has happened before? Is it still alive?"

He scowled. "*She* is no longer alive, no. This isn't a matter I'm comfortable discussing with a stranger."

"You've practically taken up residency in my bedroom. I'd hardly call me a stranger to you." She cocked her head to the side. "Aww, Elis, I didn't know bloodthirsters could blush, but here you are doing it."

This was the most confusing encounter he'd ever had. "I can't remember you."

"I know. That's why I'm here."

Pushing off him with her boots, she twisted to the side and headed across the room towards the couch where she'd thrown her purse. She reached into it and after a moment of searching, pulled out a small paper sack. "This is mugwort and rose hips tea. Take it before bed and it will help you remember your dreams, which, by the way, I happen to star in."

He took the bag from her. "I don't normally drink anything besides... I don't drink tea."

"You do tonight. Don't worry. Just because it didn't get emptied from anyone's veins doesn't mean it will kill you. Seriously, it's fine. My mom makes me drink it all the time."

"Hmm. How is it you know what I am and I don't even know your name?"

"My name is Sybille. Sybille Esmond. As for how I know you..." She tapped the bag of tea. "Infuse one teaspoon in eight ounces of hot water for ten minutes. Drink it all, go to sleep, dream. I need you to do that because, honestly, I've already told you how I know what I know and I'm not going to do it again. You need to remember all on your own, bloodthirster."

Sybille's phone chimed. Digging it out of her bag, she ignored Elis while she checked her messages. "That's work. I've gotta jet, but I'll be back tomorrow. We'll see how this goes, okay? Oh, and since Spirit Elis will remember every moment of this." She stepped up on her tippy toes to look at him right in the eye...or in the lips rather. "You're going to have to earn that lip nibbling you want me to give you so badly. Be a good boy and drink your tea."

With that, she slid out of the door.

Elis thought about stopping her. He could make her stay with him, force her to explain how the hell she knew he'd been fantasizing about her sinking her teeth into him, rather than the reverse.

One of his first clear thoughts when he'd become a soul incarnate bloodthirster had been the desire to find a replacement for Juliana. For two years he'd searched, but no one had come close to what he was looking for. No one made him feel the pull that Juliana had. Then this woman had to come along and destroy all his expectations.

The pull was certainly there. She could yank him right off a ledge if he wasn't careful. If he had to spend the rest of his life with her, though, he'd either be the happiest bloodthirster ever, or he'd be begging for the stake within weeks. It was clear that there could be no in-between with this Sybille Esmond.

He opened the bag of tea and sniffed at it. His eyes watered.

"Disgusting."

Shaking his head, he tucked the tea into his jacket pocket so that he wouldn't forget to bring it home with him at the end of the day.

CHAPTER NINE

DEVIN HAD WARNED HER THIS WASN'T GOING TO BE AN EASY GIG. IT TURNED out, her gentle giant Nate was some sort of bloodthirster gang leader in Low Hollow. Her knowledge of the Low's underworld and come to think of it, its above world culture, was limited at best. Devin knew more than she did, having been there numerous times for work, but he was missing critical pieces of the puzzle if he hadn't known Nate was a crime boss until his contact told him. The gaps in his knowledge weren't so surprising. No one was an expert in the Low, because if you found yourself there often enough to really get to know it, you were no longer in a position to be an objective observer.

Devin kept his trips to the Low as short as possible. He knew what he was doing, but still Sybille worried about him. The Low wanted things from anyone who entered its domain. Sometimes she wondered what it sought from Devin. Beyond that, exactly how much of himself would he be willing to give to it in exchange for what he took? The Low loved its thirster inhabitants, and Devin's job was to remove them, not just from the Low but from the Now World. They were undead with no claim to remain in the land of the living as far as she was concerned. The Low, champion of keeping the undead Earth-side, however, wouldn't look kindly upon Devin for doing what Sybille sent him there to do.

She cringed as her thoughts strayed to the terrible predicaments she put her field agent in. Yes, it was his job. Yes, he was compensated for his efforts, but if something ever happened to him while working for her family in the Low she would no doubt have a heart weighed down to the ground with guilt.

Sybille spent the afternoon at her cousin Zareen's house, helping clean up after the illness that each of her family members had succumbed to one by one. After several restless nights in a row, Zareen was in a foul mood. Hindsight being what it was, it had not occurred to Sybille to wait to tell her about Elis until she was well-rested and in a more reasonable frame of mind.

"He sounds like a huge creeper to me." Zareen swept chunks of meatballs and half-eaten spaghetti noodles off a highchair and into a waste bin. "Can spirits be creepers? I mean, if they can be, he totally is one. One incredibly hot pervert."

"I never said he was good looking!"

"I used my imagination, and I can tell by your fake outrage that I'm totally right. Maybe he's not a bloodthirster at all. Maybe he's one of those incubi!"

Sybille laughed. "No one's ever been able to prove those are real. Besides, I know he's a bloodthirster. I went and talked to him."

"You what?" Zareen threw down the rag she'd been preparing to scrub the counter with. "Hell no, Sybille. That's what field agents like Devin are for. We're not supposed to approach bloodthirsters and for good reason. Your mother taught you that when you were an itty bitty."

"This one is different."

"Said the bloodthirster snack."

Sybille took the rag Zareen had just discarded and tackled the counter herself. Better to keep her hands busy and feel useful rather than focus on the look of disapproval she was certain was clouding Zareen's face. "I know how it sounds, but I'm serious. I can't tell you what it is exactly but trust me, it's better that I met with him in person."

She scrubbed furiously at the counter until it was sparkling clean, then tossed the rag in the sink and swung around to confront her cousin. She expected to be met with defiance, but Zareen's upturned lip and expectant eyes made her appear more bemused than anything else.

"I can see the wheels spinning, Zareen. I know what you're going to say, but I'm not a fool. I'm aware that he's dangerous. I keep my focus. I watch my six."

"You watch your six? What are you, SEAL Team Sybille?" Zareen laughed. "I trust you Syb...but that doesn't mean I understand whatever game it is you're playing." She reached across the kitchen island and motioned for her cousin to step forward. Sybille complied, and Zareen put her hands on her shoulders. "Let me know if you need backup or not. You know I'm good for it."

"Of course, you are. I can't tell you how much your support means to me. I just need more time on this one. You probably think I'm being reckless and maybe I am, but I still need you to give me the benefit of the doubt."

Zareen squeezed her shoulders, then let go. "Always. Hand me the mop, will you? You wouldn't believe how crusty the floor gets after just one meal. We need to get a dog."

Sybille could have cried, she was so relieved to have Zareen by her side. Whenever she felt at all unsettled, she could always depend upon a visit with Zareen to restore the balance. Zareen was like a big sister to her. Growing up on the same block, they'd been thick as thieves as children, despite the five-year age gap. She'd been maid of honor at Zareen's wedding to Trevor and had been present at each of her children's births. She'd helped test Adelaide, the oldest girl, for hierophant tendencies. The two cried together, tears of both joy and sadness, when the tests had confirmed that the little girl had inherited her mother's gifts.

Zareen might have her opinions regarding Sybille's involvement with Elis, but she'd support Sybille nonetheless. This assurance was a lighthouse beacon guiding her through a stormy sea.

Zareen's house was spotless by the time Adelaide and her brother and sister woke from their naps. An hour later, it was dirty again, floors scattered with brightly painted toys, board books and various toddler accoutrements. Still, Sybille had yet to receive that coveted call from Devin. She did her best to pretend this didn't worry her at all.

Patrons were the bane of Sybille's existence. Unfortunately, this secret society of one percenters with an unholy interest in all things paranormal were also the Esmonds' bread and butter.

Growing up in a hierophant family, Sybille had had occasion to get to know many Patrons—so many that she could probably write an in-depth Patron guidebook (or perhaps a cautionary tale) to benefit future generations of psychics. She doubted any of the basic facts about them would change over the next few decades. For instance, in blatant disregard for the march of time, Patrons' attire—long brown robes with hoods that hid their faces—never changed. Even worse than their get-ups, upon being initiated as a Patron, they were all trained to speak in an archaic and stiff manner lacking contractions. She'd yet to meet one that didn't sound like a character from a poorly written fantasy novel.

Patrons may be insufferable, but damned if their wallets weren't stuffed to the brim with cash. Since Patrons were as inevitable in a hierophant's life as undeath and taxes, Sybille made the best of it by imagining how much money she could make if she revealed their existence to major news outlets. Unfortunately, if she wished to continue feeding her family, outing the Patrons was ill-advised. Instead of inciting an anti-Patron revolution, she settled for humiliating them in her mind.

The Patron she'd been dealing with for the past year or so, known only by his *not-at-all-pretentious* alias Celebrimbor, sat with Margot and Peter at their dining room table, slurping tea and staring at the chair he'd been told the spirit of Nathanial Atkins sat in. Celebrimbor had no psychic powers to speak of, only an obsessive desire to experience the paranormal. His job was to make sure Sybille's family delivered on their promises of bringing the hidden world to the Now World so he and his Patron cohorts could have a sip of it. As much as he might harp on about ridding the world of the cursed bloodthirsters and how wonderful it was that he could have a role in it, being on the right side in a battle of good versus evil was secondary. It was that taste of the supernatural he truly craved. This was the driving force behind all the Patrons: proof of a world beyond the Now World. Proof of something more.

Despite how obvious this was to Sybille, it wasn't something you mentioned out loud. She'd made this mistake as a teenager, calling out her mother's Patron for making Margot perform four possessions in six days.

Exhausted but afraid they'd lose their biggest source of income, Margot had obliged, while Sybille watched on, arms wrapped around her, face red with rage.

"Do you enjoy seeing my mom suffer for your own amusement? Why does that have to be the shit you Patrons get off on?"

The Patron hadn't taken kindly to Sybille's sass and the resulting paycheck drought nearly destroyed their already tenuous finances.

Having a Patron here hour after hour as they waited for Devin to report in was a test of Sybille's level headedness. If Celebrimbor, or Bore as she preferred to call him, asked her for one more palm reading, she was tempted to tell him she saw violence in his immediate future and then smack him in the face.

That, of course, would not earn them next month's mortgage. She did her best to keep herself occupied, which consisted mainly of binge-watching old reruns of some of her favorite shows on her tablet all evening. Soon, Bore had to come and ruin that diversion as well.

"I have no doubt that thou art watching *Supernatural*, my dearest lady. Which episode have you arrived upon?"

"It's *The Love Boat*, actually. The one where Julie—"

"I have consumed every season of *Supernatural*, which as you know, is no small feat. He sat next to her on the couch, moving his hood back just a tad to see if she was really watching what she said she was. "Now I have the privilege of viewing *The X-Files* for the seventh time. It was with boundless joy that I consumed the newest season. I cannot get enough of Dr. Dana Scully and Agent Fox Mulder. Be that it is fiction, you still perchance to glean a great deal of knowledge regarding matters of the invisible world. Do you not agree?"

Sybille removed her earbuds and put her tablet into sleep mode. She had no idea what he was going on about. "I bet you're just like a paranormal agent now, Bore. You should have your own show."

"With whom do you refer...is it I?" Hand to his chest, slight wheeze as he inhaled. "Come now, my dear Miss Esmond, Patrons must always stay in the shadows. To reveal our true identities would be to undermine the system that keeps thou safe."

"Well, a *secret* agent then." She winked at him and even with his ridiculous hood draped across his brow, she could tell he was blushing.

"Sybille, dear, do you want a slice of lasagna?" Standing at the dining room table, her mother held a metal spatula at the ready over a pan of steaming noodles and meat.

"Ugh, Mom, you know I can't eat until after the possession. Not unless the Patron here wants to have regurgitated tomato sauce sprayed all over him."

"I know, I know. I just had to offer. What kind of a mother would I be if I didn't at least try to feed my daughter? The possession could still be hours away, after all." She dished out a piece to Peter and another one for Celebrimbor. "We'll save you some. You can microwave it later."

"Thanks, Mom."

She turned her attention back to the Patron, who clearly wasn't going to leave her alone anytime soon.

"Is there something more I can help you with, Secret Agent Bore?"

"As I understand the situation, thou hast a criminal in the guise of a client."

"Head criminal, according to Devin." She shifted so that she was near enough to make him quiver in his robes. "This is a big one for you, Bore. This is the score that's going to make you the Patrons' golden boy."

"Do you imagine so? Of course, I have no desire beyond helping to save thy beautiful world." He straightened his hood and took another sip of tea.

"Yes, but I hope you know the risk you're putting us in. Things easily could go badly for Devin and I'm expecting a fight with that one." She stuck her thumb out in the direction of Nate, who smiled at her amicably. "You know how much a possession takes out of me, but Nate here? He's a really mean spirit. Nasty. I'll be lucky to get through tonight unscathed."

"Thou art the pinnacle of bravery and grace." Celebrimbor tentatively put a hand on her knee, patted it and then took it back. "I myself could never perform the acts that thou hast put upon thy shoulders."

She shrugged. "I'm just doing my job. It's important, the work that we're engaged in, you and I. Saving the world one demon at a time. I'm so thankful that you make it possible for me to do what I do. We make a wonderful team." She put all her teeth on display, eyes wide, expectant, innocent.

"I shall continue to do just that. You deserve a bejeweled crown for thy noble efforts, Lady Sybille. You deserve the keys to the kingdom."

"Aw, you're the sweetest."

A buzzing sound ended Celebrimbor's praise fest. All eyes, even Nate's, turned to the coffee table where Sybille's phone lay. She checked the message.

"Get that crown ready, Bore. It's show time."

CHAPTER TEN

Nathanial Atkins was proving to be a pain in Devin's ass. Hackles raised as though he was already facing his opponent, blood pumping—animal instinct told him Hocus was the Blood King's domain. Charlie had led him in the right direction, of that he had no doubt. Finding Atkins had never been in question, though. Devin had tracked many a bloodthirster. Normally, it wasn't too difficult, even with the Low working against him. He was good at what he did.

This time it had taken some doing, but now he was closing in for the kill. Or circling the drain, depending on how things played out. Drawing Atkins out into the open, ashing him so his undead body imploded, leaving only a heap of dust, that was the part that set Devin on edge. This guy wasn't just going to roll over and ask for a stake through the heart. Devin was treading dangerous waters here.

Hocus: a wood paneled, beer-stained, seedy shithole bar. Had it been anywhere else in rural America, Hocus would've been nothing more than a small-town honky-tonk staring in the rearview mirror in the hopes of glimpsing its better days. Gaunt, unkempt men with cigarettes dangling from their lips. Waitresses with circles under their eyes wearing bright red lipstick and short shorts. Twangy, repetitive music playing from an old jukebox. The smell of stale beer, if your nose could detect anything through the thick smoke clinging to the room like a smile on a beauty queen. It was the sort of rundown tavern you'd expect to find in a place like the Low.

Devin tried but failed to hate the place, which offered him an unwelcome, sentiment-inducing trip down memory lane. He'd grown up in a *respectable* establishment similar to Hocus, his father tending bar, his mother tending to the ass slaps of his father's clientele. Everywhere he turned in Hocus, he saw his family's dysfunction. What a twisted fuck he must be to want to park himself on a barstool and revel in it.

Maybe he'd spent too much time in the Low. Work sent him here at least a couple of times a month. Plus, there'd been that time in his youth, a time he tried not to think about, where desperation had led him to the Low's morbid embrace. That experience had been a waste and now it had led to this. Maybe its weird dark magic pull was starting to mess with his mind. If that was the case, he wasn't sure he wanted to know. There'd be nothing he could do about it anyways.

Smoke assailed him from all angles. His fingers twitched. The feel of a cigarette between them reawakened in his imagination even though it had been almost eight years since he'd kicked the habit.

"What'll I get ya?" The bartender looked but didn't look at Devin as he approached. Typical Low interaction. Eye contact inadvisable, especially between strangers. He had to wonder what sort of horror the Low folks thought would come to pass if they looked directly at each other. He wondered, but not enough to test out the theory.

"I'm here on business."

"Oh yeah? What kind of business?" Head still down, feigning disinterest when clearly, he was interested. His attention stayed glued to his hand as it moved an old rag around the shiny brass surface of a beer tap.

"The kind that involves your boss, not you." He thrummed his fingers on the edge of the wooden counter. "Be a good boy and go get him."

The bartender sneered, but he did as Devin commanded. That was the only way to get what you wanted in the Low—by using unabashed force. Devin had learned early on that asking for things drove you right into a dead end. You had to start with the expectation that you were entitled to whatever it was that you wanted. If you could pull that off, you stood a chance. Half of a chance, at least.

While he waited for the bartender to inform Atkins of his presence, he leaned against the counter and cased the room. A hall leading to the bathrooms to his left, double doors opening out to a beer garden on his right, the main entrance directly across from him. Everything was vaguely familiar, though he was certain that it was just its resemblance to his father's bar that he was recalling. There was a term for that… Transference. That's what a shrink would say it was.

Of course, he had *heard* about this place. It's not like there were loads of bars or any other sorts of businesses here in the Low. But this was a *human* hangout. Beer was on tap, not blood. There hadn't been any reason for Devin to come here until now. This, of all places, was one for Devin to avoid.

Bloodthirsters preferred the human population of the Low to be strung out—and not just on the cosmic crud they breathed in every day. Hocus was a drug front—had been for years. You couldn't just order the shit the bloodthirsters were selling at the bar, but everyone knew someone here could get it for you. Charlie's parents probably got it here or bought from someone who did. They didn't even try to hide their addiction from their daughter. He'd already heard her make references to it, like it was no big deal. Like she knew that would be her someday because that's just what adults do.

Devin shut down that thought. He had a job to do. He couldn't keep thinking about that little girl, didn't want to imagine her ten years from now, bat shit crazy, all doped up.

Dammit, he hated the world sometimes.

He walked over to the table nearest the double doors and sat with his back to them. Should he text Sybille now? He hoped he was close to finishing this job, but it was going to take more than this happy hour meet-and-greet to do it. He needed Atkins alone in order to send him to the World Beyond without Devin himself being taken down by the Blood King's entourage.

He was going to have to go in deep, play a role he didn't want to play. The thought set his blood pressure to boil, but there was nothing to be done about it. He couldn't leave without achieving his aim.

Normally, Devin was able to stay inconspicuous in the Low. He didn't want people to know who he was—that would make his repeated hunts in their terrain increasingly dangerous. Maintaining a low profile wasn't usually a problem. Bloodthirsters kept to themselves. There were opportunities to find and kill them without having to come out of the shadows. And most of the time, no one missed the little cocksuckers. A staked bloodthirster's body disintegrated within minutes. There was little evidence left behind once the deed was done. Since they weren't the type to move in packs, it might be months or even years before someone realized one of them had disappeared, if they ever did. Maybe there was no such thing as the perfect murder, but staking a bloodthirster in the middle of a forest came pretty close. Not that it was *murder* per se. You didn't murder monsters; you put them down. That's what Devin did. That's the job he was paid to do.

The bartender was taking his sweet time. Phone in hand, Devin brought up Sybille's picture in his contacts list. He texted her, let her know to get things started but also warned her that it would most likely take longer than usual. She was going to be pissed—not at him. She was smart enough to know Devin wouldn't prolong a mission unnecessarily. But the longer this took, the longer she'd have to play hostess to the Patron, and that guy was a total dick.

"Is that your girl?"

Nearly dropping his phone, Devin shut off the screen and stood up, awkwardly turning around to face the mammoth man standing between himself and the doors leading out to the patio.

The Blood King.

So much for being aware of his surroundings.

"She's just a friend."

"Women like that are never just friends." Atkins stood with his thumbs looped into the arm holes of a leather vest, a casual stance attempting to mask his at-the-ready demeanor. Turquoise and silver rings circled each of his tattooed fingers. "Why do you think you have the right to call me up like I'm the leg of lamb you're purchasing for Easter dinner? Who are you, anyways?"

Devin swallowed.

"I'm a businessman, just hoping to do business. Should I take it elsewhere?"

"That depends on what this business is that you're hoping to do." Atkins took a step around him and swung a chair so that its back was facing the table, then sat straddling it. He ordered two of his men to frisk his guest. When they came up weaponless, he motioned for Devin to take the chair across from him. "Spill."

Devin would spill all right. He was working on a hunch here. If he was mistaken, he could kiss his ass goodbye. Out of all the things he'd gotten wrong in his life, though, his hunches usually proved good. As Charlie had said to him before pedaling away earlier that afternoon, "Everyone does business with the Blood King." That business? To sell Low's human population Crave, an addictive drug that when consumed made their blood extra tasty. Addicts, of which there were many, were too strung out to object to being fed upon by the local bloodthirster population.

"You've built something here in the Low. You have a solid thing going. Solid, but not huge. It could be, though. Don't you think it's time to expand?"

"Are you saying I don't know what I'm doing?" Atkins leaned in towards Devin, grinning. Red stained teeth the texture of tree bark, breath like a dead cow rotting in a sunny field—they'd had toothbrushes when this clown was a human, right? Devin did his best not to heave.

"No! God, no." Devin patted his own chest. "Why would I say that? I wouldn't even think it! I know you have your reasons for staying within the Low. I'm just saying that if you wanted to expand, I'm the man to help you do it."

Grin departed, Nathanial's hundred-mile stare blazed a trail over Devin's skin. "And why would that be? I don't know you, don't know your name or who you run with. All I know is that you're human and you seem to know I'm not. I gotta say, that's suspicious. Most of the humans I'm around every day don't have a clue what I am. Hell, even the ones I feed off of aren't so sure."

Devin had to bite his tongue not to reply to that. The Low went a long way to muddy a person's mind, but beyond that, the Blood King made sure they were more concerned with how to get their next fix than with what sort of person provided that fix. Drug addicts didn't tend to ask a lot of questions. Their misgivings ended when flame hit pipe.

Devin needed to be extra careful. One false note and who knows what sort of frenzy Atkins could get worked into. Perhaps some fuzzy half-truths would do the trick. "My sister was a volunteer donor for a number of years. She used to live here." No lie there, just not the whole truth. "I know because she knew."

"And where's your sister now?"

Devin shrugged, hoping the nonchalant movement would stop his fists from clenching and his arms from swinging in the direction of Atkin's face. "She moved on."

"Ah, always a shame to lose a donor." The Blood King wrapped his knuckles on the table. Whether he was buying Devin's story or not, there was no way to know for certain. "That doesn't explain why you've taken an interest in my people."

"Money. It's as simple as that. Bloodthirsters maneuver through the world undercover. Humans believe you're no different than themselves. But I know better, and I see where we can work together for each other's benefit. I'll make money and you'll be expanding your interests. I'd call that a win-win."

"If you know better, then you know that the Low is our protector. The outside world doesn't come knocking; it doesn't bother us here." He narrowed his eyes at Devin. "At least, not very often. Do you really expect me to move outside of its protection at the suggestion of a stranger?"

Here was his in. "I don't have to be a stranger." He rolled up his sleeve, letting his bare arm fall onto the table in front of Atkins. "I wouldn't expect you to align yourself with me without getting to know me a little better first."

The Blood King remained still, his eyes in assessment mode, while Devin cursed himself. He was being too obvious, too pushy. Then again, anyone mad enough to propose a partnership with a bloodthirster was bound to act like he didn't know a good decision if it came and knocked him on the head.

Come on, take the bait.

Atkins pushed Devin's arm away. "Not here. Let's go to my office."

The Blood King motioned for Devin to walk ahead of him. "Last door on your right." His guards followed, then stationed themselves on either side of the door. If the office didn't have windows, Devin would be screwed.

Inside, door closed behind him, relief hit. Not only was there a window, but a door that looked as though it led to the outside world.

Atkins retrieved a small metal box from a drawer in his desk, then motioned for Devin to have a seat on the leather couch across from it.

"There are easier ways to get dosed than approaching the Blood King with a business proposition." He sat next to Devin and handed him the box. "If this is all an elaborate plot to get a fix, you're the stupidest, most unconvincing junkie I've ever met."

"Would you even be sitting here with me if you thought I was a junkie?"

"Would you be offering me your arm if you weren't?"

Devin paused for a moment, then opened the box, watching Atkins and his well-practiced poker face out of the corner of his eye. "I want you to know you can trust me. And the best way I figure I can do that is if I show you that I trust *you*." He tapped the box. "So here we are."

"Here we are." Atkins reached over, pulling out a spoon, a lighter, a narrow glass tube, and finally a small translucent green block. Crave reminded Devin of unpolished amber, the more imperfections in its composition, the more beautiful. And the more desirable.

Handing him the tube, Atkins placed the square of Crave on the spoon and ignited the lighter. Within seconds, the block had melted into a syrupy goo. A flowery aroma with the slightest hint of pine wafted towards Devin. His mouth watered in anticipation, as though Crave was a juicy quarter-pounder instead of the harbinger of a hellish existence. As Atkins lowered the flame, Devin brought the tube down to the spoon, breathing in through his nose.

The world became a watercolor painting. Purple, green, orange blotches of obscured light...a foggy brilliance. Devin's tongue thickened like a fluffy pancake, tasting as though it had been coated with maple syrup. He slid back and rested his head against the couch, eyes closed, breath deep and even. It had been a long time since he'd been under Crave's thumb. Long, but not long enough. It was the most pleasurable sensation in existence and he hated it.

Devin was only partly capable at the moment of envisioning what the days of withdrawal would be like. The cramps, the nausea, the brain-splitting headaches.

The desire to do it all over again.

It would be worth it though. It had to be. This was one of the last fully sober thoughts he had. *His plan had better fucking work.*

CHAPTER ELEVEN

Margot lit candles while Peter cleansed the downstairs rooms with a smudge stick. The aroma of dried sage soon permeated every corner, bringing with it memories of summer nights camping in arid backcountry.

Sybille was supposed to be meditating, preparing to open the channel for Nate, but instead she found her mind blipping like a heart monitor hooked up to a caffeinated rabbit. Celebrimbor's presence didn't help. He was a hoverer, poking his beak nose into her personal space and disrupting her concentration. For someone who got off on seeing her possessed, he sure knew how to hamper the process. Then there was Devin's last text, telling her to get started, but cautioning her that they'd have a long night ahead. That meant things weren't so cut and dry this time around. He never complained about the danger his job put him in, but it was apparent that this one was harrowing.

What horror had she gotten him into? Not that it was her fault exactly. He could say no, but he wouldn't; he never would. He had a history with the Low, something dark in his past that he'd alluded to but wouldn't speak about directly. He hated the Low, yet he couldn't stay away from it. Sometimes she wondered if he'd find a reason to go there on his own even if he didn't work for her. Although he complained about spending time "in that hellhole," the place seemed to hold power over him. The more she thought about it, the more it worried her.

Crave had to have something to do with it. She shivered despite the room's stifling warmth. A possession was taxing enough on its own without Crave being involved. When this was over, she'd have a talk with Devin, get to the bottom of it. His reports were never very detailed when it came to the bloodthirsters' last moments. This one wasn't bound to be either, but she would call him on it. This time, she wouldn't let it slide.

Last on her list of men determined to rile her nerves of steel was Elis. This possession and release was bound to take forever, maybe even most of the night depending on what was going on with Devin. While she had come to accept Elis' regular appearances, Sybille hoped he would skip tonight. There was no way she'd have the energy to deal with him after giving Bore his show and sending Nate off to the World Beyond.

"Bore, I'm going to have to respectfully ask you to park your ass on the couch." She fingered a black tourmaline crystal and lifted it into her palm. Celebrimbor had bought it for her believing it would help her focus her powers. That was highly doubtful, but it was still calming to have something with which to keep her hands occupied. Besides, if it didn't help center her, she could always throw it at his head.

Thankfully, it only took Sybille's friendly brush-off plus a stern look from Uncle Peter to get him to retreat. "The lady needs her space, Patron." He guided Bore to the living room. "Possessions are a tricky thing—almost as much an art as a skill. You know that, son. This isn't your first rodeo either."

Bore mumbled his acknowledgement and Sybille proceeded to tune him out, instead concentrating on the circle of twelve candles arranged on the table. Margot was already seated directly across from her. She reached her hands towards her daughter, who set the crystal down and then grabbed on and squeezed.

Margot nodded. "Let the show begin, my dear."

Nearly all the possessions fell upon Sybille's shoulders now. Zareen hadn't done more than a handful since becoming pregnant with Adelaide, and Peter had never been particularly skilled at them. His strength was in creating the right atmosphere, one that was conducive to a spirit-ready mind. Without Peter's skill at incantations, she would be far less successful. Her mother, a powerful medium in her day, had backed off years ago in favor of letting Sybille take the lead. Sybille tried not to let this irk her. Margot, more than anyone, knew what it took out of a hierophant every time she gave herself over to a spirit. But still, she let Sybille carry the brunt.

"You are far more skilled than any of us," she told her daughter on a regular basis, trying to appeal to Sybille's ego.

That may be true, but it didn't make the toll she paid any less.

While the women were preparing themselves, Nate sat to Sybille's left, absorbed once again in the patterns on their tablecloth.

"The candlelight makes things pretty." He fingered the lace with reverence.

"Yes dear, but you must be quiet now." Margot spoke in the sing-song voice she normally reserved for Zareen's young brood. "Sybille has to focus, or you will not receive your proper sendoff."

"Right. Sorry, Sybille." Nate turned to her, his brow pensive as he tore his gaze from the table. "What do I do, just jump into you or something?"

For the love of Mike. "No, Nate, you don't... Look, sit there and wait, okay? It will happen organically. Imagine that you're tied to me by a rope. When you feel me pull on it, don't resist. Let yourself be brought in."

He agreed to it and the room fell silent. Celebrimbor and Peter sat turned to the back of the couch so that they could peer over it at the spectacle. Peter's hand remained firmly on the Patron's shoulder to keep him from jumping up and returning to the dining room.

Finally, Sybille found herself able to center. The candle flames held her in their golden caress, letting her open the channel separating herself from the overlapping plane Nate resided in. She may have told Elis she wasn't able to be hypnotized, but that wasn't strictly true. Her family learned guards against the sort of mesmerizing Elis excelled at. However she was more than capable of putting herself into a trance state—the sort of state that would allow her own consciousness to be tucked away while Nate's temporarily moved in. When that happened, she would become an observer, able to watch everything that happened but unable to control any of it.

This was the part of being a hierophant that sucked ass.

It happened over an endless stretch and also in the blink of an eye. Her mind folded in on itself, making more room for its visitor. She was barely hanging on, barely able to squeeze her mother's hands or shift in her seat, when *he* came.

Elis.

"What the hell?" He stood next to her chair, in between her and Nate.

"Not really a good time, Elis."

"Oh, is this the man you were talking about?" Her mother smiled at him. "He's handsome, Sybie!"

"You were talking about me?"

"No, I was…well yes, you're part of my job and…"

"Sybille, I feel a tug!" Nate's hands clasped in front of him as though he was climbing an invisible rope. *Damned literal-minded spirits.*

Elis' attention shifted back to Nate. "You *do not*. Stay out of her head."

Sybille snorted. "You're one to make that demand. Stand down, Elis. This is what I do. If you insist on being here, you're going to have to join our other eager beaver on the let's-give-Sybille-her-space couch." She narrowed her eyes at Elis, who narrowed his eyes at Nate, who narrowed his eyes at the tablecloth.

"Fine then, but I'll be right there." He pointed to the living room.

"And I'll be right here, and Santa Claus will be right at the North Pole. Jesus Christ, Elis."

"Honey, what do I always tell you about men?" Her mother stroked Sybille's palms with her thumbs, attempting to sooth her.

Sybille took a deep breath. "That they all have a maiden-in-distress fetish. Just ignore them and save yourself because the harder they try the more they end up messing up."

"I can hear you, you know." Elis placed his hands on his hips.

To be fair, his current state of agitation wasn't totally his fault. He was brought here through Sybille's mind and so he couldn't help but feel how it was being threatened, made tinier by the second. And that threatened *him.*

"I don't know if I'll be able to stand watching you be taken over by that moron." He tapped his fingers against his sides and seethed.

This wasn't the sort of disturbance Sybille needed. Elis, as well meaning as he may be, had damaged her state of calm. That meant this possession would take more energy, more time, more effort. She put thoughts of him aside and returned to the candlelight. Nate still pulled on his imaginary rope beside her. He was doing his part. The least she could do was hers.

The next thoughts she had were not her own—a woman in a high-collared lace dress running ahead on a trail through a forest, laughter fading, and then red.

Red, nothing but red.

Eyes rolling back into her head, she moaned as another's memories drowned out her own. Her mother held fast to her hands, spoke soothing words she couldn't make out. Nate's rope pulled tight. He became her. His will was all that mattered. And he willed quite a lot.

"I want out!" Sybille's mouth, Nate's voice.

Elis flew from his perch on the edge of the couch and was back in the dining room within seconds. "Then leave. Now."

"You have no say in this, Elis." Sybille's mother spoke in a hushed murmur. She struggled to hold onto her daughter's hands as Nate pushed against the confines of a living body. Sybille danced like a marionette, her limbs jerking taught and then collapsing without warning.

Elis growled but said no more. He was only a spirit anyways. Nate was more present than he was. How could he possibly help?

"I hate this," Nate howled. "I want to leave. For one hundred years, I've wanted to leave."

"And you will soon, Nathanial, dear." Margot tried to maintain eye contact with him. How she could see her daughter like this—writhing like a fish in a net, her skin grown pale, her eyes bloodshot and hopeless—was beyond him. "Please, do be gentle with my daughter's body. She'll need it after you've left."

"No!" He shot up, hands separating from Margot, who cried as though she'd been struck. "You made me a promise, but my beast still lives. Why?"

"This hast been what I hath long awaited! To see her swallow such a beast and yield to its strength. Thy Lady Sybille, ist there no end to thy extraordinary talent!"

Ellis stared in disbelief at the weird guy sitting on the couch in a monk's get-up, sputtering butchered prose. This must have been one of the Patrons Sybille had talked about, some kind of pervert, getting off on spirit possession. A medium groupie. Elis had been so focused on Sybille, he hadn't noticed the Patron's ridiculous presence until now.

"Doest thy fair Lady Sybille perchance to flit and flutter above her mortal coil whilst the beast dances with it? It hast struck my humble person that, though I may be apprenticing yet in the ways of the Powers, I do indeed feel her energy riseth out of her. Is it not so?"

No, it wasn't so. Elis narrowed his eyes and sulked. Sybille was trapped in a little corner of herself, probably totally pissed off, not floating above this hell like a benevolent angel unable to feel or even care what was happening to her.

He waited for someone to call the Patron out, tell him what a fool he was, but no one said a word. No one could, he supposed. They needed the Patron to be pleased. They put up with him because he paid the family, which essentially made him their boss. Elis' non-existent stomach turned thinking of Sybille having to go through this horror show just to pay the bills.

His attention returned to the dining room where Sybille's mother was doing her best to keep Nate from working himself into a tizzy.

"Your beast is being dealt with presently. That's why we've begun the possession. Don't you remember, dear heart? You agreed to this." Margot lifted a corner of the tablecloth and showed it to him. To Sybille. Damned if it wasn't confusing watching Sybille move, her mouth forming words, knowing it wasn't her at all.

Nate studied the tablecloth. For a second, the tension in the room subsided. Then everything became a blur of lace and flames as he pulled the covering away from the table. The fabric caught fire. He screeched until the walls shook, everyone but Elis clamping their hands to the sides of their heads to keep their eardrums from bursting. Nate screeched until Sybil's throat must have been raw, then sank to the ground, wrapping himself in the blazing cloth.

Margot and Elis both screamed.

"My God!" the short, balding man Elis assumed was Sybille's uncle, Peter, sprang to his feet. Pulling an afghan off the back of the couch, he rushed to Sybille's side. As he threw it over her, he turned his head away from the heat and smoke. The blanket did the trick, dousing the fire in seconds. He placed his arms around Sybille's body and brought her close. "Stop this, Nate. Stop it! We're trying to help you. We can't do that if you kill your host. You must be patient."

Margot's shaking form appeared at Elis' side, her forehead dripping with sweat. "She said this one would be a challenge. My Sybie is never wrong."

Cursing for the millionth time that he wasn't physically present in the room, Elis could do nothing but stand there trying to make sense of what was happening. "I don't get it. He was so docile."

Sybille's body continued to heave as it rocked back and forth. Peter held on to her as best he could. Every few seconds a low groan escaped her lips.

"Are you sure you don't understand what's happening here?" Margot stared at him, raising one well-manicured eyebrow. "Sybille tells me quite the story about you. I don't know if I should believe it or not. I'm not even sure she does. But if it is true, you know exactly the struggle Nathanial is facing right now."

Elis shook his head. His re-souling had been a grueling, violent affair, yes, but this wasn't the same thing. "I wasn't possessed by a spirit. When I was brought back into a body, I was coming back to myself. You must see that this is different."

Margot continued to tremble. "I wish I had time to dissect what exactly you are because truly, you should not exist. At the moment, however, we have a more pressing issue to deal with."

She walked over to her daughter, put a hand on the back of her bent head and whispered something to her. The groaning became louder for a bit and then receded until it was quiet enough to hear the grandfather clock ticking from the alcove a room away. Even the Patron seemed unable to come up with one of his ill-conceived, brain-damaged Shakespearean phrases. Margot and Peter exchanged a nervous glance.

Finally, Peter spoke. "Part of this is normal." He stroked his niece's hair. "And that part you should be able to relate to, Elis. Nate has been without a corporeal form for many years. He's unaccustomed to moving within the limitations of a living form."

"But…"

"But beyond that, the aggression and level of agitation we're seeing indicates that his bloodthirster is particularly strong-willed and violent. Nate's spirit is all that his bloodthirster isn't, but now that he's within a physical form, those elements of himself are rushing back to him."

"Imagine living a hundred years without a single violent experience," Margot continued as her brother began to mutter words Elis couldn't make out in Sybille's ear. "And then all of a sudden, you're dropped into a war zone. If he hadn't nearly burned my daughter to death, I would pity him."

One hundred years of peace was something Elis could never imagine. He'd been living that span of time in the mental war zone this guy had only been introduced to twenty minutes ago. Nate should be grateful for what Sybille was doing for him.

"How long is this going to take?"

"The possession lasts until the bloodthirster is killed. At that point Nathanial will be freed. He will leave Sybille's body, leave the Now World. And when that happens, he will be fully and truly dead, just as he wishes. Either that will happen, or…"

Elis waited but she seemed unable to finish her thought. "What happens if your field agent doesn't kill the bloodthirster? What then?"

Margot looked at her daughter's blanketed form, carefree persona crumbling entirely. "Then? Then we pray."

CHAPTER TWELVE

THE HARDEST PART WAS KEEPING HIS MOUTH SHUT. FIGURATIVELY AND literally. Cravers drooled more than a Saint Bernard. Even though the only other person in the room was going to be dead soon, Devin still resisted the idea of salivating all over the place. Drool was hardly his biggest problem; Crave made him want to share every thought in his head. Loose lips sank slayers. He couldn't afford to start talking about his past, neither the distant one that involved the Low, nor his recent past under the Esmond's employ.

His slipup with the phone had already given Atkins a glimpse of Sybille. That fact was unsettling enough to keep Devin semi-present. Well, that and the Strike he'd injected before entering Hocus. That serum couldn't fully counter the effects of Crave, but it went a long way to shorten their duration, and it would help him deal with the Blood King, who wasn't expecting Devin to be a walking caldron of witchy drugs.

Taking the glass tube back from him, Atkins wiped the spoon on a rag and returned the paraphernalia to his box. He placed a long strip of cotton gauze next to Devin...*for later.* "Feeling good, are we?"

Devin nodded slowly. It was hard to stay too concerned. The room had a soft glow to it now, like the Sleeping Beauty nightlight his sister kept by her bedside as a kid. You'd expect something uglier from a monster like the Blood King, but there it was.

"Your office is pretty, like a princess's room."

Atkins chuckled. "You're officially wasted. This place is a dump. Not a princess in sight, except for you, Your Highness."

Then they were both laughing, Devin continuing semi-hysterically until his eyes watered, until his lungs ached and his stomach grew taught. He was long overdue for a good laugh. After everything that had happened, he was entitled to this bit of borrowed joy. He shouldn't have to experience the fear his sister had in the Low all those years ago. Or the fear he himself had felt when he'd come searching for her…

There was no reason for him to be anything but happily numb as Atkin's dagger-like teeth pierced the vein in his wrist so he could drink his fill of Devin's Crave-enriched blood.

By the time he stopped laughing, Atkins was already slumped against him. Devin pushed him off, watching as the thirster collapsed onto the couch. He peeled back the Blood King's eyelids; glossed-over black irises peered blindly out at him. They reminded Devin of an alien. Shivering, he closed the lids again.

"And so it goes, Blood King." A mighty tree of a beast, taken down by less than a pint of tainted blood.

Devin picked up the gauze the Blood King had supplied for him and wrapped it around his wrist to stanch the flow of blood. The thing about Strike was that it didn't just mitigate Crave's effects. It mixed with Crave and created a substance that was harmless to humans. But to Bloodthirsters? Not so much. Strike's existence was only known to a small group of people. This group included Devin and its creator, Peter Esmond. Its lethal properties were a well-guarded secret for the obvious reason that if bloodthirsters had no clue it existed, they had no reason to fear it.

He felt Atkin's neck for a pulse, waiting a full minute to make sure there wasn't a single beat.

Was this kill too easy? This question popped into Devin's mind but departed just as quickly. Simply because the method of a kill was easy didn't mean it was the wrong course of action to take. If Strike helped him finish this job, then so be it.

Knowing Sybille would be too far into the possession to use her phone, he sent Peter a one-word text:

Done.

Struggling into his jacket, he stood on wobbly legs and made his way to the back door. It took a good bit of shoving to work it open. As it gave way, a high-pitched squeal pierced the night.

"Shit!" Of course the Blood King would have armed this princess palace dump of his. Drugs, money, secrets—all reasons for Atkins to keep the place secured. If Devin wasn't half-baked, he'd have thought things through before triggering a brain-imploding alarm. He staggered out the door. Too late for regrets.

Devin circled the building. Screams and the pounding of boots merged with the blaring alarm. Someone shouted, angry words he was guessing were aimed at him. He took off running in what he hoped was a relatively straight line towards his vehicle, hands fumbling for the keys in his pocket. Just as he reached his truck, someone came up behind him and slammed him against it. His jaw ignited as it scraped against metal, the force of the impact sending his keys flying. While his attacker was busy banging his head into the truck for a second and then a third time, Devin managed to tighten his fingers around the wooden stake he kept wedged between a spare tire and a toolbox in the truck's bed.

Perhaps the Low yielded miracles after all.

Had his pursuer seen him grab it? Hard to tell. It was dark and Devin was quick. Maybe not quick enough. Before he could do anything to free himself, the man had Devin pinned to the truck, his staking hand—thankfully not the one currently wrapped like a mummy with two puncture wounds in his vein—trapped between himself and its door.

His assailant pressed into him harder. "What did you do to him?"

Devin worked his jaw, trying to determine if he'd be able to use it to speak. This thirster was getting desperate. Better see what he could do.

"All I did was give him what he wanted—Craved-up human blood. But then he passed out and I didn't know what was wrong with him. I thought I'd get blamed, so I panicked and ran." His chin was on fire now; it burned even with the Crave still working its way through his system. Still he kept talking. "I'm sorry, okay? But it wasn't me, it was just a coincidence that I was there. I wanted to work with him, I swear to you! Why would I kill someone I thought I could make money from?"

"Maybe he turned you down. Maybe you got mad." Even as he was arguing his point, Devin could feel the man wavering. He wanted to know what had happened to his boss and now he wasn't totally sure Devin was the one to blame. Devin was good at planting seeds of doubt.

The thirster eased up, just enough for Devin to twist to the side. He swung and Devin ducked, using the attacker's momentum against him by pressing his free hand into the back of his elbow. The man yelped in pain and tried to hit Devin with his other hand. Moving the thirster's arm up to block this attack, Devin saw his opening. Stake at the ready, he plunged it into the beast's heart. He sputtered, staring at Devin with eyes cycling through a range of emotions—shock, bitterness and finally, relief, before falling lifeless to the ground.

No one else had followed the man from the bar, but the commotion building within Hocus was sure to explode outward into the parking lot at any moment. Devin had to get out of there before anyone else came for him. Feeling for his keys in the darkness, it took a few long seconds to find where they'd become wedged in the gap between the hood and the windshield. Thanks to Peter's serum, the effects of the Crave were rapidly wearing off, enough so that he was confident he could drive without ramming himself into a tree. He scrambled into his truck. Vaguely wondering whether it was the blood loss or Strike's side effects or the blows to his head causing the waves of nausea rolling through him, he held his bleeding wrist above his heart as he sped away through the dark and endless forest.

He continued until he had cleared the Low. Even when he was well beyond it, he refused to stop to rest. Five hours later, eyes barely opened, gauze bloodied, jaw still pounding, whole body throbbing, Devin pulled up in front of Sybille's house.

Only when he saw her would this night be over.

This was turning out to be one hell of a long night.

Nate had proven himself an obnoxious houseguest, straining Sybille's body until she was sure she would be joining his spirit in the Beyond. If she did survive, it seemed he was hell-bent on leaving the place totally trashed. Her back was already blistered, the ends of her hair singed. And she was reasonably sure he'd come close to dislocating one of her shoulders in his maddening attempts to display his displeasure at what was happening to him.

All she could do was hope Devin succeeded in his mission soon. Then she'd be able to send everyone away, including Elis. When that happened, she planned on sleeping for a solid day. The thought of this made Sybille pine for complete unconsciousness. She could have it, too. It would be so easy to let go, to let the night pass without her being present to what happened during it. She wouldn't let herself do that, though. That sort of release came with its own set of dangers. It was enough that she was letting the disincarnate spirit of a monster poke around in her body. She couldn't just check out while it did what it was going to do. She had to play witness to it, as terrible as the experience may be.

Nate, sweet and gentle Nate, was more wrathful than she would have imagined possible. His bloodthirster must be one son of a bitch. Nate struck out at her family whenever they tried to comfort him and, point in his favor, he pummeled Celebrimbor right in his snout when the hooded twit was stupid enough to get in his face.

"No!" His nose became a blood faucet when the punch landed. "I was just trying to see into your eyes to find out if Sybille… I mean… I doth desired to ascertain whether thy fair Lady Sybille was still to be found. Why'd thou… Dammit, why'd you have to do this, you *freak*?" Voice set to screech-mode, he dabbed the blood away with the sleeve of his robe. Sybille had never seen Bore, or any of the Patrons for that matter, break character before. If she'd had the ability to control her own lungs and mouth at that moment, she would have laughed.

Elis glowered at them from the corner of the dining room. "Of course, she's still there." He sounded to Sybille like he was trying to convince himself. "Where would she go?"

By that point, Margot and Peter had conceded that the spirit was going to do as much outward destruction as he was doing inward damage. Nate pounded the floor, the table, he left fist-sized dents in the dining room walls, and of course, the tablecloth was completely unsalvageable. Her mother would not be pleased about that.

"You have a lot of pent-up rage, don't you?" Keeping his distance, Peter examined the line of salt he'd placed in the archway leading to the living room, put there so Nate would confine his damage to one room.

"I hate you!" He threw a wine glass at Peter, who ducked to the side. The glass bounced off the couch and crashed onto the floor.

Margot gasped. "That was my mother's!"

Elis snorted. "Kind of a bad idea to have it out during a spirit possession, don't you think?"

She shrugged. "If it's the price I must pay in order to be able to enjoy a few glasses of wine through this ordeal, then no, it's not a bad idea. I suppose we could start drinking out of jelly jars, though, like the kids do nowadays."

Elis reached down to pick up a large sliver of broken glass, swearing when his hand went through it. "Why is it that I'm walking on the floor like I can really feel it, but I go through everything else like it's not there? Did you ever wonder about that with ghosts?"

"You only think you feel the floor, dear." Margot continued to stare at her ruined glassware. "It's all in your head, really. You *could* learn to influence the material world, moving things the way poltergeists do. It takes a great deal of practice, but it's—"

"Why are you talking about this? None of it matters! I need you to do what *I want*! I need…" Nate's words faded. Sybille shook in the tiny corner of her brain as his panic grew exponentially. "Something is happening."

About time. Finally, the bloodthirster was being dealt with. His death would bring on the possession's grand finale, then Nate would be free of the world, and Sybille would be free of him.

Peter guided Bore, now holding a damp towel to his face, towards the table again. "I just got a text from Devin. This is it."

It was indeed. Clearly, Nate didn't know how to process what was happening. Not surprising. Spirits, for all their desire to be freed of the Now World, were often horrified when that moment came. It meant letting go to the last vestiges of their earthly existence. What had seemed so desirable in theory, became something to rage against, futile though it may be.

This was the money shot of the spirit possession, the final act that made Bore wet and left his wallet wide open. As Nate rebelled against his own deepest desire, Sybille's body rose off the floor until she was levitating just above the table, her arms ridged at her sides, the glow of a thousand lanterns shining from deep within her belly. Groans and growls and obscenities spewed from her mouth. She couldn't stop them, couldn't stop any of it.

"My god, she looks…" Elis' ghostly hands waved through her floating legs. "She looks like she swallowed the sun."

The Patron, Celebrimbor, knelt next to the table, hands folded reverentially, head lifted towards Sybille as though he was venerating a long-forgotten deity. "May thy spirit pass beyond this world. May thy spirit pass beyond this world." His chant echoed through the room as he repeated the phrase.

At Elis' confused expression, Margot leaned towards him and whispered, "I told him someone needed to chant that in order for the spirit to be released."

"Is it true?"

"Truth is subjective." She shrugged. "It makes him feel needed, which makes him feel happy, and a happy Patron is a generous Patron."

Sybille's floating body continued to light up the room. Even though his eyes weren't physically there in the Esmond's house, Elis still had to shield them from the sight of her. She was newly fallen snow on a sunny winter morning.

Her body began to rotate, slowly at first, then faster, until it was spinning like a top. Light shot out of her, and all the while, Nate screamed. The humans in the room, even awestruck hierophant-groupie Celebrimbor, moved away, clinging to the wall to keep themselves out of the path of the possessed woman whirling at the room's center.

Elis gaped at the scene in horror. Sybille was like the center of an out-of-control Ferris wheel, spinning so fast now that she'd become a blur of hands and feet, her red dress like an origami windmill set ablaze.

With a wail and a shudder, the light spun its way from Sybille's center up into her chest, then her throat before being expelled out of her mouth into the room, where it bounced off the walls, everyone ducking to keep out of its way. Finally, it twisted and twirled like a column of DNA, spiraling up through the ceiling. A crackle like distant thunder shook the walls and then it was gone.

The room dimmed.

Sybille's body slowed, tottered, and fell. Peter managed to catch her head before it crashed against a metal platter, one of the few dinner trimmings still left on the table.

"Is she okay?" Elis glided over to her. Already, her skin had regained some of its former color, but her cheeks were still sunken and even in unconsciousness, her expression remained pained.

"No." Margot stroked her daughter's forehead. Sybille didn't respond. "She never is after a possession and this one was particularly harsh. She just needs time. She'll be…" Margot froze, her gaze turning from shock to sorrow as she focused on something beyond Elis.

Elis turned, seeing for himself what Margot was so appalled by.

It couldn't be.

Nate stood a foot away from them. Ignoring their shocked expressions, he peered at Sybille as she lay motionless on the table.

"What happened to Sybille? And where'd the tablecloth go?"

CHAPTER THIRTEEN

Margot's expression when she opened the door was enough to make Devin's breath catch. Nate's spirit must have put up quite a fight.

"Where is she?" He pushed past her and made his way into the living room. Sybille lay face down on the couch, her arms wrapped around a pillow. Peter crouched over her exposed back, applying a gooey salve to it.

He sat on the floor in front of her. "Is she burned?"

Sybille opened her eyes. "Still in the Now World, Devin. You can talk directly to me. Also, you've got a pretty good view of my back. So, kind of a dumb question."

At least she hadn't lost her snide sense of humor. He grasped her hand, warm and soft. She squeezed his fingers, then pulled back.

"What happened, Sybille?"

A short gurgling laugh ensued. "Shouldn't I be asking *you* that?"

"What do you mean? I went to the Low, found the target. Took him out."

"I think there's a tad more to the story. You look like hell, by the way."

Devin bit his lip, weighing his next words carefully. He glanced up at Peter, who refused to make eye contact. He'd be no help. Peter kept some of his riskier chemical endeavors under wraps. He didn't want his family to know that he was Strike's inventor. Margot had always found her brother's interest in bloodthirster drugs unsettling, so he had hidden Strike's origins from her and subsequently from Sybille as well.

Devin was on his own trying to explain what had happened, but he preferred not to say exactly how he'd killed Atkins. Taking Crave wasn't something she'd approve of. Besides, if she thought he was an addict, there was a good chance she'd decide not to keep him on her payroll.

"It wasn't the easiest assignment you've ever handed me, but what does it matter? Nathanial Atkins is dead."

Peter snorted. "Nathanial Atkins is sitting right over there, staring at what's left of my grandmother's lace tablecloth." He pointed towards the dining room.

Devin shook his head. "Uh-uh. That's not possible." He stood and wandered towards the empty chairs situated by the table. The tablecloth lay on its scratched surface in a charred bundle. "I killed him. I saw him die. I checked his eyes, his pulse. I'm certain of it."

Margot placed a hand on his shoulder and studied the wound on his jaw. "Of course, dear. And you must have seen him turn to ash?"

He shrugged off her touch and rounded back to the couch. "No, I... I had to make a run for it. But I know he was dead. *He was dead*, Sybille. I swear to you!"

Sybille struggled to prop herself up, hugging a towel to her chest. "I believe you. I saw his spirit leave; we all did. But he came back, Devin. Somehow, he managed to, well...to not stay dead."

Devin ran his fingers through his hair. "How is that possible?"

"I don't know, but I know someone who might."

"That Elis guy, right?" Weird freak of nature. Still, he might know how this other weird freak of nature may have come about. "Is he still here too?"

Peter scooped up his healing supplies and deposited them into a leather satchel. "Elis' spirit can appear to us only when his body is asleep. He's otherwise tied to his bloodthirster. Claims to be part of him, in fact. 'Rejoined' is the word he used." The two men exchanged their first glance of the morning and then Peter headed for the staircase. "When Sybille's done with you, Devin, come upstairs and let me assess your wounds."

"Devin." Sybille braced her head against the back of the couch and took slow deep breaths. "I need to ask you for a favor. Are you up for it?"

What he was up for was a hot shower, the antibiotics he was hoping

Peter had stashed in that medicine bag of his, and bed, not whatever she had planned. "Of course. What is it?"

"I have an appointment with a certain supernatural hypnotist. It looks as though I'm not going to be able to fill it, so..."

Devin snorted. He shifted his weight and began tapping his foot against the Esmond's hardwood floor. The last thing he needed after the night he'd had was to deal with a bloodthirster he wasn't allowed to kill. Anything but that. "No. No way."

"Don't be difficult. We need his help. Besides, he can rid you of that nervous tic of yours."

Devin stopped tapping. "I don't know what you mean."

She handed him a slip of paper with Elis' business address on it. "If you tell him Sybille sent you, maybe he'll give you a discount."

Elis woke.

Bits and pieces of his dream life worked their way to the surface. It wasn't wishful thinking; he remembered. Perhaps it was somewhat of a jumble right now, but they were memories—*his* memories. Candles burning lace. Unearthly screams. Something that was supposed to happen not happening. Devastation followed by hollow acceptance.

Elis didn't want to spend the day conjuring away his client's addictions. He was sick of these humans with their petty issues and their unrelenting neediness. His one solace was that Sybille might show up, though why that thought should bring him any peace, he couldn't really say.

Or maybe he could.

It had been two years since his soul was rejoined, two years since he finally admitted that Juliana could never be his again, two years since he began searching for someone capable of taking her place.

Isn't that how he perceived Sybille, as infuriating as she may be? Juliana had been maddening sometimes as well. But he loved her just the same. And now this woman, this woman who knew what he was and wasn't afraid of him, she had captured his attention. If his mostly unremembered dreams were about anyone, they were about her. As for his jumble of memories, she was at the heart of every one of them.

Elis had an early morning appointment, a woman struggling with an addiction to opioids. After sending her on her way, he had a block of time free. This was when Sybille showed up yesterday. She said she'd come back today. He had little choice but to take her at her word. He waited, tapping his pen against the desk, checking his phone even though she'd never once called or texted him. He began to pace, an old nervous habit he should probably have hypnotized away as soon as he'd gained the ability. He gave his watch more than a few apprehensive glances.

When the doorbell finally chimed, he nearly jumped out of his skin. Half an hour before his next scheduled appointment. *It must be her.*

But it wasn't. A man leaned against the railing of his front stoop, trying to look like he was being casual about it. Sandy blond hair trimmed close and day-old stubble covering a long, angry welt—Elis had a feeling he should know who this guy was. His fingers tingled. *He smelled like her,* like Sybille. Not just her, though. The acrid scent of bloodthirster saliva wafted towards him. Someone had been feeding off of him recently. What the hell was his connection to Sybille?

The man kicked off the railing and stepped forward, mouth open, about to tell him what he already knew.

"Get inside," Elis growled, opening the door wide.

Once the man was in, he closed the door and rounded on him, pushing him back against the wall. The man was injured, not just his jaw, but the side of his head as well and a soiled bandage peeked out from the cuff of his shirtsleeve. He could guess what sort of injury that was covering up. Whatever happened with him and the bloodthirster who drank from him, there had been a struggle. He pressed his arm under the man's chin. "Have you done something to Sybille?"

Holding his hands up, the man didn't resist Elis. "I would never do anything to her. Can you ease up a bit? My jaw's already been busted once today."

Elis pressed harder. The man swore. "I'm here because Sybille sent me. She says she needs you and unfortunately, I have to agree it's a possibility she does. So, *let go!*"

Elis dropped his arm, but he kept his opposite hand firmly on the man's chest. "Did something happen last night? She gave me this tea for my memory and I—"

"She did what? She's been here already?"

Elis gave him the cockiest smile he could muster. "We had a long conversation. Right here on my desk."

The man swore again. "Whatever. It doesn't matter right now. We need your help."

"Why would I help you?"

"You wouldn't, obviously. But you'll help *her*, won't you?"

Elis stayed silent, but he gave Devin a little more breathing space. Devin made use of it.

"My name is Devin, by the way. Maybe Sybille mentioned me to you. You or that night-roving spirit of yours. I work for the Esmonds."

He nodded. "Of course. You're Sybille's servant."

"Well, I...what?" Devin narrowed his eyes. This guy knew how to get under his skin. If only he could just take a stake to him right now. Sybille would be beyond pissed, though. "I'm Sybille's *employee*. The family's field agent. And you're right, something happened last night. Something bad and...really weird, frankly. Do you seriously not remember anything?"

"Some things. Clearly not enough."

"So, not the part where Sybille called you a jackass and told you she'd rather date a Craver than be with you?"

"A Craver...as in *you*? You're the Craver she supposedly would rather date?" Elis sniffed the air around him. "I can smell it in you, you know. The Crave and something else."

Devin stiffened. He should have known he wouldn't be able to hide Crave or any of his other secrets from this thirster. Dammit. "You've got it all figured out, don't you?"

"Only when it comes to simple-minded humans. I have a feeling Sybille wouldn't like knowing her employee indulges in Low drugs."

"I don't *indulge*. I did what I needed to do to take out someone dangerous, which I *did* do. Only now he's back."

"Back as in..."

"As in, returned from the dead."

Elis raised an eyebrow. "How long have you been acquainted with our kind? You do realize that that's what we do. We die and then we return to life. Such as it is."

"Yeah, I'm not an idiot, bloodthirster. I mean, he was already one of your kind. Had been for a century. I killed him, but he didn't stay dead."

Elis rubbed his chin. "The *undead* undead."

"Something like that. Look, are you going to help us or not? Sybille says we can use you, and that may be true, but after dealing with you for the past ten minutes, I'm prepared to muddle our way through without your help."

He headed for the door. Sybille had to be wrong about this guy. True, he hadn't tried to mesmerize him to get answers even though he'd had plenty of opportunities. But instead he was taking potshots at Devin because of his connection to Sybille. You'd think a man over three centuries old would have matured beyond schoolyard drama by now.

"I'm not sure you are what she thinks you are anyways, Mr. Tanner." He reached the door, only to find Elis blocking it.

Devin spun around, confused. "How did you…" *Shit*. He glanced at his phone to confirm what his gut told him had just happened. He couldn't have been in this office more than ten minutes, but according to his phone, almost a half hour had passed. There could be only one explanation for the loss of time he'd just experienced. "You fucker."

"My apologies. I needed some answers you weren't likely to give without a little persuasion." Elis zipped up his coat. "Don't worry, I promise I didn't make you cluck like a chicken. Shall we go?"

CHAPTER FOURTEEN

SYBILLE SLIPPED INTO HER MOTHER'S SILK BATHROBE. ITS UGLY GREEN AND purple vertical stripes clashed against ill-placed gaudy magenta roses. The robe was as old as Sybille herself and she detested it. Still, the lustrous material cooled her blistered skin. The thought of wearing anything else turned her stomach.

Her mother made her a mushroom and spinach omelet and watched as she ate it along with a glass of orange juice, her expression much more serious than Sybille was accustomed to.

"I'm fine, Mom. You can stop with the puppy-dog face. It doesn't suit you."

Margot held her hand to her chest. "Am I not entitled to be concerned by the fact that my daughter almost died last night? Honestly, Sybille, there's only so much a mother's heart can take."

Please. Her mother's heart was a steel cage swathed in Christmas wrapping and tied with a fancy gold bow. Everyone else might think she was refined and lovely, but Sybille knew what was underneath—not something bad, but something a lot harder than what she appeared to be on the surface. Nothing was going to break those steel bars of hers.

"You know what, Mom, you're right. I've been thinking about myself, but here you are, having to go through such an ordeal only to have me scorn you. Uncle Peter headed off to bed. I can see you're just as exhausted as he was."

She plopped herself on the chair opposite Sybille and let out a long sigh. "Like you wouldn't believe. It's just so hard seeing your own child go through this. You wouldn't know about that..."

"Here we go again," Sybille mumbled and turned her face away so that her mother wouldn't catch the summersaults she was making her eyes do. Twenty-four years old and Margot had already been passive-aggressively insinuating Sybille needed to produce children. No husband or boyfriend in sight, but that hardly mattered.

"Your cousin Zareen, now, she would get it, three times over!"

"I'm sure she would. Mom, as your undeserving daughter, my gift to you is to let you get some rest. Devin will be back with Elis soon and we'll formulate a plan."

"Well, I suppose I could justify a few hours of shut-eye. Let me know what you decide, though, okay pumpkin?"

"God, Mom."

Margot kissed her forehead and headed off to bed. Never once did it occur to her to ask how exhausted her daughter was. Being possessed took a whole lot of energy, as her mother well knew, and last night's possession hadn't exactly been run of the mill. If Sybille thought about it, which she was trying not to do, it was worse than the last five possessions combined. Something was very wrong with Nate's bloodthirster. All she could do now was hope Elis was able to help her figure it out.

Now, with her mother and uncle upstairs, the house was too quiet. Her mind kept wandering to places she didn't want it to go. She almost wished Celebrimbor was still there just so that his annoying presence would provide some welcome distraction. He had left in a huff, partly panicked, partly vexed, according to Peter. "The Patron didn't appreciate how the show ended tonight. He said something like this 'has never happened to any of the other hierophants' and then he stormed off...without paying us."

That last part burned Sybille worse than the flaming tablecloth had. She'd endured all of that for nothing. Nate's spirit was still trapped, his bloodthirster still walked the earth, she'd been burned and had her insides rearranged, and they had zero to show for it. She was going to have to dip into their dwindling savings account just to pay Devin.

Leaning on her side to avoid putting pressure on her wounds, Sybille was calculating in her head her family's next month's worth of expenses when Devin showed up, Elis in tow.

"Good Lord, Sybille." Elis pushed passed Devin and took a seat on the edge of the couch. "Devin filled me in on the parts I can't remember, but he didn't mention you'd become a fashion victim as well. That robe is truly hideous on you."

She fingered the edges of the offending garment. "You sure know how to make a girl feel good, asshole."

Devin cocked his head to the side. "He does have a point. It looks like something MC Hammer's backup dancers would have worn in 1991."

Why they should both choose this moment to taunt her was beyond Sybille. There were more pressing issues at hand.

"Sorry if it's an affront to your refined aesthetics. It happens to be the only piece of clothing that doesn't make me want to scream when it comes into contact with my skin. It's either this or…" She shimmied her way out of the sleeves, ignoring the pain the movement caused as the garment fell around her waist, exposing her naked body from the belly up. "Or I walk around nude."

Both men froze, their eyes decidedly focused south of her face.

Devin swallowed. "Definitely the second option."

Elis quickly changed the subject. "I don't remember much from last night. I don't even remember you getting burned."

Sybille slumped. "My tea didn't work then, I guess."

"No, it did. But my mind was resistant. I remember far more than I have before. I can recall snippets from my other visits with you too. Maybe a few more doses will bring it all back."

She sat upright again and leaned forward. "Maybe. What matters is that you're here now, you and your spirit. Together. Which is a fact I'm still trying to wrap my head around."

"Impossible things only stay impossible if they never happen. It happened to me. *I happened.* So here I am, a thirster with a soul." He paused. Opened his mouth, closed it again, then finally spit words out of it. "Are you going to put that robe back on? Not that I…it's just…"

Sybille resisted drumming the tips of her fingers together Mr. Burns-style. How devious it was for her to be enjoying both of their reactions this much.

"We have more important things to attend to other than what I'm wearing or not wearing."

Both men shifted their glances. Finally, Elis spoke again. "Devin keeps saying you need me to help solve your case, but I don't see how. I don't know how Nathanial Atkins managed to come back. I don't know what's different about him from other thirsters. I don't know how to stop Nate there from losing what's left of his sanity." He gestured in Nate's direction. The spirit was now holding the ruined tablecloth, his face betraying a hundred years of sorrow. "Because it's pretty apparent to me that he's on his way to crazy town."

⚒

"Wait, you can see him?" If Devin hadn't been so preoccupied with Sybille's surprise disrobing, he would have had the brain capacity to put towards feeling disgusted. Elis could see spirits, just another advantage this stupid thirster had over him.

For once, Elis didn't seem smug about one-upping him. The corners of his mouth turned downwards. "Seeing spirits isn't exactly a choice I'd make if I were to be given one."

Devin did his best to avoid gawking as Sybille slid back into her robe. "I do need you, Elis. Margot and Peter don't want us to pursue this, but I can't let it rest. This deal with the Blood King…something is very wrong and the way I look at it, we don't really have a choice but to figure out what that something is. What if what happened is related to Crave?"

Elis shook his head. "Crave has been used in the Low for over ten years. When a bloodthirster gets staked, they stay staked. It's never caused this sort of thing before."

"As far as you know it hasn't. I don't know, maybe something's changed."

"I might know something about that." Devin shifted his weight, forcing himself to look Sybille in the eye. Elis studied him, no doubt wondering how much he was about to reveal. *More than you even know, buddy.*

"What do you mean, Devin? Spit it out."

"Well, Atkin's death, I mean his supposed death…it wasn't a normal kill."

She narrowed her eyes. "You mean you didn't stake him? Then how? Decapitation, burning?"

"Poison."

She sat back, then winced and leaned forward again. "You used Strike, didn't you? But that's only supposed to work if…Jesus Christ, you let him feed from you."

Devin braced himself. "It's worse than that. I…"

Elis interrupted him. "He took Crave, just like he used to."

Sybille closed her eyes. "Thank you, Captain Obvious."

That reaction managed to surprise the bloodthirster. "You knew?"

Devin sat forward in his chair, arms on his knees, hands folded together. "Sybille, look, Atkins was one dangerous dude. I did what I had to do to take him out."

"Which should have been to separate him from his security and then stake him."

"It wasn't that simple."

"Really? Are you saying you didn't have the opportunity? Are you sure about that, Devin? God, you're making my head throb. What were you *thinking*? Strike has too many unknowns. I've never even known anyone who's seen it, much less actually used it. Where'd you get it from?"

"That doesn't matter right now." Devin scooted his chair so that he was in front of her. "Look, you don't understand, Sybille. You weren't there!"

"Hey, back off." Elis thrust an arm out against his chest, the force causing his chair to tip backwards. Caught off balance, Devin tilted sideways and then managed to stand. He glared at Elis before taking a step away from him.

Ignoring them, Sybille continued to put the pieces together. "So, when the Blood King drank from you, he was consuming blood laced with both Crave and Strike, and that killed him, or so you assumed. It's not like Strike's been well tested, you know."

"It *did* kill him, I told you that and believe me, it works."

"Whatever." She eased herself off the couch and was standing for less than a second before she began to wobble.

"Careful there." Elis caught her arm, brought her towards him so she wouldn't collapse. Devin bit his tongue to keep from swearing out loud. He should have been faster, should have been the one to have Sybille leaning up against him. Though on second thought, she'd probably stomp on his foot or kick him in the balls if he tried to get near her.

Sybille took a long, steadying breath. "Okay, last question, Devin. Have you ever killed a bloodthirster using this method before? And don't think I won't figure it out if you're lying."

He reached a hand towards her, despite the fear of it getting slapped. She moved to avoid his touch.

"I wouldn't lie to you, Sybille."

"No, but you'd withhold the truth, wouldn't you?"

He put his rejected hand into his pocket. He didn't want to talk about this, but she'd given him no choice. For ten years he'd kept what happened to himself. Not even his parents knew the whole story.

"I've done this before. Only once, a decade ago. And I had a good reason." He stared down at his feet, imaging long blond hair whipping in the wind, a smile that always broke through his callused heart. It had been for *her*.

"Out with it, Devin." He raised his head and Sybille's face softened. He must look pathetic.

"It was my *sister*. Can't you understand? I couldn't stake her. I couldn't do that." He shrank back onto his chair, head down, no longer caring how Sybille would view him for what he was revealing, or what Elis thought about him going from badass slayer to basket case in under two minutes.

His body stilled as he waited for Sybille's response.

"I've been waiting for you to tell me about the demons in your past for a long time, Devin." The steadiness of her voice called him back from the brink. "Now maybe we can get started on fixing this."

CHAPTER FIFTEEN

DEVIN STUDIED A DIME-SIZED STAIN OF BLOOD CRUSTED ONTO THE CUFF OF HIS shirt. He thought he'd have trouble speaking his story out loud. Until now, it had remained a silent tale told to himself in the confines of his mind, but now the dam had broken and the words flowed. His throat ached with the force of them.

"It feels like I've known about bloodthirsters my whole life, but I was grown before I found out they were real."

"Most people never find out." Sybille nodded.

"I wish I hadn't."

"You and me both." She reached her hand out again, this time resting it on top of his knee for a moment before pulling it back to her lap. "How did you find out? What happened to you?"

"It's not what happened to me. It's what happened to Raelyn. My little sister. When she was fifteen, she ran away from home and ended up bloodthirster food."

"Holy shit, that's young. I'm so sorry." She leaned in, trying to establish eye contact. He kept his focus on his blood-stained sleeve.

"After searching for almost a year, a friend of hers told me Raelyn had contacted her. Raelyn had named the place she was living—Low Hollow. I'd never heard of the place and had no idea what I'd be walking into but that didn't stop me from going there immediately. I was fearless in my ignorance.

"From what her friend admitted to me, it was obvious she'd gotten mixed up in something bad. So it wasn't a total shock finding her living in a rusty trailer in the middle of the backwoods, totally strung out on Crave. Of course, I didn't know anything more about Crave than I did the Low at that point. She kept talking about blood. That's what I remember most. And how she'd sniff the air like she was a coked-up hound dog."

Sybille groaned. "Some sick fuck turned her."

"Only I didn't know that. How could I? I was naïve. 'Raelyn,' I said to her, 'come home with me. We'll get you in treatment. There's hope.' Only there was no hope and Raelyn knew it. She was with her kind now, so for her, she was already home.

"That's when she played me, convinced me that yes, she was an addict, and sure, maybe she'd leave with me, but not until I understood."

"Understood what?"

"How she felt on Crave. Being a bloodthirster meant she preferred her Crave mixed into the veins of a human, but that was more information than I had at the time. She wanted me to sample her stash, understand— truly experience what she felt. Then she'd go with me. She promised."

"And so, you did it."

Devin finally looked up from his wrist. "In order to save my sister? Hell yeah, I did. Don't look at me with those judgy eyes of yours."

"You took a highly addictive drug that you knew nothing about."

"If it was Zareen in Raelyn's place, wouldn't you do the same?"

Sybille responded with silence and Devin continued.

"That night, I got blitzed out of my mind and my sister got a Crave blood cocktail. In the morning, she thought I'd wake up ready for more. Brother blood mixed with Crave whenever she wanted."

"That's one fucked-up family dynamic."

"Thing is, I didn't wake up wanting more Crave. I woke up angry. Confused. My sister had pierced my skin with honest to God *fangs* and drank my blood. I pretended to be asleep until she slipped past me and went to take a shower, then I left as quickly as I could. I was still fucked up, but I had to get away from her. I sped down icy roads, my vision blurry as the Crave finally wore off. I couldn't believe what had happened. I'd found my sister, but she was still lost."

"Something tells me that's not the end of the story."

He hesitated for the first time. If he could spare them both this next part, he would. But Sybille deserved to know and now that his burden was half unloaded, he needed to finish the job.

"I couldn't go home until I'd understood what happened to Raelyn. What had happened to *me*. I rented a motel room in a town just east of the Low and then I researched. Blood lust. Blood sucking. Search terms I never thought I'd be using.

"The search results all lead to the same place. My sister was a bloodthirster. She didn't have a disease, she *was the disease*. None of the forums I scoured gave me hope, but there was a man, very active on several of the sites I joined. An expert of sorts. Said he was a scientist and claimed to have formulated a drug that could combat bloodthirsters. I didn't know what that meant exactly, but I messaged him and he got back to me right away. He agreed to meet me the next morning at the café across the street from where I was staying."

"No way! Are you saying you met the guy who invented Strike?"

Devin cringed. *The guy.*

"On the forums, he went by the handle ag47vulpes."

Sybille snorted. "Ag47vulpes. Silver fox. He sounds like a proper nerd."

"In real life, he introduced himself to me as Peter Esmond."

The room fell so silent, Devin imagined he could hear his own eyelids blinking. Sybille slouched back in the couch, composing herself before daring to speak.

"I'm surprised but somehow feel like I shouldn't be. God dammit, Uncle Peter."

"I'm sorry I kept this from you, especially the part about him."

She shook her head. "It's Peter who needs to apologize for involving you with Strike, but I don't have the energy to unpack all of that right now. Finish your story."

Unfortunately, the rest of the story was going to do some of that unpacking for her. "First, Peter examined me for signs of Crave addiction. 'I'm not sure why your withdrawal symptoms aren't far more severe,' he told me. 'One time is usually all it takes.'

"I couldn't rely on that situation to hold. If I took Crave again, I'd probably be hooked. And hell, I *wanted* to do it again. Crave is like a present wrapped up under a tree just waiting to be opened. I wanted it to be Christmas morning every morning for the rest of my life.

"That's when Peter handed me a vial containing a pale-yellow fluid. Strike. It was meant to lessen the duration of Crave's high. And it would decrease my desire to have the drug again.

"'You won't crave Crave.' He promised me that. And then followed up with the fact that he was only pretty sure because it hadn't been tested yet."

"Great, so he made you a lab rat too."

"It was my choice. Blame him for lying and keeping things from you but don't blame him for that. Or for what came next."

She sighed. "That doesn't sound at all ominous."

"According to Peter, Crave and Strike would combine into a lethal cocktail within my bloodstream. He had the rationale all worked out, saying 'remember, there is no salvation for that bloodthirster that inhabits your sister's body. But there is hope for your sister herself. Kill the bloodthirster and your sister's spirit goes free. Kill the bloodthirster and the curse is lifted.'

"I took what Peter offered and I drove back to the Low. Only now, I knew better, like a child able to decipher lines on a page as letters and words and then whole sentences. I eyed everyone with suspicion. How many were bloodthirsters? How many were humans who willingly fed them? It was that day that I fully realized the Low was fucked to holy hell.

"I found Raelyn and told her I couldn't live my normal life knowing she was here without her family. I'd stay. I'd do what she wanted. I offered my wrist. She offered me a spoon.

"Because of Strike, the high was different this time. Less intense, but the colors were still deeper than a Hawaiian sunset. Raelyn's rundown trailer, its stained bed sheet curtains, its walls dotted with mold blooms—I might as well have been living in a watercolor painting.

"My sister was part of my hallucination too. She was a monster hungering for her own brother's blood but she was also a memory. She was a little girl with pigtails, making up pretend games up in our attic."

"Pretend games?"

"We played them together when we were children, and even though I was only remembering that time when we were little kids, it played out as though it was happening in the present.

"'I'm a spy in this scene, Dev.' She always called me Dev. 'I've tracked a double agent to Russia. He thinks he's gotten away with it, but he's so wrong!'

"I laughed. 'Let me guess. I'm that double agent?'

"Then the memory broke apart. I was back in her trailer, my wrist in her hands, her fangs out. 'I'm sorry, Dev. It's who I am. You'll get used to the pain.'"

Sybille breathed out, long and even. "Jesus."

"I was more of a double agent than Raelyn would ever know. It took a few minutes, and then she was gone. I'd killed her. Except, she was already dead. I had to remind myself of that.

"As soon as I'd checked to make sure she was gone, I left. Strike made it easier for me to focus, but the drive out of the Low was still like winding my way through a nightmare. When I got back to the motel, I slept it off. In the morning, I called my parents to say Raelyn was still lost but that I'd reached a dead end.

"It wasn't a lie."

Sybille's gift of foresight was patchy. Likewise, she had the least control over the ability to see into someone's past. She had glimpsed unintentionally into Devin's past many times—*his* memories somehow sucked into *her* consciousness. It was one of the reasons she'd kept her distance from him. Something of life-changing importance had happened to him before they'd met, something that connected him both to the Low and to Crave.

Today's confession from Devin confirmed everything she'd feared. The sister part was new, though. He'd never talked about her, nor could she relate any of his fragmented memories directly to her. She'd assumed Devin was an only child. He'd mentioned that his parents had sold their business a few years back and were now living abroad, but that was all he'd ever said regarding family.

Devin had a heart that would never heal. If her mother's heart was a giftwrapped steel cage, Devin's was an open box, nothing but a flimsy sheet of paper tissue between himself and the world that taunted him.

She fought the urge to question him more about her uncle's

involvement in all of this. What the actual fuck? She was certain Margot hadn't a clue that Peter had helped manufacture Strike. Zareen she was less sure about.

Peter's closet of secrets was a lot deeper and darker than she'd imagined it to be. She would explore this more, but not now. Now, Devin was suffering. He needed to be met with kindness, not a game of twenty questions. She could give him that much—after she'd asked him one last thing.

Devin closed his eyes as he ended his story and allowing Sybille to slide onto the couch next to him. He didn't protest when she draped her arm around his shoulder, stroking his forehead. She waited, her question swirling around in her mind. Finally, he opened his eyes and glanced around the room.

"Where's Elis?"

Sybille did her best to keep her hand gentle upon Devin's head. He leaned into her touch.

"Don't you remember? I sent him to gather some supplies I need for my clairvoyance session."

"Right. I knew that. See, I was just kind of hoping he'd walk in right now." He gave her a half-smile.

She ignored his attempt to lighten the mood. "Devin, I have to ask you something. Please forgive me, but I need to know. When Raelyn died, did you stay until she ashed?"

What a shit friend she was, making him dwell longer within the worst moment of his worst memory. She hoped he understood she was only trying to gather clues so she could understand the Blood King's miraculous resurrection.

"I lit the trailer she was living in on fire and I watched it burn to the ground." He rubbed his eyes and pulled away from Sybille's embrace. "Either way, she's ash now."

CHAPTER SIXTEEN

WHAT THE HELL HAD HE GOTTEN HIMSELF INTO WITH THESE PEOPLE? ELIS HAD done more head shaking today than he had in the last hundred years. Bloodthirster Crave addicts who couldn't die, hierophants who spoke to dead spirits and glimpsed the future, heartbroken clods who got high and let thirsters drink from them. He should be hightailing it straight out of Port Everan. He could make a living in any city anywhere in the world. He didn't need this, didn't need any of them.

Sure, Sybille appealed to him. More than that, she resonated with him in the same way Juliana had. This was new—being able to admit to himself that he wanted her. The crazy world she was part of, her strange and wonderful abilities...all of it should have been a turn off; instead he could barely think of anything else.

Sybille was the one he had been searching for these past two years. He wouldn't find her in another city. She was right here. If she wanted him to go grocery shopping for a bunch of items she claimed would help her see into the future, then he was going to pretend that didn't sound ape-shit crazy and get her whatever the hell was on her list.

This brought him to Food-n-More, where they had her brand of rainforest certified coffee beans but not the organic fair-trade eighty-five percent dark cocoa and chili bar she had specified. It took several more stops to find that. Then, steeling his resolve, he headed for The Psychic Palace, a woo-woo store run by clueless hippies.

Elis hated these sorts of shops. Even though Sybille had assured him that the owner didn't know about bloodthirsters, he was still hyper aware of her gaze as it followed him around the floor past rows of incense and tarot decks. He'd hoped he'd be able to find what he was looking for without her assistance, but Sybille wanted a chakra opening crystal and he had no idea how to identify the specific one.

Finally, he resigned himself to asking the owner, a short, plump woman with long braids, wearing a salmon-colored shift and a necklace made from turquoise beads.

After stumbling over the name of the crystal he needed, he showed her the shopping list Sybille had written out for him.

"Oh, phenacite! Of course. You know, I felt it when you first came in the door—right in my heart center, I felt it. I said to myself 'that man is touched with the spirit. I wonder if he realizes it.'"

"You have no idea… So, about the crystal?"

"I'll show you." She came around from behind the counter and walked him towards the back of the store, a cloud of patchouli-scented air trailing behind her. "I'd love to do a reading for you, if you have the time."

"I don't actually. My friend sent me to get this and she—"

"Say no more. If she's asking for a phenacite then I have a feeling I already know who we're talking about. Strange, though… I sold her one only a month or two ago."

"Maybe it was someone different."

The woman stopped abruptly in front of a table littered with rocks and gems of various colors and sizes. "Could be."

She laid her hands on the crystals, running probing fingers over the surface of each one as though she was petting a favorite cat. Finally, she picked up a clear white crystal about the size of a golf ball and handed it to Elis.

"It will open that third eye of yours right up! Practically jumps out of your hand when you hold it—all those vibrations. Can you feel them?"

Not really. "Sure. How much?"

They walked back to the register, where Elis handed over more than any rock should be worth.

"Do you need a grounding stone? She really should have a grounding stone if she's going to use a phenacite. Black tourmaline would work nicely. I can throw it in for ten percent off."

Not on the list, so not going to pay for it. "I think she already has one of those."

"Okay, well, if you're sure." She closed her register and began fiddling with the red laughing Buddha statues lined up in the case next to it. "I meant what I said about a reading. Do come back. There's much you could learn about yourself."

Elis did his best not to narrow his eyes. He knew a charlatan when he saw one, possibly having some experience in that arena himself. "Maybe. See you."

He left before she could smudge him with sage as some kind of spiritual cleansing ritual. That, after all, had already been tried on him before.

As worn out as she was from the previous night's events, Sybille found it impossible to sleep. Instead she tucked Margot's afghan around Devin's sleeping form, chatted with Nate about early twentieth century logging practices, and then headed up to her bedroom. Instead of lying down, she sat against her headboard, legs crossed, following her breath in and out.

She would need to concentrate to do what she was about to do. It was now or never. If she was going to get even a tiny glimpse of what was to come, she required a stretch of uninterrupted time. Margot, Peter, and Devin would sleep for hours. That left Elis. Elis, the king of distraction. If he remained out of the house on that psychic scavenger hunt she'd sent him on, she might be able to do this.

The human mind contained a jumble of pathways. Some were well-worn routes walked every day. Some were less frequently traveled. The majority were hidden.

Soon Sybille had achieved a trance state that would have made Elis jealous. In that state, hidden roads were unveiled. Paths that reached beyond Sybille's consciousness, beyond the Now World, opened for her. The challenge wasn't in finding a path; it was in choosing which one to walk down. The road to the disincarnate world where disembodied spirits dwelled was one she was familiar with. As odd as it may be, it was a path she herself had built.

What she wanted to do now would take a great deal more deliberation. She let thoughts of the Low come and go. Thoughts of Nathanial Atkins, Crave as a user inhaled it, damaged minds and broken bodies. A land of rambling brooks and deep virgin forests. The Low with its relentless pulsations, constantly wearing away at the minds of its human inhabitants until they decided to take drugs before the craziness hit. Not that the drugs would stop the insanity; it would simply make them care less that it was happening.

She let these thoughts flow, let everything Devin had told her surface. She clung, not to a rock or crystal for guidance, but to the picture of Raelyn Vargas that Devin kept in his wallet. In it, she appeared with a big toothy grin. Young, sweet, innocent. She was everything the Low had taken away from her.

Eyes closed, Sybille held the photo in her cupped hands and she pushed herself along the path she hoped would lead where she needed to go. She pushed Raelyn forward with her, first a fifteen-year-old girl running away from her past, then a few steps down the road. Sixteen-year-old Raelyn taking refuge from that past by obliterating her present. She walked with her as her health deteriorated, as the addiction grew, and she remained by her side when the fragility of her human existence ended so that a new life with a new addiction could begin. Before she knew it, Sybille was there with Devin as he let her feed from him.

The path Sybille walked was on fire, Raelyn's spirit dancing in the flames. Sybille witnessed Raelyn's death through a haze of thick smoke.

And then?

Resurrection.

Perhaps it was her connection to Devin that opened the past up to her in such a clear way. It wasn't normally like that, not at all. Things were usually more jumbled and a lot less detailed. Yet, ten years went by and Sybille was still on the same trajectory. Raelyn had faded—to where, Sybille couldn't say. All she knew was that she hadn't left the Now World the night Devin set her trailer on fire. She was still here, somewhere.

Now it was Nathanial Atkins she saw. She traveled with him down a murky path. From what she could gather, he'd killed the thirster who'd run the Crave ring before him. His own rule was brutal, with more human deaths than had occurred in all the time the thirsters had dominated the Low.

Her mind spun, Atkin's obsessive desire for control and his rotting teeth making her want to break her trance long enough to puke. Never had her glimpses of the past been so focused, so coherent. This wasn't the time to give up. She forced herself to stay on the path long enough until Devin appeared, bearing a heavy dose of guilt along with that Crave-Strike killer combo package of his and again, the death/not-death of a bloodthirster.

That brought her to the present, the most malleable of time. It was being experienced now, now, now. It, in fact, had no time. If she was to see into the future, something that didn't exist, it was the present that would have to be manipulated. The best she could hope for was to see the most likely possibility. It was inadequate, but it was better than nothing, which was pretty much what they were currently working with.

She took the now and she folded it like a shirt. Sleeves smoothed and turned inward, everything bent in half and half again. A neat square of overlapping fabric.

Sybille reached for the strongest overlap and, hoping that it would show her something, she folded herself into it.

Nate was in his customary spot, hunched over the dining room table, when Elis returned from running his bazillion errands. While the spirit mumbled to himself about a beautiful white dress and how sorry he was for bringing someone he called Mary to "that bad place," Devin lay on the couch in the living room, a red and orange granny square blanket spread over him. Neither spirit nor human were present enough to acknowledge Elis' return. He climbed the stairs and ventured down the hallway, shopping bags in hand, surprising himself when he knew Sybille's room was the third door on the right. It appeared he remembered more from his dreamtime spirit travels than he realized.

He found her sitting up in bed, reading another one of those trashy historical romances she loved so much. He tossed several bags onto the bed in front of her. "It wasn't easy, but I got you everything on your list."

Sybille dropped her book and with a gasp started rummaging through what he'd brought. "Even the chocolate bar? Where is it?"

He reached into a red sack and handed it to her. "I had to go to half a dozen places to find this."

"They have them at Organic Market."

Elis went still. "Yeah, I discovered that. After searching for it at five other stores first. You know, you could have told me where I'd be able to find it before I left."

"Oh my god." Ignoring him, she tore open the wrapper and bit into it. "Nommm. It's so good, thank you."

"Don't you have to save that for your, you know, your clairvoyance session?"

She licked her lips and took another bite. "No, I just really like these. They're my favorite."

Elis did his best to keep his jaw from dropping. An old cartoon came to his mind wherein a character was so angry, steam blew out of his ears. "Are you serious? You didn't need this impossible-to-find organic vegan fair-trade Wildlife Federation certified free-ranged chili chocolate for your fortunetelling?"

"I really don't care for the term fortunetelling. There are a lot of negative stereotypes associated with that word."

"Such as doing psychic work in exchange for pay?"

"Well…" She shifted under the covers. Even with a mound of pillows supporting her, Elis was betting her back was still sore.

He sat on the edge of her bed. "You know, you and me, we're not as different as you may think."

"Please. We're completely different."

"Why? We both give people what they want. We both provide comfort for the bereaved. We both put on a show in exchange for money."

Sybille rolled her eyes. "Fine, Elis, we're two peas in a pod."

He smiled. A moment of silence followed, a moment in which Elis became aware that they were alone together in her room, both sitting on her bed, Elis no longer just an ethereal presence.

Ignoring where his thoughts were starting to linger, he dumped out the rest of the contents from their bags. "Let me know when you're ready to get started. I'd love to understand how you utilize these items. Would you like me to lay them out in some sort of ritualistic pattern?"

"The coffee can go in the right-hand cabinet above the dishwasher. Pile the candles and matches on the kitchen table. I'll put them away later. Let's see, that crystal can go in my mom's study. She'll be thrilled to have it—loves all that crystal magic lore. Oh, and the 'fortunetelling—'" She gave the word air quotes with the hand that wasn't still clenched around the remains of the chocolate bar. "I already did that."

"You *what*?"

Wiggling her fingers, she made her voice quiver like the narrator of an old black and white horror flick. "I already *glimpsed into the future.*"

Elis paused a moment, trying to make sure a logical sentence escaped his lips rather than a slew of semi-coherent obscenities. "What was the point in me getting this stuff? It took me all afternoon!"

"The point was that it took you all afternoon. I needed peace and quiet."

"You could have just asked me to leave."

"And you would have left without a fight? Or would you have insisted you could stay without causing any problems?"

She had him there. "But didn't you need that crystal to open your third eye?"

Sybille's cheeks dimpled as she grinned. "You've been talking to Larkin at The Psychic Palace, haven't you? Isn't she a sweetheart?"

"Sybille!"

"I already have a phenacite. I bought it from Larkin a while back because her landlord upped her lease. Even though our budget is tight, I can't stand to see that place close. They have the best incense in Port Everan." She flicked a bit of fuzz off her robe and took another bite of chocolate. "Anyways, I never use it. My mother carries at least three different kinds on her at all times but to me, crystals don't do much. I like having them around because they're pretty, but that's about all they are. They're just rocks. Pretty rocks."

"Do you know how much that pretty rock cost me?"

"Think of it as good karma. Larkin is saving up to attend yoga teacher training in Bali next spring!"

Elis sighed. "You really are unbelievable."

"Not the first time I've heard that."

"The word I used was 'impossible,' which you are too, by the way."

Sybille laughed and then a moment of silence filled the room again. Elis' head spun. She had already had her vision, or whatever she wanted to call it. Was she going to tell him about it or keep it to herself?

"So, about that fortunetelling of yours…did you see anything?"

Sybille put down the now-empty candy bar wrapper, her face grown solemn. "I did. I saw our future, clear as day."

He waited for her to continue. "Well?"

She leaned in towards him, eyes wide, voice hushed. She gripped his hand.

"Elis, we're all going to die."

CHAPTER SEVENTEEN

FOR MANY MONTHS, JULIANA HAD THOUGHT ABOUT FINDING HIM. MAYBE SHE would devise a way to punish him or at least ask him why he had run away. As she stewed in her discontent, she remembered fondly the time before he left. There had been something calming and beautiful about the purposefulness of Juliana's existence during the years when she had been searching for Elis' spirit. After so many decades of floating along directionless, having a mission provided her with a solace she hadn't thought was possible in the Now World.

Now she was floating again, floating and wondering what the point of it all was. Elis, both the beast and the soul, had rejected her offering. That left her in the same predicament she'd found herself in since she'd been killed by that priest as a young woman—she was trapped. Her existence was torturous in its tedium. There was no drive and almost no spark remaining, but still she existed. It was like being put in suspended animation without the advantage of unconsciousness.

The only thing she could do to break out of her stasis was to find Elis, and yet she hesitated. She had wanted his bloodthirster dead so badly, but now that bloodthirster was more than just a monster. Was it wrong to kill him if his soul existed alongside his beast? The spirit had been an innocent, like her. She had felt a kinship with him. Juliana deliberated, changing her mind again and again. Two years went by and she was no closer to deciding what to do.

Then the shift occurred.

It came upon her without warning, a cruel certainty spreading through her ethereal body. Juliana was merely a disincarnate spirit, but if she'd occupied a physical form, her gut would have twisted, her heart would have ached.

Something had changed. Something had broken. It wasn't until she'd felt in her metaphorical bones a severing of her bond with Elis that she realized she'd still had a strong attachment to him. She experienced that bond's absence like a death—not the kind of death she'd suffered as a young woman, but the kind that most people knew. Something final. A point of no return.

Elis still walked the world. He drank his microwaved blood, he paced his floors. This she knew, but she also knew that the love he'd maintained for her, carried all these years since she'd plunged a stake into her own heart and even after she'd tried to kill him, was finally, irrevocably...gone.

There must be a reason for this shift, but damned if she knew what it was.

Juliana had her purpose then. She made her decision.

Elis needed to be found. He was guilty of so many wrongs, she had a million reasons to justify what she wanted to do to him, both to the beast and the spirit who had chosen to align with evil. She would locate Elis and discover the reason why he had stopped loving her. When she found out what that reason was, she would make sure it was destroyed along with him.

Humans possessed the ability to help Juliana. This was unfortunate—not that they could help her, but that they were human. The more years that separated Juliana from her humanity, the more she felt a gulf of indifference bordering on loathing for that species. They were weak, succumbing to diseases both of the body and the mind. In a certain regard, it could be said that all spirits were imprisoned as long as the hearts of their physical bodies remained beating. Every soul on earth was trapped, just like she was.

These were her darkest thoughts, the thoughts that arose when Elis' betrayal came to mind. What good were any of them, really? The Juliana of years past would never have thought in these terms. That Juliana, the one searching for Elis' spirit, was a hopeful Juliana, a spirit who still believed everything could be set right. She had loved and admired people. They were still kin to her.

Now, they were only a means to an end. Eventually, they wouldn't even be that, but at present, she still needed them. Laurence wouldn't help her anymore. His experience with Elis had left him frightened and useless. She'd pestered him endlessly, but it did no good. He couldn't be swayed.

"What happened is meant to be," Laurence told her. He poured himself another shot of bourbon and downed it. "We must accept it. His end will come when the Universe wills it. I'll have no part in it. Not anymore."

Juliana had rolled her eyes. Stupid man with his stupid *Universe wills it* crap. What about *her* will? What about what was fair, what was moral?

If she'd been able to, she'd have upended a few tables, taken a knife from his kitchen and bled him until he agreed to help her. She could do none of this. All she could do was float around, screaming and moaning and gliding through him, something he particularly loathed.

In the end, she'd left him to seek out someone with less understanding of the situation. Someone who she could tell her story to and who could receive that story without bias, someone who'd have no reason to think that she wasn't anything but completely right.

Finding that someone wasn't easy. Juliana, despite her determination, was still a spirit, and an old spirit at that. Not to mention that she was a bit of an unusual case, what with her choosing to stick around in the Now World even after her bloodthirster had perished. All she was, really, was thought. Ceaseless consciousness. It would have driven lesser spirits to insanity, but Juliana was no lesser spirit. She was a spirit with renewed determination. She wouldn't give up until this was over.

Few humans possessed the ability to connect with spirits. Those that could often fled from their gift, terrified by it, drowning it in liquor and other mind-altering substances. The rest embraced it. These were the people she was looking for. They practiced their talent by reaching out into the ether, where the spirits who had not passed on dwelt, purposely putting themselves at risk to connect with the disincarnate.

Juliana was even closer to these people than other spirits. She'd been called from the ether for over one hundred years now. She was able exist amongst humans. Only the thinnest of veils separated them from her, and anyone with a capacity to call spirits would be able to see her, no ritual or meditation or magic spells necessary.

If there had been more of these *spiritual savants,* as she liked to think of them, it would have been quite easy to find someone to help her, but they were needles in a haystack. All she could do was float and float and float and hope to run into one of them, the way she had with Laurence.

⚷

The playground was still crowded with children, despite the briskness of the November afternoon. It had been raining for days, but now the storm had passed, making way for brilliant, frigid skies. Or so Juliana imagined them to be. The children were well bundled, except for a few who had escaped their homes in shorts and t-shirts, ill-prepared for the weather. It was amazing to her that so many of these creatures made it to adulthood.

As Juliana passed by, she stopped to stare at the screaming, laughing throng. No playgrounds existed when she was a child, but still she remembered what it had been like to play. She'd found a stick once and used it to sketch patterns in the dirt until her father had caught her and beat her with it for neglecting her chores. The next day, she'd found another stick and drew with it again, only this time, she'd been careful to rub out the images with her feet before her parents noticed.

Amongst the clueless, happy children at the playground was a girl of five or six in a fluffy pink coat and a knitted hat with bunny ears. The girl, chasing a friend in a game of tag, stopped abruptly, her dark eyes set upon Juliana.

Juliana glanced behind her but there wasn't so much as a squirrel that could have caught the girl's attention. She hadn't expected to find one so young, not that it was too surprising. Children could be just as perceptive as adults, if not more so.

Juliana floated over to the girl, who stared at her, unflinching.

"Well now, little girl, I bet you didn't expect to see someone like me here."

The girl shook her head. She wasn't scared, but she was cautious. Rightly so.

"Do you know what I am?"

This time the girl nodded. "You're one of them."

"One of *them*?"

"My mommy tells me not to play with you until I'm older."

"And do you always do what your mommy says?"

She giggled, but then her face hardened. "Are you a bad one?"

"Whatever could make you think that?" Juliana smiled, hoping that her tone and countenance came across as benign woodland fairy rather than demoness of the night. "In fact, I'm here because I'm hoping to find one of the bad ones. He's dangerous, you see, and I want to take him away so that he won't be able to hurt anyone. Would a bad spirit want to help get rid of the bad guys?"

The girl opened her mouth to respond, but another voice spoke instead. "Adelaide!"

A woman with the same glossy black hair and full heart-shaped lips as the little girl came up behind her. "I was wondering where you'd gone and now I see." She spoke in a hushed voice so that no one else could hear her. She turned Adelaide to face her. "What have I told you? Never summon spirits, especially when I'm not around."

"But Mommy, I didn't! She was just here. I didn't call her!"

Adelaide's mother raised an eyebrow at Juliana, who nodded in confirmation. "She tells the truth. I was already here."

"Who called you? Wait, never mind. I can't do this here." She handed her daughter a backpack, pink to match her jacket. "If you need my assistance, follow us back to our house. It's only a few blocks away. I can help you, but there will be a price for that assistance."

Juliana's glow deepened. "Whatever it is, I will gladly pay it."

Devin awoke to panic—panic in the form of a bloodthirster pounding down the stairs, growling out obscenities with every step, eyes wild and, much to Devin's alarm, glowing bright red. Something had set Elis off.

"Sybille had her vision. She says we're going to die—all of us. *All of us* —that includes *me*!"

Scratching his head and yawning, Devin sat up. "Did she say how these deaths were going to occur? Or when?"

"She didn't say anything specific. That's not how her visions work, you know that. She just said it would happen."

"That we'd all die."

"Yes."

"Maybe not right away, but eventually."

Elis bit his lip. "Right."

"The fate that awaits us all, man. Even you, bloodthirster. Someone's going to stake that rotten heart of yours eventually." Devin grimaced as he stared at Elis. "Do me a favor and blink a few times until you've got yourself under control. Save the glowing devil eyes for someone who cares."

Much to Devin's surprise, Elis did as he'd instructed. Soon his eyes returned to their usual grey stormy seas. He was calm again, but not happy. "She's fucking with me."

Devin nodded. He would have found Elis' predicament hilarious had it not been for the fact that he'd been in the same position not that long ago. Sybille had this effect on men, both living and undead. "Don't feel bad, she did the same thing to me when I first started working for her. Had me watching over my shoulder for days, and when I finally asked her if she could please find out what specifically was going to kill me, she looked at me like I was the world's biggest dumbass."

"So, she didn't have a vision that we're all going to die…imminently."

Devin shrugged. "I doubt it."

"You doubt *it*, or you doubt *me*." Sybille made her way downstairs and joined them in the living room. She'd traded her mother's hideous robe for a loose-fitting checkered blouse and black leggings.

Devin's gaze followed her as she stepped closer. "I would never doubt you."

"Give it up, man," Elis muttered under his breath. He turned to Sybille. "Honestly, Sybille, I don't know why I'm still here. First you send me on a wild goose chase, then you incite panic with your fake prophecy."

"You make it sound like I yelled 'fire' in a crowded theater." She gave him a puppy dog face.

"Cut that out. That…that face you're making won't work on me. I'm a vicious bloodthirster!"

She kept it up and threw in a bit of eyelash batting for good measure.

"You're a vicious bloodthirster with a soul. That makes you special, and a special soulful thirster should be able to take a joke."

"I can take a joke. What I can't take is the fact that you're deflecting. Whatever you saw, you don't want to share it, so you decided to divert my attention with one of your games."

"Hmmm, that does sound like something I would do. Only in this case, I didn't do it. I messed with you for the pure pleasure of it. No ulterior motives there. And," she paused long enough for both to lean in towards her, "I can tell you exactly what I saw."

Elis paced the floor. Again.

It had taken several minutes for Sybille to recount the contents of her vision. Nothing she relayed had been very reassuring. "I thought you said you hadn't seen any of our deaths."

Sybille grabbed his hand, forcing him to come to a halt. "This is true. I didn't. I said she was about to kill me. She hadn't actually done it yet. Come, sit down."

He did as she asked, plopping himself next to Devin so that the sliver of satisfaction he got watching the slayer observe Sybille's fingers entwined with his own would counter the terror threatening to undo him. Anxiety was a long-forgotten enemy that had returned with a vengeance along with his soul, and it made him even more anxious that he felt anxious in the first place. What was happening to him?

"Tell me again what you saw in your vision. Leave nothing out."

"Again, really?" Sybille sighed, but she squeezed his hand and nodded. "We were in the Low. All three of us. There were people there—humans—but they were sick, not whole somehow. I don't know, maybe they were on Crave, but whatever it was, there was this hopelessness radiating from them.

"Then suddenly, Devin was gone. Not dead gone, but I think I'd sent him to do something, something we needed done. You were still there, Elis...and then this woman was with us as well. A spirit. An old spirit."

Elis swallowed. *An old spirit.* "And she said something to you?"

"I think so...no, she said something about me, to you."

Elis swallowed. His mouth was dry and he realized he had been so wrapped up in all of this that it had been far too long since he'd eaten. The sweet, woody aroma of cinnamon permeated the air around him. *Why the hell did she have to be so tempting?*

"What did she say?"

"It didn't make any sense, Elis. Like I said, she's an old spirit. All of them are pretty much nuts."

"*I'm* an old spirit."

Sybille shrugged. "She said, 'she will be deserving of this. How can you even bear to smell her?' Whatever the hell that means. Do I smell bad?"

"No!" both men answered in unison.

"See? She's crazy. After that freak out, she raised a knife and aimed it at my heart. That's when the vision ended and you brought me my favorite chocolate bar."

⚔

"So, all of that…" Devin pried himself out of the couch, keeping his back turned to them. "And you got nothing on Nathanial Atkins. Nothing?"

"I'm pretty sure the strung-out humans were his clients, so there's that." She looked down to her lap, finally sliding her hand away from Elis. "But no, nothing more specific. I'm sorry, Devin."

"Yeah, me too."

If they were going to figure out what was going on with the eternally eternal Blood King, they were going to have to go on a fieldtrip to the Low —they didn't need a vision to tell them that. The hard work would have to be done in person. But if she was going to put herself in harm's way, Sybille still needed one thing answered.

"Elis, that spirit spoke to you as though she knew you and that's because she does."

Elis stared straight ahead saying nothing.

"I recognized her. She's the woman from the portrait in your office. Before we go any further, I need to know. Who is she to you?"

Sybille let the question hang in the air. Even with him facing the other direction, she could tell Devin was waiting for the answer as well.

Finally, Elis turned to her, his eyes red again, but now there was no glow to them, only the bloodshot, heavy-lidded dullness of someone whose pent-up misery was about to burst free. "She was my wife for well over two hundred years and my torturer for one hundred more. A couple of years ago, she tried to kill me. I thought I'd escaped her, but now it seems she's been searching for me again and if your vision is correct, then she has a new plan."

Devin turned back towards them, his arms still crossed in front of him. "Which is what, Elis?"

"She wants to torture me again—that's nothing new, but now she's going to do it by killing the only other woman I've built an attachment to."

"Dammit, Elis." Devin's eyes narrowed. "Sybille, I'm not going to let that happen.

Elis grabbed for her hand again. "Neither am I."

The men's attention was on Sybille now. Both had that alpha-dog look, the one that presumed a woman was endangered unless a strong man was there to protect her. For all her mother's faults, she'd nailed that maiden-in-distress fetish dead on. "For fuck's sake both of you, take a step back. You don't seriously believe I haven't come up with a plan, do you?"

CHAPTER EIGHTEEN

Sybille hadn't anticipated having to add 'deal with a bloodthirster's tragic romantic history' to her to-do list, but here she was.

After a century of mourning and two attempts on his life, Elis finally decided he was done with Juliana. Even then, he admitted, it hadn't been a clean break.

"She's responsible for giving me back my soul, Sybille. She made me a bloodthirster and then she made me a bloodthirster with a soul." He'd confessed this to her earlier in the day during the few minutes where Devin had given up chaperoning them in favor of a hot shower. Elis' shoulders stooped as he spoke, his usual bravado shrunken inward. Then he straightened, puffing up his chest, voice clearing. "Not that I'm *not* over her though. Of course, I'm over her. Completely."

She nodded rather than calling him out on this lie; the only one he was deceiving was himself. He may no longer love or long for her, but her influence upon him would be with him until his death. He would never fully escape her.

Perhaps Sybille wouldn't either.

The fear of Juliana killing her was real enough. Sybille had downplayed it for Devin and Elis—she needed them functional and strong to carry out her plan, not wasting their time and skills babysitting her. It wasn't like her visions were destined to happen. There was no such thing as destiny. There were only choices and consequences for those choices. Her vision had been a warning, a call to arms. It didn't have to happen, but it would if they weren't careful.

As for the plan she had so boldly told them she already had, well…it wasn't exactly rock solid. They didn't have to know that though. As long as she acted confident, as long as she led them on this mission hoping for the best, she'd see them all through this. They would simply have to roll with the punches.

This, if anything, was her plan: improvise.

It was hardly comforting to realize the only thing standing between herself and Juliana's vengeance was a façade of confidence and a knack for quick thinking.

Well, if it was all she had, it would have to do.

Juliana floated near Adelaide and her mother, the little girl's hand peeking out of her bright jacket as she grasped onto her mother's coat sleeve. The woman wore an infant strapped to her back. The baby gurgled, bringing its mitted hands together in a silent clasp. She couldn't tell if it was looking at her or simply staring mindlessly at shiny moving objects. Juliana made a face, sticking out her tongue and bulging her eyes. The baby laughed and wiggled its legs.

A whole family of hierophants, then.

She began to think with greed about what sort of power this mother might possess.

They turned onto a tree-lined street with compact two-story homes, modest but well kept. Juliana glowed with delight. There was so much intuitive energy surrounding them. It was exactly what she'd been searching for.

"You are not the only ones of your kind here?"

Adelaide turned to stare at Juliana. The woman stopped walking. "My children and I are certainly not the only humans able to communicate with spirits. Most who claim to have the ability are nothing but frauds and thieves, though. You're lucky to have found us."

An answer, but not an answer. Like her daughter, the woman was being cautious. Juliana took note of that. Humans were as a whole an idiotic, self-destructive lot, but there were exceptions. She wouldn't be able to play this person as though she was nothing more than a townie about to throw away a month's salary playing rigged carnival games.

The woman proceeded to a house nearly at the end of the block. Children's toys littered the otherwise well-tended lawn. They entered, removing scarves and hats and jackets. A man with a neatly trimmed beard and glasses appeared, holding a third child, aged somewhere in between the other two. The child clung to his father, cheeks flushed, eyes glazed.

Adelaide's mom put her hand on the boy's forehead. "How's he doing?"

The man swayed a bit as he held his son. "The same. Lots of coughing. At least the fever isn't any higher."

"Still, maybe we should take him in to urgent care. The tea I made isn't helping."

"I'm going to put him down for a nap. Eleanor too. We'll see how he is when he wakes up."

Juliana floated in front of the man, who looked through her to his wife. "He can't see me, can he?" She waved her hand in front of his face.

The woman scoffed. "Obviously not."

"What?" The man looked momentarily confused. "Oh, is there a spirit with you?"

"She followed us back from the park. I've got to see what I can do for her. Will you take Adelaide up with you too, maybe read a book to her while Simon and Eleanor nap? I'll check in with you in a bit."

He nodded. "Of course. Bye-bye, spirit. Adelaide, tell the spirit, 'bye-bye.'"

Adelaide rolled her eyes. "Daddy, I'm not three!" She turned to Juliana. "Be a good spirit, okay? Evil spirits suck!"

Adelaide took Eleanor from her mother. She carried the baby up the stairs, followed by her father. When they were gone, the woman turned to Juliana. "Sorry about that, but it is true. Evil spirits do suck. I have no reason to assume you mean any harm, but I need to be extremely careful." She led Juliana through the kitchen into a back room that she explained had been the farmhands' quarters back when this was a farm house surrounded by corn fields instead of a sprawling city. "I want to warn you: I have children and a husband to protect. My work can't be allowed to negatively impact them. You understand."

"Of course!" Strangely enough, she did. She never had children and never wanted them, but she did remember Elis as a child. She remembered wanting to protect him, to keep him from harm. It's all she ever wanted for him, actually. If only he had understood that, none of this would have happened. "I would never wish any injury upon your family. I know you can't know that, but it is the truth."

Mostly the truth, at least. She needed this woman and there was no sense doing anything to jeopardize her plans regarding Elis. She would be very careful with this hierophant family, at least until she'd achieved her aim.

"Maybe, maybe not." The room they were in was tiny and dim, heavy drapes obscuring the late afternoon sun. A round metal table was set up in its center, two folding chairs pushed in around it. The woman slid one of them out and sat in it, her gaze never leaving Juliana. She lit a candle in the middle of the table and from its flame ignited a stick of incense. "Why don't you tell me why you're here. I'm almost one hundred percent certain you're the spirit half of a bloodthirster. Your type tends to gravitate towards my family. Do you want me to find and destroy your thirster? I can call someone who will help us—"

"No!" Juliana uttered the word with such vehemence that the woman stopped speaking and stared at Juliana with the same narrowed, suspicious eyes her daughter had back at the park. Juliana calmed herself and then spoke again. "Please don't misunderstand me. I'm grateful for the work you do. Believe me when I say that destroying bloodthirsters is of particular interest to me. But the truth of the matter is, mine has already been found...and destroyed."

The woman finally unfroze herself. She set the burning incense upright in a bowl of dried rice. "What? How is it that you're still here then?"

Juliana proceeded to explain how she'd sacrificed her own freedom to find the spirit of her husband so that that spirit too could be liberated and its beast obliterated. She explained that things had gone wrong, so wrong that now a new creature had been created, one in which thirster and spirit mixed to form a monster unlike any the Now World had seen before.

Juliana expected the woman to scoff. She was fully prepared to be met with disbelief, to have to explain it all several times over again to make herself understood. After all, what she was saying seemed outlandish, even to herself. Instead, though, the woman not only took it in stride, she threw in her own outlandish proclamation.

"No effing way!" She put her hand over her mouth the way humans did when they believed something unbelievable. "I know who you're talking about. It *must* be him!"

"You *know* him?" Juliana did everything she could to hold herself back. She couldn't scare this woman off, not now, but the urge to wail, to scream and shake and lose herself was nearly over powering.

"I don't, but I know someone who does, and if what you're saying is true, she's in danger, isn't she?"

"She? Who is this?"

The woman bit her lip, perhaps realizing she'd revealed too much. "It doesn't matter. The only thing that does is that we stop Elis before he hurts her, or anyone else."

Elis. This woman, this stranger knew his name. It *was* him then. He was close and this human could take her to him. This could all end now. She took a moment to calm herself before she spoke, each word measured as though she were Scrooge weighing coal for the fire.

"You may not realize it, but you're helping free the world of something so dangerous, no one is safe until he is gone. You, your husband, your children… If this woman you spoke to is close to him and also to your family, well…I can't emphasize enough how dangerous this situation has become. We need to fix this…" Time to drive it home. *"For your children's sake."*

She floated towards the door, ready to slide through it. "Take me to my husband. Now."

CHAPTER NINETEEN

THE AIR STILL SMELLED FAINTLY OF PETER'S SAGE SMUDGING RITUAL. DEVIN SAT on the Esmond's couch trying to let the aroma soothe him as he contemplated the shit show he'd somehow become a part of. He couldn't believe he was going back to the Low less than a day after he'd fled the damned place in fear for his life. If it was up to him, he would never return, and he certainly wouldn't contemplate bringing Sybille there. Elis, on the other hand... Devin was perfectly willing to throw that guy to the wolves. The monsters of the Low were Elis' kind of evil, anyways. It would be fitting to make him figure out what was going on. Meanwhile, Devin and Sybille could sit back, drinking a Johnny Walker Red neat (for him) and a triple espresso made from magic rainforest-preserving beans (for her) somewhere well away from the Low's reach. It's not like they'd miss him if he died attempting to solve their little mystery.

Well, Devin wouldn't, at least.

Regrettably, Elis wouldn't be traveling to the Low all by himself. That dream had died for Devin as soon as Sybille declared she would be leading their little expedition into hell that very night. The Low was a dangerous place for her under normal circumstances. Factor in the Blood King, a drug ring, and an environment increasingly hostile to people like her, then top it all off with that craptastic vision of hers—they were just asking for trouble. Sybille was not to be swayed, however.

"How else are we supposed to figure this out, Devin? Do you have a better plan?"

"Wait here for Nathanial Atkins to figure out where we are. At least we'll be on our own turf, he'll be out of his comfort zone, and your vision won't have a chance to come true. I'd call *that* a better plan."

Sybille wasn't having it. "Do you seriously want him to find out where I live? Just down the road from Zareen and her kids, in a neighborhood filled with innocent people? We can't let him have the upper hand like that, home turf or not. We have to go in, Devin. *I* have to go."

"She's right. As much as I'd like to avoid the Low, we need answers that can only be gotten there." Elis had slipped inside the front door in time to hear their conversation. He sauntered over to them, dropping a duffle bag on the coffee table. Inside were a few items he'd gathered from his house in case they needed to remain in the Low for a few days. "You know, I've always stayed away from that place. Newer bloodthirsters aren't my thing, though I do envy them for designing such a perfect environment in which to attract willing donors."

"I'd hardly call them *willing*." Devin zipped up his own pack, stood and slung it over his shoulder. "Would you say a woman given date rape drugs was willing?"

"Of course not!" Elis held his hands up, a look of genuine befuddlement on his face, like he couldn't believe Devin of all people had been able to call him out on his own assholery. His eyes shifted to Sybille and then back to Devin, who did his best to look like he wasn't happy as hell that Elis had unintentionally showed his amoral side. "That was the old Elis talking. The Elis without a soul. Current Elis thinks the Low thirsters are a sick bunch, of course."

"Whatever, man."

"Cut it out, both of you." Sybille buttoned her jacket and pulled a blue knitted alpaca hat down over her ears. "I knew boys like you back in middle school. They kind of sucked. In fact, middle school all around sucked for me. Stop reminding me of it with your senseless bickering."

"Middle school was not a thing that existed when I was young. You realize I'm three hundred and forty-nine years old." Elis picked at a loose thread on his bag.

"Start acting it then." She hesitated. "Or act like you're in your mid-one hundred-twenties, at least. A *mature* mid-one hundred-twenties."

"We've got food for the road," Uncle Peter called from the kitchen. After waking from their all-day naps, both he and her mother had begrudgingly agreed with Sybille's assessment: the three of them—Sybille, Devin and Elis—should head to the family cabin in the Low tonight and start figuring out first thing in the morning what was happening there.

Peter and Margot wandered out of the kitchen now, Margot continuing the feeble protests she'd carried on most of the evening. "Darling, I know it might be necessary for you to go to that dreadful place, but I am worried about you. After the possession, well...and the Low is such an unseemly corner of the world for people like us. I'd feel better if you stayed home." Margot futzed with the collar of Sybille's jacket as though she was a preschooler.

"So, you'll go in my place? You and Uncle Peter?"

Her face fell. "Honey, we would never be able to figure all of this out. We aren't like you. Oh, I wish we were, you know I do, but we simply aren't. I hate the sacrifice you must make for this family, and if I could lift that burden from your shoulders, I would, but the Universe blessed you, Sybie, and with that blessing comes a responsibility which can't be redistributed. You know how sorry I am."

Of course, she was. She always was, but that hardly changed anything. And in this case, Sybille wouldn't have let them go in her place. In a way, her mother was right. No one else was quite as qualified as she was to deal with this situation. Maybe Zareen, but she had the kids to think about. What did Sybille have? She looked at the two men staring each other down and sighed.

She had both more and less than what she wanted.

Her uncle handed her a small cooler filled with iced tea, cheese, and four different kinds of cold cuts. Sybille kissed him on the cheek. "Keep Nate out of trouble while we're gone, okay?"

Poor Nate. He really was sweet, when he wasn't possessing her. It wasn't his fault his bloodthirster was so fucked up. If they didn't find a way to destroy the Blood King, Nate might be staring at lace tablecloths until the sun went supernova.

She took the basket her mother offered her and peeked inside. It was filled with muffins, sandwich breads, and various assorted carbs. "You do remember there's only two of us who can eat all of this, right?" She breathed in the yeasty, gluten-rich goodness. One thing that could be said of Margot and Peter—they'd never let Sybille starve. She latched the basket closed and turned towards the front door.

"Come on boys, let's get going. We've got a long drive ahead of us."

Elis shouldn't be letting the human drive. His vision was better at night, his reflexes quicker. Devin insisted, however, and Sybille backed him up before Elis was able to mesmerize the weakling into giving him the keys. He'd settled into the cramped back seat of Devin's truck where he could stare daggers into the back of the man's head.

In all honesty, Devin wasn't so bad for a human. He was resourceful, he was of moderate intelligence, and Sybille thought highly of him.

Too highly.

That was it, then, the reason Devin annoyed him so much. It burned him that he could be petty enough to become involved in a human love triangle, if that's what this was. How was it that he was thinking of Devin as competition? It was pathetic.

Elis had chosen Sybille. Clearly, she was into him too. But she had known Devin longer than she'd known him and there was a connection between them Elis couldn't just write off. He'd thought about killing and eating Devin when Sybille wasn't looking, but his spirit half had been quite insistent that that was not an appropriate solution to this problem. It was wrong and he knew it. Plus, if Sybille believed any harm had come to Devin at Elis' hand, she'd never consent to what he wanted her to.

On this point, he was insistent: Sybille must give her consent. He wouldn't turn her by force. That's the sort of thing a soulless thirster would do. It's what had been done to Juliana and it's what she had done to him. He wasn't like that; he would never be like that. Never.

Elis was an enlightened bloodthirster. Or as close to one as the world was ever going to see. He wouldn't turn her unless she let him, so it was simply a matter of convincing her. It would take time, of course. He wasn't going to rush it, but it would be at the back of his mind, waiting to whittle its way out to the front of his mind when the time was right.

Heading to a bloodthirster haven to confront an immortal drug kingpin was probably not the right time.

It rained gently the whole way. Sybille and Devin chatted about inconsequential human things while they slowly made their way towards the Low, a damp breeze and the scent of fallen leaves permeating the truck's cab through its cracked windows.

Devin gave them both progress reports as they went along. "About an hour out. Almost there—five miles or so from the Low's border. Here we are, Sybille...Sybille?"

Elis jerked awake at the sound of Devin's panicked voice. He immediately reached for Sybille, shaking her arm.

"What's wrong with her? Dammit, there's no shoulder on this road, I can't pull over!" Devin shot his gaze back and forth between Sybille and the road. "Her eyes are open. Why isn't she responding?"

"I don't know." Elis scooted as close to her seat as he could get and gently turned her face towards him. "Sybille."

He patted her cheeks. She was immune to his hypnotic abilities, but perhaps his voice would still have some effect on her. "Sybille, come back. Wherever you are, we need you here with us. Come back."

As though she'd been drowning, Sybille's body shook and she took in a strained, choking breath. All the time he'd spent with her and this was the first moment he'd ever seen her look truly scared.

"That's it. Breathe, breathe. Easy now, love."

"Is she okay? What's going on? Is she breathing?"

"You can hear her, can't you?" He stroked her hair. "That's it, that's it."

Her eyes closed, then opened, then closed again. "God dammit," she whispered.

"What is it?"

"My mother." She caught Elis' hand and stilled it as he pressed it against her face. "She was right. The Low is no place for our kind."

It had started as soon as they'd crossed into the Low. Most people wouldn't have noticed anything, but Sybille wasn't most people and she noticed everything. It was a pull—that was the best way to describe it. Something or someone was pulling on her as though she was a chunk of space debris being drawn into the planet's orbit. She knew how that would end. The debris would be sucked closer and closer until it burnt up in the atmosphere.

That was how it felt. She was being pulled by something that wanted her, something that *welcomed* her, but it would kill her if she let herself be taken by it. It would use her and then discard her. She would burn and burn as she fell to Earth. Even the ash would dissipate, floating away on the slightest wind until there was nothing left of her to reach the ground.

To Sybille, she'd experienced this horrendous pull and nothing more. To her traveling companions, it had been something much more startling. Elis described it as a trance. It had taken Elis and his charming, ancient thirster voice to bring her back.

"That was scary and fucked up, Sybille," Devin said as they continued towards their destination. "Do not do that again, okay?"

"Yeah, well..." she replied noncommittally. It must have been lack of sleep. In the past thirty hours or so, she'd been possessed by a violent spirit, gotten burned in more ways than one, glimpsed into a potentially deadly future, and had put up with well-meaning but pain in the ass friends and family. And now some unseen force wanted to kidnap her, snatching her consciousness from her body so that it could do who knows what with it.

She was exhausted, and that meant her resistance was down. This was not the right place for her to be off her game. "How far are we from the cabin?"

Devin squinted at the darkened road. "We'll be there in ten, maybe fifteen minutes. Can you hold out that long?"

"I guess I'll have to."

They rode the rest of the way in silence, Elis' hand pressing her shoulder every few seconds to remind her that this place—right here, right now—with these two troublesome, troubled, troubling men was where she needed to stay.

CHAPTER TWENTY

SYBILLE COLLAPSED ONTO A COT NEXT TO THE FIREPLACE, LETTING ELIS DRAPE an old moth-eaten army blanket over her while Devin brought the fire to a roar. The Low's influence barely registered within the cabin's walls, though it had been pressing against her right up until the moment she'd crossed its threshold. The sudden lack of a struggle was as relaxing as a thousand cups of chamomile tea. As soon as she was horizontal, it became impossible to keep her eyes open.

Uncle Peter deserved the credit for the cabin's haven-like feel. During his days as a field agent, he traveled to the Low as often as Devin did now. The only way he could handle its strange pull was by creating a space that would repel it. Lucky for her, his powerful charms hadn't diminished over time.

When Sybille was in her teens, Peter had had enough of the Low's torments. He and Margot found a string of hired help to do their slaying for them. This revolving door of field agents swung around for years until Devin finally came along. Sybille was sure he didn't stay because of the meager amount her family paid him or because it put his life in danger. She refused to think about the real reason he remained. By her side. Whenever she needed him.

Sybille refused to think about anything. Even thoughts of Peter's shadowy past dwindled quickly once the cabin had surrounded her in its magical embrace. Thoughts were overrated. Soon, there was only the scratchy blanket tucked beneath her chin and the slowly growing warmth of the hearth.

Sybille was safe, for now. She stopped forcing her eyes open and let herself rest, thankful that between Peter's spells, Devin's loyalty, and Elis' intuition, she could let go for just a few hours.

What in the blasted hell?

"You have got to be kidding me. Elis, what are you doing here?"

Elis looked around. He could have sworn he was at the Esmond's cabin in the Low last time he checked, but now he was in an alpine valley on the sunny side of a mountain. Birds twittered to each other from nearby trees. Sybille stood before him dressed in a tank top, shorts, and hiking boots, a faded green canvas backpack slung over her shoulders. She carried a walking stick in one hand and a water bottle in the other.

He turned around again trying to make sense of everything. "I don't even know where 'here' is."

Sybille pointed her walking stick at him and tapped him in the shin. "You're in my mind, asshole. You're asleep and your stupid roaming spirit decided it wasn't spending enough time with me during our waking hours, so it came and invaded my dream. *My* dream. Dammit." She turned around and started walking away. "You are going to be in so much trouble with me when I wake up."

"Look, it's not like I did it on purpose." He jogged to catch up with her. "It just happened."

"Nothing just happens with you, Elis. You must have been thinking about me while you were falling asleep." She turned and stared at him. He couldn't help the wave of heat rushing over the surface of his skin.

Sybille scowled. "Ugh, you *were*! There you go again, blushing. That's your tell, you know."

"Is it so awful that I would be thinking about you?"

"No. Yes." She shifted the weight of her pack and sighed. "I don't know, okay? What I do know is that I needed a break—a total break from everything in my waking life. *You* are part of that waking life. Here you are, though."

"Here I am. Just you, me, and the mountain."

"Stop smiling like that. You already know you can't mesmerize me."

"No, but I can charm you in the more traditional sense of the word, can't I?" His smile fell. "I can, can't I?"

She turned and walked away again. "Go have your own dream, Elis. Maybe I'll join you there later. Maybe I won't. Don't wait up."

"A little late for that!" He watched her hike along the trail until it twisted to the left and she was lost among the spindly pines. Sniffing the air, he tried to make out the warm, tingling scent of cinnamon that always accompanied her, but it had faded away just as she had. He *could* run after her. He wanted to, but it was best not to push Sybille Esmond. He knew when to do as he'd been told.

Elis headed away from Sybille, down the mountainside. The trail weaved along a river heavy with water from the mountain's thawing snowcaps. He followed it until it weaved past the shaded woods and instead abutted a wide sandy beach, finally merging with the ocean. Calm blue waters sparkled in a bay under clear skies. He turned around hoping to see Sybille's dark twist of hair bobbing down the path behind him, but the mountain, the pine trees, even the trail itself—all of it was gone. Instead, there were rows of palm trees and a tiki shack with a sign on it that read "help yourself."

"Don't mind if I do."

In the shack, Elis found a tiny fridge and searched its contents for the one thing he wanted, but there was no blood, only cans of pop and a bottle of margarita mix. He took the latter out, found the tequila and triple sec behind the bar and got to mixing. Strange. He'd never had a margarita. He didn't even know he knew how to make one, but there he was doing just that.

The glasses on the counter were already rimmed with salt. Lime wedges sat in a tray off to the side. He poured his concoction, squeezed in some lime and brought the glass to his lips. Sweet and sour flavors danced on his tongue. It had been too long since he'd tasted anything like this.

"I hope you made enough for both of us."

Elis almost dropped his glass. Sybille stood just outside the shack dressed in a blue string bikini, a hat with a floppy brim perched atop her head.

She looked down at herself. "Apparently I'm in *your* dream now. What am I wearing? You couldn't even give me a beach wrap or something?"

"What for?"

No wonder there'd been two glasses prepped on the counter. He poured her a drink and she took it from him.

They strolled out to a couple of beach chairs that hadn't existed five minutes ago. There they sat, listening to the gentle lap of waves gracefully hitting the shore as they sipped their drinks.

"We don't have time for this, you know." She placed her glass in the chair's cup holder.

"We're asleep. We have time for whatever we want."

She looked away. "That's not what I mean."

He slid his hand behind her neck, gently rubbing her shoulder.

"This. This is what I mean." She tensed up but didn't stop his fingers from working over her skin. "You're complicating things for me. My life is already complicated. So is yours. What we're trying to do is complicated. And dangerous."

"We're not in our lives right now. We're outside of them. I'm not asking for anything from you." He was of course. Or he wanted to, but for right now, he wanted nothing more than to be here with her. He refused to think beyond this beach and the sand and what they could do in it.

Slowly, she responded to his touch, leaning towards him, letting him move in front of her so that he was kneeling between her thighs, his face dangerously close to her own. Her breath caught as his lips brushed her neck.

"None of that, thirster."

"No teeth, I promise. Only lips. And tongue."

She slid her hands over the bare skin of his back, tucking them inside the elastic band of his swim trunks, feeling the muscles tighten as he pressed himself against her. "Just because I'm letting this happen here doesn't mean I want it in our waking life. We can't have this. It can't happen."

"You're not awake yet."

Those words were spoke against her lips as his found hers.

"You need to wake up. Wake up!"

How were words still coming out of his mouth when he was kissing her? It made no sense. Stupid dream. "How are you still talking?"

Wait, how had she said that if she was kissing him back?

"Sybille, wake the hell up! We have to go!"

Darkness fell and the beach slid away. Sybille bolted upright in her cot. Her family's dimly lit cabin came into focus. Devin had both hands on her shoulders. "Were you shaking me?" Already missing the feel of warm sand under bare feet, she shivered and wrapped her blanket around herself.

"I had to. You wouldn't wake up."

"I was...I was dreaming. Why are you waking me anyways? It's not even light out yet."

Devin frowned. "I've looked everywhere. I can't find him."

"Find who?" There could be only one person he was talking about, of course. Her stomach tightened. Suddenly, the warm sand and salty ocean breeze weren't the only things she was missing. Sybille's eyes darted around the room. No one else was there besides the two of them.

Elis was gone.

CHAPTER TWENTY-ONE

It was entirely possible that Juliana was being deceived. If so, her new human psychic assistant made an excellent liar. Zareen appeared as disconcerted as Juliana.

"No, no, no, they have to be here. They couldn't have left!"

Juliana floated next to a shaking, cursing Zareen in the alcove of a house a few doors down from where Zareen lived. Aside from a more vibrant color palette and the questionable decorating aesthetic found here, the homes were very similar—both bungalows with a living room leading through a large archway into a dining room, a kitchen visible behind that. A staircase stood off to their right and under it was an open door which appeared to lead to a small den cluttered with boxes, papers and craft items—bolts of fabric, yarn, and a random assortment of discarded, half-finished projects.

A middle-aged man and woman stood in front of Zareen and Juliana, blocking the short hallway leading to the den. They were both spiritists and both were aware of Juliana's presence.

"Dear heart, Sybille doesn't *have* to be here. And she *did* leave. With Devin and Elis." The woman put her arm around Zareen's shoulders and, one eye on Juliana, led her to a chair in the living room. "Why so upset about it?"

The man, wearing an atrocious paisley vest that made Juliana's ghostly eyes sting, sat on the couch near her. "We don't have time to catch you up on all of the details, Zareen, but you know your cousin. She wouldn't have made the decision she made if it wasn't the right thing to do."

Zareen leaned in towards him. "That may be so, Dad, but this spirit knows Elis. She's known him his entire life."

The man, Zareen's father, raised an eyebrow. "His *whole* life?"

Juliana hovered close by. Not wanting Zareen to speak for her, she could no longer stay quiet. Who knew how her story would sound filtered through a human's mouth? "I was married to Elis. We were both bloodthirsters for many years."

She proceeded to tell them the cleaned-up version of her history with Elis. It pained her to talk her way through the most wretched moments of her existence for the second time in an hour, but there was no avoiding it. If she was to find out where Elis had gone, she needed them to believe her.

Unfortunately, neither of them was won over quite as easily as Zareen had been. The woman was particularly suspicious. Juliana gathered that this was Zareen's aunt and the mother of Elis' pathetic crush. The woman's words seemed intended to invoke Juliana's ire. "You are his estranged wife then? You parted *badly*?"

That was the century's most grand understatement. "Yes, we did, but that doesn't negate the truth of what I'm saying. Elis is dangerous. Your daughter is in danger as long as she's with him."

Playing the mother-daughter sympathy card seemed to work, at least to an extent. A flicker of doubt crossed the woman's face. Her brow furrowed in concern.

The man handed Zareen a cup of tea. "We don't expect you to understand all of our family dynamics… Juliana is it? The thing is, out of all of us, Sybille is by far the most powerful. She's capable of handling a lot, and she's also an extremely good judge of character. Perhaps the Elis you knew is gone now. His soul has reattached itself to him, after all. Quite literally, he's been reincarnated. That's bound to change someone."

"But we don't know how it would change a bloodthirster, do we, because it's never happened before." Zareen placed her tea cup on the coffee table. "Sybille told me about Elis before all of this business with Nate started. She said he came to her every night for weeks. Not when she had opened herself to spirits, but afterwards. He invaded her personal space, her *very* personal space—her *mind*. Don't you wonder why?"

No one offered any suggestions, though Juliana could imagine exactly why he would do such a thing. It seemed Zareen could as well.

"Whether he's got his spirit back or not, he's still a thirster—an *old* thirster. You've seen the way he is when he's with her. Doesn't he come off as obsessed? Margot, come on, this is your daughter's life we're talking about!"

"He actually seems quite reserved." Margot fussed with a button on her cardigan. "Besides, I always imagined she and Devin would eventually... you know."

Devin. That name had been mentioned before. Juliana stored it away at the back of her mind. Another potential love interest—a potentially jealous one—could be of use to her at some point.

"Devin? Maybe." Zareen laughed. "Until a sexy thirster on the lookout for a sexy eternal life partner shows up and starts making goo-goo eyes at her."

"All right, enough of this." Zareen's father crossed his arms. He was anything but an intimidating presence—short, mild mannered, with a receding hairline, thick glasses, and terrible fashion sense. Yet when he spoke, everyone listened. "Zareen, your cousin is the most capable person I know, but Margot, that doesn't mean Elis doesn't pose a threat to her. She's already going into a dangerous situation. Devin is good backup, but he's only one person and his position there has already been compromised."

Zareen sat forward in her chair again. "What position? Where? Wait, do you mean... Holy crap." She looked at Juliana. "I know where they are. I can take you there."

Her father stood. "Absolutely not. *Zareen!*"

Already out of her chair, Zareen led Juliana back to the front door. Her father followed her. "You can't go there. You know that."

She paused, her hand on the doorknob. "If it was anyone besides Sybille, I wouldn't do it. But it is Sybille. You can understand that, right? She's like another daughter to you."

He paused and exchanged a look with Zareen's aunt that Juliana couldn't interpret. She had all but forgotten how messy human relationships could be. And they dared to judge *her* interactions with Elis as strange! She had to admit, though, such familial dysfunction provided a certain amount of entertainment value.

Finally, the man nodded. "I'll prepare some salts and herbal blends. Get your things together and then come back here. You can take my car."

A smile spread over Zareen's face. Even Juliana, as detached as she was, could tell that her father's willingness to help both surprised and pleased her.

They headed back to Zareen's house, where she gathered some essentials and aptly lied to her husband about a benign spirit needing her help in a safe, gentile town fifty miles to the East.

She kissed his cheek. "I'll be back in a day. Two at most."

He didn't complain, but instead pressed her to him and gave her a proper sendoff. Juliana could barely watch, thoughts of all those years with Elis threatening to undo the tenuous calm she'd worked so hard to maintain.

"He's used to it, me having to do weird things I can't really explain at the last minute. I don't like lying, but I also don't want him to worry," Zareen whispered to her on their way out so that her husband wouldn't hear her. "It pays our bills. Sort of. We both get to spend a lot of time with our kids. It's never enough, though."

That she understood. Time was something that could be stolen away. All it took was one choice for your entire future to be undone.

"I rest my eyes for five damn minutes!"

"You can stop panicking any time now Devin." Sybille threw on a sweatshirt and twisted her hair into a messy bun at the back of her head. "He's all right, wherever he is. I mean, he's still alive, at least."

"Okay, A: how do you know that; and B: do you really think I care whether he's alive or not? Jesus, Sybille!" Devin waited for her by the front door, nervously twirling his keys around his fingers. "What I care about is that he took off on us. On purpose. For all we know, he's playing on the Blood King's team and he's lured us to the Low so we can become bloodthirster ritual sacrifices."

"That's absurd. Bloodthirsters don't have ritual sacrifices. They only have the regular kind. You're being paranoid."

"Am I? Did you know that Elis mesmerized me without my permission the other day?"

This made her pause. She studied him for any telltale smugness, but if he felt self-righteous, he wasn't showing it. The only emotion he was displaying right now was good old-fashioned anger.

"That's right, Sybille. He used his ancient thirster magic to get into my head and find out about my past so he could leverage that information against me. Does that sound like a guy we should be trusting with our lives?"

"Why didn't you bring this up earlier?"

"Well, I mean…he didn't actually end up using what he'd found out, but that's only because I told everyone everything anyways. He would have though, if it had suited himself."

"Or he gave you the opportunity to tell us things we needed to know about this case instead of spilling it himself."

"Are you defending him? Seriously?"

"I just want you to see that this issue with Elis isn't as black and white as you'd like it to be, Devin. We don't know where he is or why he isn't here. We can't go making assumptions about his guilt."

"Or about his innocence."

"Fine. Or his innocence. We need to find him and then we'll figure out if we should save him or stake him. Agreed?"

"Maybe. Answer my first question."

She rolled her eyes. "What first question?

"How do you know that he's alive? Did you have a vision?"

"In a manner of speaking." She paused. Devin wasn't going to like this. She didn't want him to know that only a few minutes ago, she'd been wrapped up in a hot embrace with the man he so bitterly detested. It would only hurt him and serve to prejudice him against Elis further. Plus, the thought of Devin knowing was unbearably awkward. Best to stay vague. "He was in my dream."

Unfortunately, those five words were enough for Devin to draw his own conclusions. "Oh God, take it back, I want to unhear that."

"Well, sorry, but he was. It wasn't that I dreamed of him, though. His spirit took a field trip into my brain again. I talked to him."

"And during the course of your conversation, did he happen to mention why he isn't still sleeping on that rug in front of the fireplace?"

She shook her head. "No but I don't think he knows that anything has happened to him. He seemed…um…" A shiver ran through her at the thought of Elis' lips upon hers. "He seemed pretty happy."

"I bet he was. Ugh, I think I might be sick." Devin turned his back to her and leaned his forehead against the door.

"I'm just saying, this indicates to me that someone took him. I don't know how, but it's what I feel in my gut happened. He must be unconscious somewhere. We have to find him!"

Devin's shoulders stilled. He took a deep breath. "At least we can agree on that."

All bundled up, Sybille stood, bag in hand, waiting for Devin to open the door. Instead, he stayed put, turned back to her and placed his hands on her shoulders. Some things must be said, and he knew he'd have to be the one to say them.

"You need to be prepared for everything not to turn out the way you want them to with him. He isn't like…" He wanted to say, *"he isn't like me."* Couldn't she see that? "He isn't *human*. Elis thinks like a predator, because that's what he is."

"So are humans." She took one of his hands off her shoulder and held it in her own. Warm, soft skin wrapped around his rough fingers. "If we choose to be. Elis has a choice too. His spirit gives him that choice."

Hands clasped, they stayed there a moment and then a moment longer, both knowing they didn't have time for this, both unwilling to break away. "Thank you, Devin."

"For what?"

"For coming back to the Low with me. For helping me figure all of this out. For helping me now, even though Elis isn't exactly your favorite person."

Here was his opening. It was now or never. "You should know that I'd do any—"

She stilled his words with a finger to his lips. "There will be time for grand declarations later."

Devin had thought he'd have more time with his sister too and look how that had turned out. Disappointment picked away at his already frazzled emotions. He pulled his hand from hers and took a step back from her touch. The chill left by the absence of her skin upon his own set in quickly, the isolation of being next to her and a world away at the same time a familiar discomfort.

Sybille was wrong. The future wasn't guaranteed and *time for that later* was a lie people told themselves to forget the pain of the present. He couldn't seem to muster the energy to argue with her, though. In his mind, he thought of a million ways to say the same simple thing to her. He thought through a million things he'd do to show her he was the one being truthful. He hoped a million times that he would have the right chance to tell her just once, and that for once, she would believe him.

CHAPTER TWENTY-TWO

SHE HAD BEEN STOLEN FROM HIM. ONE MOMENT SYBILLE WAS IN HIS ARMS, HER lips willingly—even eagerly—upon his. The next moment, Elis was kissing salty sea air.

Someone had woken her. It hadn't been him, obviously, since there was no way he would have interrupted what was going on in that dream. It must have been Devin. Had he known what they were doing? Maybe he'd woken her out of jealousy.

No, that wasn't possible. Devin was as psychic as one of Larkin's stupid, expensive rocks.

The question then wasn't why Devin had woken Sybille, it was why neither of them had woken *him*. If Sybille needed to be yanked from their sexy escapade so abruptly, why was he still here on this beach, getting drunk all alone while he stared at the sunset?

And why couldn't he wake himself up?

He was usually pretty good at that. He might not remember it when he did wake up, but his wandering dream-spirit seemed to know when it was time for his physical body to shrug off sleep and start the day.

He tried this time and got nothing. Then again, there was that margarita. Or four of them, rather. Possibly five. He had no idea how long it had been now since Sybille left, or since he'd lost track of his margaritas. The pitcher was bottomless.

It felt good to be drunk, but damned if it wasn't disorientating as well. He was trying to do something, wasn't he? He was trying to wake up.

There was someone who needed him…

Elis stared at his salt-rimmed glass. What had he been doing before this beach, before the mountain and Sybille?

He lifted the glass to his lips and the set it down again. Turning around, he walked the way he had first come, away from the beach, through a stand of swaying palm trees, their shoots heavy with ripening fruit. It didn't take him long to realize his assumption that the dreamscape would change back to Sybille's mountain had been naive. The tropical island stayed a tropical island, the trees stayed palms. There was no mountain, only a slight rise in the land that couldn't even be properly called a hill.

Elis hiked around the perimeter of the island twice before he came to the realization that this was not his dream; it had never been his.

Whoever's dream it was, they weren't about to let him leave.

Sybille tapped the car door with the heel of her boot as Devin took the truck at a snail's pace down their driveway and out onto the unpaved road beyond it. They'd already searched the property by flashlight, turning up little evidence of Elis' whereabouts.

"He must have come outside for something," she hypothesized. "Then he got grabbed and someone dragged him away."

Sybille had been sure this is what happened, but Devin couldn't find any drag marks or any other signs that a struggle had taken place. Besides, they'd have heard a confrontation if there'd been one. There were no scuffs from a body being pulled through the mud, but there were shoeprints leading from the cabin straight down the driveway. They were fresh. He showed them to Sybille who had simply said, "Let's follow them."

Unfortunately, that didn't get them very far. About fifty yards down the drive, they came to an abrupt halt. "I need more light," Devin lamented. "It's like the trail just dead ends right here."

"It will be dawn in another hour or two, but…" She bent over as though she could pick up his scent like a dog. "I don't want to wait. I have a feeling we should search for him using the truck. If we can't find him, we can come back here when it's light out and keep going."

"Maybe. But, Sybille, he could be *right here*. He could have turned into the forest and be hiding somewhere."

"Why would he do that?"

He threw his arms up in annoyance. "Why would he come out here at all?"

Sybille pursed her lips. An idea had occurred to her, but she'd kept it to herself. Devin didn't need one more reminder of why he hated Elis. Still, if it could help find him... "He might have been hungry."

Devin nodded. "So, he came out here to kill an innocent woodland creature?"

"Better than killing one of us."

Five minutes later, they were bouncing along the dirt roads, searching for a monster in the darkness.

The trees were tall, silent sentries on either side of them. The stillness of the predawn reminded Devin of one of those found-footage horror flicks. He and Sybille would drive around the Low searching for answers and no matter how far they drove, they'd never find their way out of the Low. One day, his truck would be located, abandoned in a ditch right next to a forest such as the one they were driving past right now. A video camera, found twenty-feet away, would reveal their descent into madness. Their bodies would never be found.

Shivering in his plaid jacket, Devin's fear was amplified by the night. He strained his eyes trying to see into the black abyss to his side.

"Look out!" Sybille screamed. Devin slammed on the breaks. He swerved to avoid a figure standing in the middle of the road. *A deer? Elis?*

They both breathed hard as the truck ground to a halt. "Did I miss it?"

Sybille yelped again as a hand knocked on the glass of the driver's side door. Devin rolled down the window. Relief shifted quickly to confusion.

"Jesus, Charlie, what the hell are you doing out here? I almost hit you."

The little girl snorted. "Hardly. You were driving slower than an old lady."

"Old ladies hit things they don't mean to all of the time. Now answer my question. Why are you here?"

"I was on my way to see you. I had to tell you."

"Tell me what?"

She twisted her braid around her fingers. "About your friend."

Sybille leaned over towards the girl. "Our friend. You mean Elis?"

"I don't know what his name is, but it was the man who came with you."

What sort of Horror/Disneyesque/Small World nightmare was he living in where Charlie would wander the Low in the wee hours to tell them she knew where their missing "friend" was? "Were you spying on us?"

Charlie narrowed her eyes.

Sybille hit his shoulder. "Just let her talk."

"My daddy was watching for you, waiting to see if you'd come back. Says he saw your friend come out of the house in the middle of the night and that's when he took him. He took your friend."

She hoisted herself through the open window, clambered over Devin's lap and made her way in between the bucket seats to the back of the cab. "We better go see what's going on, cuz one thing is for sure, Devin: The Blood King is set to do some ass whooping today."

This girl was like some sort of Low fae, speaking with an almost mystical assurance about things she should have no clue about. She acted as though leading people on a mission to save someone from a particularly monstrous monster was how she was used to spending her mornings and seemed quite proud of herself for what should have been her very unfortunate involvement in all of this.

Sybille both pitied and admired her. Surely her life must be very difficult here. That was not about to change considering she was aiding the person who had attempted to murder the Low's most dangerous bloodthirster less than two days ago. Yet she was utterly fearless and that bravery had nothing to do with ignorance. She knew what she was getting herself into, perhaps better than she and Devin did. This child had an inner power that Sybille was in awe of. It was impossible not to like her instantly.

"Is this the girl you were talking about, Devin?" He had mentioned a young informant, a child he'd grown to care about, one whose fate he wished to change for the better.

He nodded. "That's her."

"My name's Charlie, not 'girl' or 'her.'"

Devin chuckled. Sybille slid lower into her seat, shame burning her. She had dismissed Charlie so easily when Devin brought her up in the past. No, she'd told him he couldn't take her from the Low. That would be kidnapping. And besides that small technicality, there was the damned Low itself, always having to exert its authority over everything and everyone it claimed as its own. A child born and raised there would be considered one of the Low's. The Low wouldn't give her up without a fight. And if it wished to fight for this child, where would that leave them?

No. It was simply too risky to help the girl. To help *Charlie*.

That's how she'd felt before she'd set foot in the Low, before she'd tasted firsthand its cosmic smack-down of everyone who it felt was an enemy, before she had experienced the pull that even now threatened to send her over the edge. Before she'd met Charlie.

"Charlie, do you like living here?"

Charlie clucked her tongue. "What kind of question is that? Devin, is she stupid? Did you bring a stupid person here to help you?"

"Be nice, Charlie. Even smart people can ask a stupid question."

"Devin!" Sybille slapped his shoulder.

He laughed again. "But seriously, Sybille's about the smartest person I know. We're in good hands with her, kid."

Charlie kicked at the back of Sybille's seat. "I'll believe that when I see it."

A gap in the conversation followed. The truck's inhabitants stared silently out the windows as they drove past rolling countryside, the earliest signs of a foggy dawn just now visible to the east. A blurry gray-pink aura crept over the tops of trees like a watercolor painting with too much water and not enough pigment. Several minutes later, Charlie broke the tension. "Where are you going, Devin?"

"To Hocus."

No response.

Devin wrapped his fingers against the steering wheel. "Isn't that where we should be headed?"

Charlie sighed, loud and long. "It's a good thing you two came across me. We're not going to Hocus, we're going to the Blood King's house. And you missed your turn."

"Well, why didn't you tell me that?" Devin slowed the truck down, backed onto the shoulder and swung around. "I don't have a clue where the Blood King's house is, so you'll have to lead me there, okay kid?"

"As long as you promise never to call me 'kid' again."

"I'll do my best."

"Fine. Take a left up here."

Several more lefts and a right later, they turned down a newly paved driveway. The truck moved quietly down a stretch of curving blacktop. Lining both sides of the road, stately poplars swayed, golden leaves still clinging stubbornly to branches despite the encroaching winter. Beyond them, dark fields, barely discernible in the predawn light, loomed like wide open seas. Soon, a house came into view, as large and ostentatious as the fancy waterfront mansions back in Port Everan.

"Fit for a king." Devin gave a low whistle.

Sybille tucked a strand of loose hair into the bun at the base of her neck. "Are you sure this is where your dad brought Elis?"

"Of course, I'm sure. Devin can tell you, doubting me will get you nowhere."

"Noted." Charlie had spunk, no doubt about it. Sybille cleared her throat. "This place has got to be heavily guarded, but you told us to drive right up. I assume you have a plan? Because it's either that or you're leading us into a trap."

"Sybille, she wouldn't do that."

"I'm not saying she would *intentionally*. I'm just saying, here we are, currently pulling up to the fortified house of an immortal mobster and we," she motioned between the two of them, "don't have a plan. We're relying on a seven-year-old to lead us into the belly of the beast."

"I'm eight. Almost nine."

"See? She's eight. Almost nine."

"I'm very mature for my age."

"Devin, this is crazy. If something goes wrong, Charlie could get hurt. We should turn around, head back a ways, drop her off."

"Just leave her in the middle of the woods? It's cold out!"

"Nathanial knows who I am. I'm safer than either of you, that's for sure. Plus, Devin, you're my supplier. Why would I cut off my candy source on purpose?"

She paused, hand held out. Devin reached into his coat pocket and pulled out a chocolate bar. "You'll get another when the job's done."

"Two more. And the deal is, I sneak you in without you getting killed but after that, you're on your own. I'll still expect the rest of my payment, though, so try to keep from dying."

Devin pulled the truck over, then reached behind him, drawing his arms around Charlie. "You're the best little extortionist ever and the best little spy. You've got a future in the CIA."

Charlie hugged him back. "Please. You know what my future is going to be like if I stay in the Low. It's going to suck."

"Don't say that."

"It's the truth, though isn't it? I've asked and asked you to take me away from here and every time, you hand me an extra candy bar and change the subject. You're no help to me."

"Come on, Charlie, it's not like that!"

Charlie let go of Devin and sat back in her seat again. "I don't have time to hear your excuses. Listen up. This is not a drill. Sybille, I'll talk real slow so you'll be able to understand. Here's what we've gotta do."

After a quick debrief in which Charlie schooled them on what they were about to encounter as though they were kindergarteners, they left Devin's truck and headed through a gate and around to a ground floor entrance at the house's side.

"Last chance to make a run for it." Sybille squeezed the girl's shoulder, but she shrugged her off.

"You think they don't have cameras everywhere? Last chance passed the moment we turned into the driveway. Just follow my lead. Are you smart enough to do that?"

"Yes, boss." She gave the girl a quick solute.

Charlie rolled her eyes. "I don't get why Devin likes you so much. Guess it takes all kinds."

Sybille expected Charlie to knock on the door but instead she twisted the knob and pushed it open. The three entered a dimly lit hallway which opened on the left into a large kitchen. "This is the servants' entrance."

It seemed strange that they'd gotten this far without being met by heavily armed guards with big pointy teeth. Sybille's skin crawled. From the way Devin turned in circles to scan every corner of the room, it seemed he was feeling the same unease.

"Where is everyone, Charlie?" He opened the door of what turned out to be a walk-in pantry and then closed it again. "This doesn't feel right."

"Your definition of what's right has always been a bit skewed in my opinion." The three spun around to encounter the person speaking. A slightly built, striking young blond woman stood blocking the entryway.

"My God." Devin gasped. "Raelyn?"

CHAPTER TWENTY-THREE

IT WAS ALMOST AS THOUGH THE DARK DAYS SPENT WITH RAELYN IN HER MUSTY trailer deep within the Low had never occurred. Here she stood, healthy and vibrant, not at all like the troubled girl he'd encountered ten years ago, but also not like the sister he once loved. This Raelyn was poised, calculating. Haughty. He wanted to hold her close and also to smack the smug right off her bloodthirster face. He could just make out the edge of a fang where her lips parted.

She was alive, though. Or she was...*something*. She existed. It took a moment for him to compose himself enough to speak.

"Raelyn?" Saying her name somehow made the moment real. Perhaps he'd been given a second chance. Perhaps all was not lost. He took a tentative step towards the woman, who stood her ground, her eyes retaining their cold bemusement. The pain from the night he'd burned her trailer to the ground was a fresh ring of heartbreak around him. His grief was laid open to her, and yet she responded with a sneer.

Sybille stared at Devin's long-lost sister. He'd convinced himself he'd killed her ten years ago, but Sybille's vision hinted at a different reality, a reality she'd chosen to secret away until she could confirm it. Now, the truth stood in front of them both and regret flooded her. Devin had bared himself to her and she'd repaid him by letting him keep believing a lie.

"You're…" Devin staggered back a step. "I watched you die."

"Yet here I am. And good thing for your little tour guide." She pointed at Charlie. "But we don't have time for a family reunion." Raelyn turned on her heels. "How's that quote go? 'Follow me if you want to live.' Good advice."

Charlie took Devin's hand and Sybille gently pushed him forward. She didn't like the idea of putting their fate in the hands of Devin's runaway-junkie-thirster sister, but if they were to find Elis, they needed an insider's help. Besides, Charlie seemed to trust her.

They slipped through the empty kitchen and down a long corridor. "I set the cameras to loop so your arrival would go unnoticed, but it won't hold forever, not with that one here." She pointed over her shoulder at Sybille.

Devin gave both the women a nervous glance. "What do you mean?"

Sybille sighed. She'd forgotten she'd been keeping her status as Low bait from him too. "The Low knows I'm different. It's an effort to keep it at bay. Anyone in tune with the Low can sense that push and pull."

"So, every bloodthirster in the Low…"

"Will eventually be able to tell I'm here. No wonder my mother and Peter kept me away."

By now they'd arrived at a large steel door. Raelyn paused, key in hand, and sniffed the air. "She smells like the Christmas cookies I used to make with granny. Like cinnamon."

"Gross, Raelyn."

"Whatever. I'm just saying, there won't be a single thirster who isn't trying to hunt her down and drink her dry by day's end. You need to get her out of here." She twisted an old skeleton key into the lock and pushed on the door with her shoulder. It groaned open into a chasm of darkness.

She felt the side of the wall until locating a switch. A long staircase appeared as a light bulb flickered on. They began their descent.

Sybille couldn't stave off her suspicion. "Why are you helping us? If that's actually what you're doing. Otherwise, why are you leading us to our deaths? Is it because Devin tried to kill you? Because that was a long time ago and I'm sure he feels badly about it. Don't you, Devin?"

Devin glared at the back of his sister's head. The fact that she was alive, here with him, must be quite a shock. Sybille nudged him until he broke free of his stupor. He shook his head. "Every day I wish there'd been some other way."

"I don't." Raelyn paused again. "I understand why you did what you did. Besides, it was easy to forgive you when I realized what I'd become because of what you'd done."

Devin clung to the railing so he wouldn't collapse. Sybille grasped his hand and squeezed. How awful for him to have to relive the night he'd killed / not killed his horrible, beloved sister.

He steadied himself. "What exactly is it that you've become?"

She smiled and turned away from them, resuming her descent. "Invincible."

CHAPTER TWENTY-FOUR

THE BREEZE CARRIED SALTY SEA AIR AND MEMORIES OF THIRST.

Elis was sure now that it had been a monstrous thirst that had led him out of the security of the Esmond's cabin, back before this dream world had come along. He remembered lying there awake after Devin and Sybille had both drifted off, Sybille because she'd needed sleep desperately, and Devin because Elis had grown sick of the human's sullen stares and obvious displeasure at having to be in the same vicinity as Elis. Five seconds of mesmerizing and Devin was snoring away, allowing Elis to focus on the all-consuming thought of Sybille's bare neck, blood coursing under supple flesh.

He hadn't desired anything so ferociously in a long while.

Would it have been so terrible for him to drink from Sybille and turn her? He would have her then, have her for all of time, perhaps. Sure, she wouldn't have a choice in the matter, but he hadn't had one either and it all worked out for him. More or less. She'd be angry at first, but eventually she'd come around.

Getting up, he stretched his long limbs and crept over to the cot where Sybille slept. Moonlight poured in through a nearby window, illuminating her in pale blue. In that light, it seemed death had already touched her.

Elis turned away so he couldn't see the pulse in her neck; he shielded his nose from her mouthwatering aroma. No, he couldn't do this, couldn't steal her human life away from her without her consent.

Stupid soul and its stupid moral code.

He made a dash for it, outside, away from the cabin, down the path and out into the driveway, deciding that he would track a deer or a raccoon or a squirrel. *Anything.* He needed to taste the blood of a creature whose heart was still beating. His own slowly pumping thirster heart skipped in anticipation. Fangs out, he envisioned piercing flesh, imagined the first taste as warm liquid, salty as the sea, slid down his throat.

Midway between the cabin and the road, he sensed it. A large mammal. Elis stopped to sniff the air, to listen for its movements.

That's when that large mammal must have struck him from behind. He remembered someone catching him as he collapsed, and after that there was a mountain and a beach and an island with no way off. There was sleep that both wouldn't come to him and wouldn't cease, and a life that had been taken from him, a life he just realized, for perhaps the first time ever, he would miss bitterly.

Invincible.

There was nothing they could say to that. Both Devin and Sybille knew what Raelyn meant even if neither of them could fully comprehend it. As much as Devin must have wanted to hear everything that had happened to Raelyn over the past ten years and as much as Sybille wanted answers, there was no time for any of that.

Raelyn led them into a small, neatly organized office. Sybille's heart fell. No Elis.

The thirster laughed at her expression. "What, did you think it would be as easy as me leading you to him, you taking him, and that's that?" She reached over a desk and turned the monitor around so they could see what was on it.

Charlie pointed at the grainy image. "There's your friend."

Sure enough, a live feed showed Elis strapped to a gurney while several people stood over him. He appeared to be asleep.

Sybille ran her finger over the screen as though she'd somehow be able to reach him through it. "Where is this? What are they doing to him?"

Raelyn smirked. If this horrible woman hadn't been Devin's sister, Sybille would have punched her in the nose. She might be invincible, she might make Sybille pay for her actions, but still it would be an immensely satisfying act. Instead, Sybille stood in silence while Raelyn explained to her how stupid she and Devin were.

"The Blood King has had his eye on Elis Tanner ever since the rumor of his existence reached the Low. Imagine our delight when we found him right here in our woods. Thank you for bringing him to us, by the way. It made things so much easier."

Sybille cringed. "We didn't bring him to you!"

"Whatever you say." Raelyn waved her off. "What matters is that we find his returned soul to be equal parts repugnant and fascinating. Our scientists are busy seeing what makes him tick. Nathanial believes he could be a candidate for a new strain of Crave—that's if they confirm what we believe, that his spirit has somehow altered his physiology."

"Wait a minute…" Devin braced himself against the desk, bringing his hand up to his mouth. "Are you saying Crave is made from bloodthirster…*blood*?"

"No, not blood, bone marrow."

"That's not any better. God, I think I'm going to be sick."

Sybille gripped the monitor like she might strangle it. "They're planning on testing him and harvesting his marrow. We have to get him out of here. Tell us where he is!"

Raelyn shook her head. "No way. You'll get yourselves killed, which you may be surprised to hear I prefer didn't happen. Lucky for you, I have a sentimental attachment to my traitorous brother's sweet blood. I promise I'll get Elis Tanner out for you, but you have to do something for me in return."

Sybille narrowed her eyes. "I'm not sure you're the sort of person I want to be making deals with."

"You don't have a choice. If you want to leave the Low alive and with your friend, you'll do as I say." For such a petite woman, her words held great strength. Even though she was too young to have any mesmerizing powers, her natural gift of persuasion was impressive.

"You really haven't changed, have you?" Devin sighed. "What do you expect us to do, Raelyn?"

"I expect you to take my daughter with you out of the Low and make sure the Low never tries to reclaim her."

Devin was silent for a long moment. When he spoke, his words came out in a croak. "Your...*daughter*?"

Charlie put her arms around him. "See Uncle Devin? I *can* keep a secret."

Devin let Sybille drive—a sure sign the events of the past hour had rattled him. Sybille was barely holding it together herself, the Low picking at her like a cat kneading its claws into her bare legs. Beyond that maddening sensation, there was a growing awareness, a *stirring*. The thirsters of the Low were awakening to her presence amongst them. The edge of their collective consciousness pressed against her, side by side with the Low's energetic assault.

If she didn't get out of the Low soon, she never would.

The road. She needed to focus on the road. Letting herself get riled up would help nothing. Devin, Elis, Charlie—they all needed her to be her usual level-headed self. She gripped the clutch and thought about everything that had happened, as well as what was yet to come.

Raelyn promised she would deliver Elis to their cabin by midday. "You should be ready to leave as soon as I get him too you. And remember, if you won't take Charlie with you, I won't hand him over. Understand?"

Raelyn said this to her as she ushered them through the house, tracing their way to the servant's entry. "I've already been away from Nathanial for too long. If I don't get back up there soon, he'll send people to find me. She gave her daughter a quick hug. "Remember...midday."

Sybille was startled out of her thoughts and back to the present by a loud sigh coming from the seat next to her.

"How could this have happened? How could she..." Devin's voice trailed off, the same way it had several times since they'd returned to the truck and sped away from Nathanial's house. Sybille could hardly blame him for his dejected state. The disappointment of not being able to confront Nathanial and take Elis back herself still sat in Sybille's mouth like a bitter pill.

She wished she could have comforted Devin, but how? She wasn't the one with any answers. His niece, on the other hand, had more than her fair share.

"Do you know what the Blood King calls my mom, Devin?"

He started in his seat at the sound of Charlie's voice, then shook his head no.

"The night you lit her trailer on fire, Nathanial was driving by. He stopped to watch it burn to the ground. He thought my mother was dead. Who wouldn't? She should have been. She was for a while, I guess, but then she rose from the ashes just like Dumbledore's bird, so he named her after it. Calls her Phoenix."

"So, he knows what happened...what I did."

Sybille completed Devin's thoughts. "He must have figured out mixing Crave with Strike was the key to this invincible state."

"Yeah...only when he tried it out on other thirsters, they just died and stayed dead."

"Little spy, you have been holding out on me."

Charlie shrugged. "It was for your own good. You weren't ready to hear it. Besides, Mom never told the Blood King who you were. She says she isn't capable of love but that's not true. She loves me and there's still a part of her that remembers loving you. She didn't want Nathanial to suspect you were the missing ingredient. Of course, he knows now."

"What the hell are you saying?"

"Oh my God, is Sybille's stupid wearing off on you? You're the reason my mom is still alive and Nathanial is still Blood King. You plus Crave plus Strike equals invincible bloodthirster. I don't know why that is, so don't be dumb and ask me."

"Shit." He banged the back of his head against the seat's headrest a few times. "Shit, shit, shit."

"Um, language? Even Mom tries not to swear around me and she's a blood sucking monster. You're not a very good role model, Uncle Devin."

Sybille was hardly less dumbfounded than he was. Devin, her completely un-mystical, psychically inept friend was the key to immortality? Poor guy, he was really getting a lot of unbelievable information dumped on him today. She patted Devin's knee. "We'll figure this out. Let's get back to the cabin, wait for Raelyn to bring Elis to us and get the hell out of here. Then we can sort through all this craziness. Together. Okay?"

"Are you going to take me with you now that you know I'm your niece?"

"My niece." Devin turned towards her. "That's another story I'd like an explanation for, but Charlie, you've gotta know, I've always wanted to take you out of the Low. It's just...complicated."

"How complicated can it be? You put me in your truck and you *drive away*!" Her little voice rose to a mighty tremor. Sybille had a feeling Charlie spent a lot of time wondering why Devin hadn't saved her from a fate she'd more than hinted at she knew would be dismal.

"What your uncle means, Charlie, is that the Low makes what should have been an obvious and easy decision into one that's much more challenging." Sybille kept her voice low and steady, hoping to calm the girl. "We're not going to abandon you here. We'll take you with us, just as we promised your mother, but you have to be prepared."

"Prepared for what? Are you going to go all evil queen on me when your magic mirror starts telling you you're no longer the fairest in the land?"

Sybille raised an eyebrow. This girl was Devin's niece all right, running around the clock on one part adrenaline and two parts sarcasm. "I traded in my magic mirror for a flat screen. So, I was thinking more along the lines of the Low deciding to put up a fight. We want you with us, but it wants to keep you."

As she drove down one dirt road after another, the Low's tendrils continued to reach out of the earth, twisting their way around her like vines strangling a tree trunk. It was maddening. Her head pounded from the effort to keep herself from giving up, from letting the Low take her and do with her whatever it wanted. Charlie may not be able to feel that, but it didn't mean the hold the Low had on her was any less. It was a mistake to take Charlie with them. But if it meant getting Elis back, she would do it. Besides, they had to at least attempt to save the girl, even if their efforts ended in disaster.

She expected Charlie to be ready with a snarky comeback. Instead, there was nothing but stillness within the truck as the trees lining the roads leading to the cabin streamed by. Finally, her little voice sounded from the back seat. Sybille had to strain to hear her.

"Thank you for trying, at least."

"Hey, hey now...don't cry, little spy." Devin reached his arm back and let her grab onto his hand. "If the Low comes for you, it's going to regret it."

Sybille bit her lip and focused on getting them to the cabin. She couldn't bring herself to tell either of them that it wasn't really about the Low coming for Charlie. The Low ran through the girl, like an incubating disease. She had lived here too long for it not to have infected her. It wasn't a question of the Low finding her, then. It was a matter of whether Charlie was strong enough to fight off that infection before it destroyed her or spread itself to everyone else.

CHAPTER TWENTY-FIVE

THE ISLAND WAS WARM, THE BREEZE PLEASANT. ELIS COULD NOT HAVE BEEN more miserable. He had no concept of how long he'd been trapped in this dream and no clue where Sybille had gone or if she was ever coming back. Something terrible might have happened to her. Maybe she needed his help.

He would never know if he continued to sit here in this horrid paradise. The question that ate away at him the most was one he'd been asking himself before this dream began, ever since Sybille first explained her vision to him: *How was it that Juliana was going to manage to ruin his life yet again?*

Elis sat with his fingers pressed around another margarita-filled glass. No matter how much he took from the little tiki shack, it always seemed to be fully stocked when he returned for more. He hadn't had blood in who knew how long, and he no longer cared. So long as his glass was full of something that would dull his unhappiness, it was fine by him.

The sun set, gently nestling itself into the horizon and then disappearing under its folds altogether. Elis remained in his beach chair, the open expanse of darkness a simple comfort against the claustrophobic thoughts threatening to undo him.

There was no sleep in this place because he was already asleep. He sat there, eyes open, until pink light crept up behind him, sunlight peeking over towering palm trees. Finally, he made his way back to the shack to grab another pitcher.

"You shouldn't drink that." Elis, mid-pour, looked up at the sound of her voice. He couldn't recall how long it had been since he'd seen her or heard her speak. His hope crumbled when he realized it wasn't Sybille. A young woman with hair the color of the sand sat on a bar stool, swinging it partway around as her hands grabbed the edge of the counter.

"Who the hell are you?"

She stopped twisting. "Not one for manners, are you?" She hopped off the stool and walked around behind the counter. Elis took a step back.

"Relax, bloodthirster. Your psychic darling sent me. I'm not going to be able to hang around and chat, so you'll need to listen to me and try your best not to interrupt."

She stared at him, her fierce expression challenging him to disobey her. Not going to happen. Having anyone show up in this place was a development Elis wasn't likely to ignore. Whatever she had to say, he was listening. He motioned for her to continue.

"You're being held by the Blood King. He knows you've let your soul back in and he wants to see if that means your bone marrow can be turned into extra potent Crave. He's got me hooked up to you so I can poke around inside that beautiful brain of yours, but what he doesn't realize is that I want to get you out of here. You and your team are the only ones who might be capable of destroying him. That's a pretty big 'might' but it's all we've got—a thirster with a soul, a powerful hierophant, and my dumbass brother who for some reason has the ability to make immortals extra especially immortal."

Elis reached for his margarita. "You're making exactly zero sense, love."

She knocked the glass out of his hand. "I might make more sense if you weren't totally blasted."

"Is that really my fault? This is a dream. I'm not actually drinking anything. Apparently, it's your lovely Blood King that's keeping me all stoppered up."

"Maybe, but you're more in control than you realize. You think you're trapped here, but it's because you *think* you're trapped that you are. If you think you need to be drunk to cope with it, you will be. I mean, it's fine if you want to give up on your own time, but you're on *my* time now. And Sybille's time. So, if you want to see her again, if you're worried about her, put down the bottle and come have a taste of something much more sustaining."

She brushed her hair away from her neck and tilted her head, exposing a curve of taught skin. Desire flared inside of him. It had been a long time since a woman had willingly offered herself.

Deep, unsated thirst coursed through him. He was on her in a second, fangs dug into flesh, warm iron upon his tongue. She tasted not of mint or cinnamon but of something he couldn't quite put a finger on, something that he'd experienced at one point in his life but had forgotten all about until many years later. Until now. It was all he could do not to break away from her and sob.

He woke to pain and chaos—pain in his chest, chaos everywhere else. His wrists were strapped to a table. He tried to struggle against the bindings with no luck; it was as though his arms were made of jelly.

The island was gone but the woman he'd been feeding from was not. She bent over him, undoing the bindings from his wrists. Her blond hair brushed over his cheeks.

A tall, broad-shouldered man appeared above him, long enough for Elis' eyes to focus and recognition to hit.

"Nate." The man turned to him, his expression cold. Elis swallowed, his throat aching in its efforts to produce sound. "You're Nathanial Atkins. I've met your spirit. Nice guy."

Nathanial's eyes turned into pools of fire. "Get him out of here. Now."

Elis let himself be lifted by the woman–it wasn't as though he could do much to resist anyways. He struggled to gain a modicum of control over his limbs, feeling like with each step he was a rubber band being pulled taught and then flicked a foot farther ahead.

The woman dragged him from the room, past thirsters with confused, scared looks on their faces. They kept well clear of Elis. Reaching the top of a staircase, the woman sighed under his weight. "You either have to make it down the stairs on your own, or I'm just going to push you over, let you tumble down them and hope you aren't too broken when you reach the bottom. Which is it going to be?"

With trembling hand, Elis reached for the railing, clinging to it as he made his way down, stair by stair. It was slow going. The woman's biting commentary did nothing to help.

"It's like I'm a hummingbird being forced to watch a tortoise cross a desert."

"I'm doing the best I can!"

When he finally reached the bottom, she grabbed him by his arm and dragged him out the front door and across a lawn to where a white SUV waited. "Get in."

He paused, bracing himself against the car's side. "Why should I? I don't even know who you are. Where are you going to take me?"

She clicked her key fob to release the lock and then opened the door for him. "I'm taking you to Sybille. Do you really need to know any more than that?"

Soon they were on the road. Elis glanced over his shoulder. He couldn't believe Nathanial would kidnap him, run a series of tests, and then release him. It didn't make sense.

The woman picked up on his unease. "There's no one following us. I assure you."

"That doesn't add up. You said Nathanial knows what I am. He had me constrained and attached to those machines. He kept me drugged. Why would he just let me go?"

"I might have told him that I had gazed upon the face of your spirit and it showed me a great darkness in which you destroyed all bloodthirsters who were anywhere near, even so-called invincible ones."

"Oh, come on!"

"He bought it, didn't he?"

"But why didn't he just kill me?"

"Because the plan is to drive you to Port Everan, drug you again, and deposit you on the nearest cargo ship heading to Asia. You're supposed to wake up somewhere in Russia a week from now. 'Let the Siberian thirsters deal with him,' he told me. Plus, obviously, killing you would be even worse than keeping you around. Releasing your wrathful spirit would only free it to set in motion the apocalyptic demise of every bloodthirster in North America."

Elis rested his head against the window. "Right. We wouldn't want that. But the apocalyptic demise of Russian bloodthirsters is okay, I guess."

She shrugged. "What, you expected him to be anything besides self-serving? Nathanial's a mean son of a bitch and he doesn't want his little kingdom crashing down around him, especially not now while he's basking in his invincibility. Did you know he had his men stake him over fifty times yesterday while everyone watched? Can you imagine how powerful he must have appeared to them? He's already Blood King; now he thinks he's Blood God."

"But he's not the only one. There's a Blood Goddess too, isn't there?" The way she'd tasted—dream or not—hadn't been like anything he'd experienced before. Everything was falling into place for him now—who and what this woman was. "Pull over, Raelyn."

She started at the mention of her name but did what he asked of her. "What is it? Why do you want to stop? I thought you were anxious to get back to Sybille."

"I am. I have one need that's more pressing, however." He brushed the hair away from her neck.

Her eyes grew wide, but she didn't ward him off. Instead, she tilted her head, just as she had in his dream. "We wouldn't want your needs to go unmet now, would we?"

CHAPTER TWENTY-SIX

Juliana studied Zareen's face as she drove them out of the city, past rolling countryside and into Low Hollow. Zareen eyed her nervously several times.

"It's weird—you staring at me like that. Cut it out."

She couldn't, though. Moving at the speed the car traveled proved to be no easy feat. She was a spirit, not a physical being who could strap herself in and go along for the ride. She had to keep a connection with the human to stay in the car and regrettably, this meant focusing on her as much as possible.

Zareen relaxed a little when Juliana explained this to her. "Okay, well, I guess that makes sense. Lowers the creep factor a notch, at least. It's just, we don't usually take spirits around for joy rides, you know. I'm not used to this."

"This is hardly a joy ride."

Zareen winced. "Tell me about it."

She turned on the radio, but it soon became apparent that they were never going to agree on what to listen to.

Juliana rolled her eyes as Zareen scanned through the stations. "I hate everything written after the eighteenth century."

"Yeah, well, the classical station doesn't get good reception out here."

Soon they were riding in silence again, Juliana vigilantly training her gaze on Zareen to avoid being sucked out of the car and left in a nearby wheat field.

Finally, Zareen piped up. "So, I've noticed you haven't done any manipulation of matter."

Juliana raised an eyebrow. "I haven't what?"

"You know, you haven't *channeled your inner poltergeist*. No chain rattling, no lifting candelabras and dancing through the room with them, no slamming doors. All those good Victorian ghostly things."

She raised her chin and sniffed. "The Victorians, such imbeciles. A nasty, dirty time. It's beyond me why humans romanticize these past eras. Would you prefer to be forced to marry an unwashed, parasite-infested man who doesn't think you should have the right to vote or own property? Disgusting."

"Jesus, I was only suggesting that if you want to destroy your hell beast ex, you should probably be able to lift a chair or two and fling them across the room. I wasn't suggesting we all start wearing corsets and ride around on those bicycles with the gigantic front wheels. You're so touchy."

She was touchy? Humans and their lack of self-reflection. Still, Zareen brought up a good point. In all her years as a spirit, she'd never gained a knack for affecting the material world. It was enough of an effort trying to stay in a speeding car. She couldn't imagine being able to grab the wheel and turn it, for instance. Though maybe it was worth a shot.

She reached across Zareen's lap.

"Hey, what the fuck? What are you trying to do?"

Juliana's fingers slipped harmlessly through the wheel.

"I didn't say you should try it now. I'm going seventy miles per hour. You want to get us killed? Or, *me* killed, at least? I won't be able to help you if I'm dead."

Juliana sighed. "As you can see, I lack the skill you spoke of."

Zareen seemed surprised. "Really? Even Nate can do a little bit, and he's a lot younger than you, plus I think we can both agree he's a tad on the dimwitted side."

"It's not about intelligence!" Juliana moved so she was right next to Zareen. "My body was destroyed. I gave up my freedom so that I could set the world right. With that, I also gave up certain abilities spirits gain over time. I'd rather have my mental capacity than be able to flick light switches." Though truth be told, being able to turn on a light would be useful too. Too many nights she'd sat in dark rooms because the humans had gone to bed.

"Okay, I get it. I didn't mean to offend you. Your sacrifice was very noble. But, how are you going to defeat Elis, then? I'm not much of a fighter, so if you expect me to stake him or something..."

"I expect you to stay out of it and let me worry about that. Get me where I need to go and trust that I know what I'm doing. I've had years to think this through." All a bluff, but a convincing one. She'd done a lot of thinking—that part was true, but it hadn't been until yesterday that she'd realized a hierophant had gotten mixed up with her ex-love. From there, though, it hadn't been difficult to figure out what she would need to do. It was perfect, really.

The journey to the Low seemed like it would never end. Finally, they crossed into its territory, thickening woods on either side of them, the sky darkening even though the morning was making its way towards midday. The strain on Juliana eased as the divisions between her plane and the Now World began to blur. It took less and less concentration to stay in the car.

She grasped at the door handle hoping that maybe she'd be able to feel the cold metal and then sighed.

"Nothing?"

"It doesn't matter." And it didn't. The only thing that did matter was that Elis and that human of his were dealt with properly. "Properly" didn't require any poltergeist skills on her part.

The farther they went into the Low, the more relaxed Juliana felt. It amazed her that she'd never come here before. She could have spent years in this place, relishing in the freedom it gave to her. Of course, it wasn't true freedom; it wasn't the total release she sought. But it was pleasant. Then she remembered what the Low was known for—a bloodthirster safe haven. A land of heartless, soulless beasts and a cesspool of humanity's worst to boot. It disgusted her to think a place that had the potential to ease her own burdens was the sort of environment she despised the most.

That confliction threatened to undo her tenuous sense of ease. "How much farther?"

Zareen laughed. "You sound like Adelaide. She hates long car trips." The woman glanced in the rearview mirror at the booster and car seats stationed in the back of the minivan. "My car needs several thousand dollars of repairs that I can't afford to make. So my dad lets me borrow this car to cart the kids around in."

It was inevitable that Zareen's thoughts would gravitate towards her children now that a dangerous situation was growing ever nearer. Juliana fought with herself not to think about them too. This woman made her own decision. She wasn't being forced to help Juliana; she'd chosen to. Of course, Juliana had been exceedingly persuasive; her argument for ridding the world of the scourge of Elis was quite compelling. Still, Zareen could have played the mother card to get out of helping: she had young children, she shouldn't put herself at risk. They could never get by on only her husband's meager part-time school counselor income if something were to happen to her.

Well, no matter. Zareen had made her choice. Juliana would not feel guilty because of it.

Zareen's eyes shifted back to the road. "It's just like my father said it would be. It's strange here. Like I'm being drugged."

"You're not going to crash the car, are you?"

Zareen gripped the wheel tighter. "No, I'm all right. I can handle it. If you see my eyes glazing over, scream in my ear."

Juliana renewed her vigilant study of her human companion, this time to make sure Zareen didn't take a turn into the Low's chasm of crazy. By the time they reached a small log cabin situated on a forested hill overlooking a crescent-shaped lake, Zareen's breath was shallow and sweat glistened on her temple, but she still appeared to be coherent.

"We're here." She parked the van next to a dark blue pick-up truck. "And so are they. What do we do now?"

"We go say hello, of course."

Juliana floated behind Zareen, her feet brushing the cold ground. It was almost like real walking, or how she remembered real waking to be.

The cabin door opened before they reached it. A woman with an oval face and sleek dark hair stared out at them, her expression flying through a series of emotions: hopefulness, confusion, surprise, and finally…horror.

"Zareen, what are you doing here?" Sybille gave her cousin a quick hug, which turned into a spin that placed Zareen behind her so she was standing between her and Juliana. "Why did you bring this spirit with you? You have no idea how dangerous she is."

Zareen tried to step out from behind Sybille, but Sybille held her back. "No, no, Juliana's not the one you have to be worried about. You've been tricked, Sybille. Elis is evil. He's a monster! He means to kill you and turn you into a bloodthirster!"

Naturally, Sybille had already thought through that scenario. She wasn't naive. Hell, she'd spent her whole life dealing with beasts. She knew their inclinations. Elis might have a soul, but he was still a thirster. He had dark desires. None of that mattered, though. Despite what he might want, he wasn't a mindless beast anymore. He wasn't the monster her cousin or this Juliana claimed him to be. He'd had plenty of opportunity to kill her and he hadn't. It was a line she felt strongly he would never cross.

"You know, Zareen, it's not the smartest thing in the world to believe the word of someone's deranged disincarnated ex."

Zareen stomped her foot. "Come on, Sybille, think about it. Have you ever known a bloodthirster who got its spirit back? You don't know what sort of power that gives it, what sort of awful things it might do with that power!"

"I do know, actually. That one there," she pointed at Juliana, "got her soul back and she went insane and killed every human within reach. That's the sort of monster you've aligned yourself with."

Zareen looked back and forth between her cousin and Juliana, who shrugged her shoulders. "I killed myself for that reprehensible act, so I think I've paid my dues. Elis, on the other hand, has not. By the way, where is he?"

Sybille put her hands on her hips. "Not here. Nowhere near here, so leave us be."

Devin and Charlie, both carrying firewood, appeared from around the side of the house. "Sybille, what's going on? Zareen, why are *you* here?"

Juliana wandered over to him. "Who's *this*?"

"Stay away from him!" Sybille yanked on his sleeve and grabbed the girl's shoulder, ushering them both inside.

Devin tossed his wood into a metal bin next to the wood burner and came back to stand behind Sybille. "What's going on? Don't tell me we've got another client already. Couldn't it have waited, Zareen? We're a bit tied up with our current case."

"She *is* our current case." Sybille eyed Juliana with distaste as the spirit wandered into the cabin, keeping as close to Devin as she could. She usually prided herself on the fact that her feathers weren't easily ruffled, yet here she was, a mere two minutes after Juliana showed up and she was already fantasizing about releasing Juliana to an afterlife featuring flames and medieval torture devices. The worst thing was that Juliana had noticed her discomposure and was playing it to her advantage.

"Devin..." Juliana placed her ghostly hands over his chest and slid them downward, exploring as much of him as she pleased. "I like that name."

"I can see you, you know." Charlie scrunched up her nose. "And it's gross. That's my uncle!"

Devin looked from side to side. "What's going on? Am I being felt up by a spirit? Is she hot, at least?"

Sybille pulled the little girl onto the couch next to her. "Yes you are, and unfortunately, she's admittedly attractive. If you like your spirits vengeful and brooding."

"Not really."

"The bigger question is," she turned to Charlie, "how are *you* able to see her? You didn't get this ability from Devin's side of the family, that's for sure."

"Hey, now."

The girl shrugged. "Maybe it's the invincible thirster mom thing, maybe it's from my dad's side. All I know is, I see her, and Sybille, seriously, don't *you* see what she's trying to do? She's trying to make you mad. Don't you get why?" The girl took Sybille's hand.

"The Low is teaching you terrible things, Charlie."

"This isn't about me. It's about you. And Elis. Stop worrying about me and worry about yourself."

"It's exhausting to be here. I hate this place." Sybille slumped back against the couch. Juliana was here in the Low. With her. Just like in her vision. This should have made her extra vigilant. Instead it left her depleted. What was wrong with her?

"I know how you feel." Zareen wrapped an arm around her. "Dad seems to have fixed this old cabin up nicely though. The Low's attack isn't as strong inside. Don't worry, Sybille. We're here to help. Elis is the reason this is happening to you, but we're going to stop him."

"You don't understand."

"You really don't." Devin crouched in front of Sybille. "I mean, I hate the guy, but what you think is going on, it's not. It's a lot more complicated than that."

"Or maybe it's actually very simple." Juliana swept over to them from her position at the window where she'd been searching for any signs of Elis. "A car is coming. I presume my husband is home at last. It's finally time to pay him back for everything he took from me."

She glided right through Devin and situated herself in front of Sybille. With her in close proximity, the Low's assault mounted anew. In her weakened state, even Peter's buffered cabin could not keep it out completely. Why was she so drained? She'd never felt this way, not even after a possession.

She barely registered it when Zareen squeezed her shoulder. "Oh my God, the bloodthirsters know you're here. Holy shit, Sybille, what have you gotten yourself into?"

That was different, all right. Bloodthirsters. Hundreds of them gathering from all corners of the Low. They were awake and making their way to her, craving her, her blood, her power. Out of all of them, some were probably old enough to be able to mesmerize. Were there enough to break through her defenses, forcing her to be powerless so she could do nothing to prevent them from killing her?

They would be here soon.

"You should leave," she whispered. "Devin, take Charlie and Zareen and get out of here."

Devin gasped. "What? No way. You're coming with us!"

"I have to wait for Elis so we can deal with this and it isn't safe anymore for you to wait with me. Please, Devin." She willed herself to look past Juliana's scornful face towards her friend. "Please. Save your niece."

"No one is saving anyone!" Juliana spun herself around Sybille who flinched when the spirit drew near.

"What do you mean, Juliana? You said you were here so that you could save *everyone*!" Zareen finally seemed to be questioning whether she'd taken up arms with the right side.

"And you wonder why I kept secrets from you people." Charlie sat with her arms wrapped around her knees, trying her best not to look scared. "Adults are all so dumb!"

A car engine purred louder and louder and then cut out. Juliana smiled while placing spectral hands on each side of Sybille's face. "It's time. Open up, Sybille. I want in."

CHAPTER TWENTY-SEVEN

"WHY IS THERE AN EXTRA CAR HERE?" ELIS TUMBLED OUT OF RAELYN'S SUV, the effort of putting one foot in front of the other while simultaneously staying upright nearly more than he could manage. If it hadn't been for the tasty meal he'd just had, he'd probably still be slumped in the passenger seat, completely spent. "Sybille?"

Raelyn trailed right behind him. He shrugged her off when she offered her arm for support. Her eyes iced over. "Got what you wanted from me, huh, bloodthirster?"

"Pretty much, yeah."

The door to the cabin flew open and Devin came running out to meet them. "Jesus Christ, Elis, this is your doing. You have to stop her!"

Fighting off dizziness, Elis hastened his pace. "Stop who?"

Devin's hands balled into fists. "I'd describe her for you but she's a tad invisible."

Dread filled his heart. *Dammit, they'd been so close to escaping.*

Seeing him struggle, Devin dragged him the rest of the way into the cabin. Elis nearly collapsed again when he realized what was happening there. A young girl sat hunched in a corner, wailing, her hands around her knees as she rocked back and forth. Sybille's cousin Zareen was pulling on Sybille's arm.... And Sybille...

He rushed over to her. Eyelids fluttering, eyes rolled back into her head, her body lay taught against the couch, neck bent at a weird angle. Hovering just above the surface of Sybille's chest was the woman he had once loved more than life itself, the woman he'd spent lifetimes with, whom he had killed with and fed on. The woman he'd mourned over a century.

"Don't do this, Juliana."

Juliana's spectral body froze. "It's for your own good, Elis. Everything I've ever done for you has been for your own good."

Sybille moaned, turning her head from side to side. For a moment, her eyes slid back into place, warm hazel pools focusing upon his own. "I don't have the strength to keep her out, Elis. Stay back."

"No! Come on Sybille, you do have the strength, you do! You have to!"

She moaned again. This didn't look good.

Elis turned to Devin. "Take the others and get out of here."

"Why does everyone keep telling me to leave? I'm not going to do that. Don't you get it? It would be just like it was in her vision."

"It doesn't matter now. Juliana will use Sybille's body to kill every last one of us, including *her*." He pointed to the young girl weeping in the corner.

Raelyn placed a hand on Devin's arm. "You promised me you'd save Charlie. I brought Elis back to you. Now you have to do your part."

"I know, dammit!" Devin punched a chair next to the door. It tottered on one of its legs before falling over.

He ran to the little girl, scooping her up in his arms. "Zareen, let's go."

Zareen hesitated, her lips trembling as her focus shifted between Devin and her cousin. "This is my fault. I brought Juliana here. How can I just leave?"

"How do you think *I* feel? I got Sybille mixed up in this mess, too. There'll be time for us both to feel guilty later. I don't want to have to explain to your husband and kids how you died because you were too stubborn to run when you had the chance. *Come on!*"

Zareen sighed, but then nodded in agreement. With one more anguished look at her cousin, she headed towards the door, Devin and Charlie right behind her. Before she could make it over the threshold, though, she froze in her tracks. "We're too late. They're here."

She slammed the door closed and bolted it.

Elis turned his thoughts from the tug-of-war possession taking place in front of him long enough to try to make sense of her words. "What? Who's here?"

Raelyn peered out the front window. "It looks to be the whole damned undead population of the Low."

Elis stayed near Sybille, craning his neck so he could glimpse through the front and side windows. A caravan of cars formed a line down the length of the driveway. More thirsters made their way toward the cabin on foot, emerging from the forest. A few pushed canoes onto shore from the lake.

They would be surrounded soon. Inundated.

Raelyn swore under her breath. "And look who's leading the charge. It seems like the Blood King's found something so desirable it trumps his fear of Elis Tanner."

The army of bloodthirsters froze. Devin, with Charlie still in his arms, Raelyn, Zareen—everyone stopped moving, nearly stopped breathing. They were trapped in a moment, stilled by a scream so terrible, it was as though the most cursed beast had uttered it. But it was no beast; it was Sybille, her final defenses against the onslaught of Low, thirster, and Juliana obliterated. As Juliana slid inside of her, her mind retreating to its cold, tiny box, the entire world paused.

When it started again, there was a new demon in its midst.

"Come on in, Sybille. I've made pie. Custard—your favorite! Didn't the meringue turn out lovely?" Sybille's mother was dressed in an orange taffeta A-line skirt over which she'd tied on an apron that read "Kiss me, I'm psychic." She held the custard pie out so that Sybille could attest to its tempting appearance.

"It smells heavenly, Mom, but you know, I'm in the middle of a possession right now, and not one that I sanctioned. I don't have time for pie."

"Oh honey, must you be so serious? There's always time for pie."

"No, I mean it, Mom. You're just an illusion Juliana set up for me to keep me distracted so I don't try to kick her out of my body. So really, I don't have time for pie, or for you either."

Her mother frowned, setting the steaming dish down on the kitchen table, then wiped her hands on a checkered dishcloth. "I suppose that's true." She looked down at her feet. "Your real mother would never wear heels while she baked, would she?"

"That would be a no." Her mother's kitchen didn't look anything like this one, either, so clean and organized and like it hadn't seen a day past 1955. Juliana had gotten her mother's love of cooking right, and the custard meringue pie too, but the rest of the details were way off. "I'm going to have to shut you down now. Any last words of fake motherly advice for me?"

Margot grabbed a knife and began to slice into the gooey custard. "Always use real butter. None of that artificial margarine crap. It's filled with chemicals. And your crusts won't come out flaky; they'll be way too dense."

"That's not very helpful."

"I doubt your real mother would have done much better." She lifted out a piece of pie, deposited it onto a plate and stuck a fork in it, holding it out to Sybille. "Are you sure you don't want a slice?"

It took all her strength to shake her head no. "Bye, Mom."

The kitchen faded and with it her mother's face as she savored a fork full of sugary butter-filled goodness on the tip of her tongue, shutting her eyes in pure delight. Then she was gone, the striped yellow, pink, and green wallpaper swapped out with walls made of heavy logs, her mother's face replaced by Elis'.

I'm still here, Elis.

But was she? She could see the cabin, but she had no control over which direction her body was turned. Hell, she couldn't even blink when she wanted to. Juliana was at the helm. All Sybille could do was try to stay conscious of the events playing out, try to remain present even though she wanted more than anything to retreat back to her mother's bygone-era kitchen and eat that entire custard pie. She didn't want to see the horrible things Juliana was about to do. Regardless, she forced herself to witness it. *Every* moment. It was the only way to keep herself from becoming so lost she would never find her way back to herself.

The hardest thing was continuing to believe she wanted to keep fighting to return to herself. Because if she didn't, soon there would be nothing left for her to return to.

Sybille's body was a marvel. Perhaps it was the fact that it had been over one hundred years since she'd had her own; maybe it was something about Sybille herself. Whatever the case, Juliana spent a moment basking in the sheer pleasure of possessing fingers and legs and eyes. While she basked, the world paused. They knew, as she did, that something extraordinary was occurring.

The Low thrummed around her. It wanted this, wanted Juliana to do this, but the thirsters waiting at the door wanted it as well. Sybille would fight them with everything she had. Even relegated to a tiny corner of her brain, Juliana could still feel the woman's strength. She wouldn't let the thirsters just take her. Not this one.

Where Sybille was desirable to the thirsters, Juliana was a powerful unknown. They would want that power for themselves, if they could get it. Even that odd thirster woman, Raelyn, was fighting the urge to open one of Sybille's veins. Only Elis seemed free from this need. His spirit must be keeping him sane, perhaps. She refused to dwell upon the hard rage pouring off of him. This woman, Sybille, had merely been a temporary distraction, a tiny blip on the endless timeline she herself shared with him. And now that blip was over, and so were they.

Elis would follow her to freedom. She could end this.

This thought concluded her moment of revelry. Juliana was ready to show them who she really was now.

CHAPTER TWENTY-EIGHT

ELIS CHANTED HER NAME LIKE A MANTRA.

"Sybille, Sybille, Sybille."

The recitation stilled the world around him. For a moment, the thirsters stopped advancing on the cabin. The others there with him paused in their panicking. Juliana paused as well. He couldn't say if this was a good or bad sign. He'd seen Sybille possessed before, he knew what it meant, that she would lose control and be subjected to whatever the spirit inside of her wanted to do. But he had also seen her fight. She'd been able to reclaim herself before.

He held onto the hope that she'd be able to stop Juliana from whatever it was she had planned. Juliana, however, had other ideas.

Sybille's body squirmed and wriggled. Elis held her wrists down. The moment of calm over, her eyes flew open. Not the warm, lively eyes of Sybille, but the cold winter ice of Juliana's.

"I always did like it when you held me down, didn't I?"

Elis flinched. *His* Juliana had enjoyed that, not this wretched spirit woman. This being was a tattered remnant of the woman he'd known.

"Don't do this, Juliana. There's no need."

She laughed, spreading her legs and wrapping them around him, drawing him closer to her. In the periphery of his vision, he caught Devin shielding Charlie's eyes, turning her away from the scene.

Juliana laughed again. "There is every need. Can't you feel that, Elis? Don't you want to devour her, your sweet psychic human? What would she taste like now, with me inside of her?" She brought her head close to Elis', craning her neck so her silky skin brushed against his lips.

He pulled back, trying to get out of her vice grip. He had almost bitten into her flesh, almost done exactly what Juliana wanted—lose control and destroy the only good thing he'd had in his life for as long as he could remember.

"I won't do it, Juliana. You need to release her."

"Oh, I *will*." She dropped him then, causing him to lose balance and tumble backwards. Before he could stop her, she was up off the couch and running towards the kitchen.

"No!" Zareen rushed at her, but Juliana swung without even having to look, planting a fist right in Zareen's face. Hitting her head against the wall, Sybille's cousin crumpled to the ground.

Devin set Charlie on the ground and nudged her towards Zareen. "Go make sure she's okay." He crept around the counter, Elis joining him, and they watched as Juliana searched through drawers until she found what she wanted.

"Just like in Sybille's vision." Devin swore as Juliana brandished a large knife, swinging it towards them until pointing it at her own chest.

"Seem familiar, Elis?" Her gaze peered into Elis' and then swung back to Devin's. "He probably never told you, Devin, but this isn't the first time Elis and I have done this dance. I killed myself once already for him. I'm not above doing it again."

Elis had a feeling Juliana would have him on his knees groveling and pleading soon. "But it's not you who you'll be killing. It will be Sybille."

She shrugged. "What's your point?"

"I thought you were above such pettiness and violence. This isn't you. You've been telling me for decades that it was the beast who did wrong, and your only mistake was being unable to control the beast while you were linked with it."

"You're right, Elis. That *was* my one mistake. Not being able to control you—your spirit and your beast. Had I not failed in that, none of this would have to have happened and your Sybille would be sitting safely at home trying to contact pathetic, forlorn spirits with her fashion-challenged family. Instead, I have her locked away in her own mind while I decide how many breaths she has left in her."

Devin moved forward, but Elis held him back as she brought the knife upwards, then dragged it back until it was once again pressed against Sybille's heart. A thin scarlet line trickled down the blade's edge. Shameful or not, Elis had to resist licking his lips as a delectable scent coiled around him—like a freshly baked pie topped with cinnamon ice cream.

Devin slapped Elis' hand away. "Let go of me!"

"Look at her, Devin. She'll do it. She'll have the knife embedded in Sybille's heart before you get to her."

"It's just a flesh wound now, but…" She twisted the knife so that the tip cut a fraction of an inch further into her. "It could be much more than that. Tell me Elis, honestly. You want to come here and lick the knife clean, don't you? I can feel your desire. It's almost too much to resist. If I tore her open, you'd drink her as she died, wouldn't you?"

He shook his head. "No!"

Juliana clucked her tongue. "You're lying to yourself. Do you think your soul makes you more than a beast? I'm proof that's not true."

The door of the cabin shook. Faces began appearing in the windows. Juliana pulled the knife away from Sybille. "Look at that, we have company."

Blood, thought Elis. She'd done that on purpose, drawing blood so that every thirster hovering around the cabin would feel the need to press in closer. If Juliana didn't twist the knife into Sybille's heart, the hundreds of ravenous thirsters would finish the job she'd started with their own teeth.

Devin and Raelyn threw their weight against the front door. It wouldn't hold for long, but it might buy them the time they needed.

"I don't believe you're no better than your beast, Juliana. I *can't* believe that. You never wanted to kill those people—that was your beast. You know if you'd had any control over it, you'd have stopped it." Even now, referring to *his* Juliana as "it" set badly with him, but he had to win the spirit over somehow.

Juliana wavered, the knife still pointed towards Sybille's heart.

"I know you only wanted to free my spirit and in doing so, to free the world of a menace. I didn't want to believe you were right. The pain of losing you was too great."

"The pain of…" She raised her eyebrows.

"Yes. Haven't you figured that out? You say you did everything for me, but all I could feel was you being gone. I couldn't accept that you were trying to keep me with you. I didn't see it that way, but I do now."

The door continued to shake as Devin and Raelyn strained against it. Howls from outside echoed through the cabin. Peter's charms and the siblings' strength were bound to fail at some point; then the last barrier guarding them all from the hoard of unhumans would be no more.

"Can you stop them?"

Juliana narrowed her eyes. "Why would I want to do that?"

"To show how powerful you are, and so that you can succeed at what you always wanted to succeed at."

"Which is?"

"To kill me, kill my beast, and release my soul. Our spirits can depart the Now World together, just as you tried to do two years ago."

She wrapped a lock of Sybille's hair around her finger. "Will you really go with me?"

He took a tentative step in her direction. "You know I will. I've missed you so much. I've kept a picture of you. After I left you with Laurence that night, I wanted a reminder of how much I loved you. So, I painted your image and kept it on my bookshelf."

"You didn't."

"Search Sybille's memories. She's seen it herself."

Juliana paused. It was an awkward affair, sorting through this human woman's memories. She didn't care for it, though she had to admit that as humans went, Sybille was less boring than most.

She brought up memories linked to Elis, finding the one where Sybille scanned Elis' office, her eyes eventually resting upon Juliana's portrait. According to the memory, Sybille had even believed Juliana to be beautiful.

That was satisfying. Juliana should have left off there, but by then, dipping into Sybille's past had become addictive. She traced her memories back to the first night Elis had appeared to her, and to all the nights since.

Her eyes widened as she realized something. "You...you *love* her."

Elis' tentative step forward became a quick leap back. "What? No! I was drawn to her psychic abilities of course. I saw that I could use them. She was a means to an end, that's all. I've known her for how long? A few months. I've known you since sixteen seventy-four. Honestly, how could she mean to me what you do, what you've always meant to me!"

Her hands shook as they grasped the knife's handle. "If you're lying..."

He kept his eyes focused on her own. "I'm willing to go with you, aren't I? I'm willing to end my life to be with you. Please, Juliana!"

Her name upon his tongue brought back so many memories, memories that where hers and hers alone, not this Sybille woman's.

"There is one thing I hate worse than what you did to me, Elis."

His eyes flickered to her chest and the weapon she held against it, then back up again. "What is it?"

"Bloodthirsters." She motioned with her knife to the faces lining the windows. "The beasts who keep their spirits trapped, who take and take from the innocent, who turn those innocents into beasts themselves. I hate every one of them."

Elis reached towards her, steadying the knife, placing his fingers over her own. His touch sent a shiver down her spine. He gave her hand a gentle squeeze. "I think that hatred needs a home. Is a psychic possessed with a seventeenth century spirit capable of taking out a few monsters in order to spend eternity in hell with her good-for-nothing, wayward husband?"

She smiled. Upon Sybille's full lips was contained all of Juliana's mirth. "I don't think Sybille would appreciate me using her body to murder anyone."

He took the knife from her hand. "Sybille's not the one who gets to decide now, is she?"

His words were a devastating blow to Sybille. It had been bad enough, watching helplessly as Juliana pressed a knife into her skin, seeing the desperation in Elis' eyes, and in Devin's as well. But now, whether he realized it or not, Elis had bargained his own life for Sybille's. First, though, Juliana was going to use Sybille to seek her revenge upon an army of undead—and there was nothing Sybille could do about any of it.

Even in her tiny box, she could feel the bloodthirsters pushing in on her where the Low pulled. She was a piece of taffy being worked over so many times she feared she would be stretched until she no longer recognized herself.

She couldn't tell whether Juliana felt any of that. If anything, she seemed to savor the Low's pull. It was an enticement to her—a welcome home party—where to Sybille it was as though the Low was opening a pit below her feet.

The bloodthirsters, however, were a different matter. Juliana loathed them. She wanted to stop them just as Sybille did, though Juliana would undoubtedly turn Sybille over to them as soon as she was done using her body. For now, however, they had that one thing in common: stop the bloodthirsters from decorating her skin with fang-sized holes.

The more she thought about it, the more she believed this shared aim could be used to her advantage. Somehow, Sybille might still come out of this on top.

That was a new, hopeful thought, the sort she hadn't considered possible since Juliana had taken charge. She'd thought about ridding herself of Juliana's command without even thinking it odd. Had she done this kind of thing before? Had she allowed herself to be controlled only to reclaim that control when the time was right? Yes. Yes, she had. In those cases, it had been easy because the spirits had been on the verge of being released to the World Beyond. They would attack her, afraid of their own freedom, but it was a futile fight and something they'd eventually come to terms with.

A departing spirit was no challenge at all. Juliana, on the other hand, would not leave until she was good and ready, which meant one thing: Elis would have to be dead first. And who did Juliana expect to do the killing?

The thought stabbed at her heart deeper than any knife could. She wouldn't sit idly by while Juliana used her to kill Elis. It was the worst thing she could imagine. She let that thought spur her on, keeping her far away from her mother's fifties kitchen.

Sybille would take back her body from this intruder. But first, Juliana would deal with the bloodthirsters for her. In the end, it would be Sybille who used Juliana to achieve her aim, not the other way around.

CHAPTER TWENTY-NINE

DEVIN WRESTLED BETWEEN STAYING CLOSE TO SYBILLE AND HELPING HIS SISTER keep the bloodthirsters out. When it became apparent that Elis had the situation under control, however tenuous, he rushed back to Raelyn. The pounding became more persistent. It was a miracle the beasts hadn't splintered the wood and rushed into the cabin already.

"How is she?" he called over to Charlie, who was bent over Zareen's prone form.

"Still breathing." The girl held Zareen's hand as though if she let go, Zareen would surely die.

"She'll be okay, Charlie," her mother crooned. "We'll all be. Your uncle's going to get you out of here, I promise."

"What's that?" Charlie looked around, feigning confusion. "I couldn't hear your promise over all of the *lies*!"

"Charlie!" Devin's head shook like a bobble head every time the bloodthirster on the other side of the door pounded on it with its fists. "Don't talk to your mama that way!"

"She has a right to be angry with me, Devin. Bloodthirsters don't exactly make the best mothers."

Devin snorted. "Or mothers at all, usually."

"I'm not usual."

The pounding stopped. In its place, a voice rose. "It's time you let me inside, Raelyn."

"Shit, my damned boss is here to say hi. That's perfect." Raelyn brought her ear to the door.

"I promise, it will be me and only me. The rest will stay back if I tell them to. Do you want me to order them to stay back?"

"Do whatever the fuck you want, Nathanial."

"What I want is for you to let me in so I can find out what smells so good."

Devin moved aside as Sybille—*no*, he corrected himself—as *Juliana*—walked to the door. "The scent is wonderful, isn't it? I've been baking bread. Fresh out of the oven. Do you want some?"

She opened the door. Nathanial stood there, his fellow thirsters gathered just a few steps away, all of them swaying silently, their eyes filled with unquenchable need.

"Won't you come in and have a seat." Juliana gestured towards the cabin's interior. "I trust you will be a thirster of your word and not allow your minions to join us. We only have so much bread to break and as you can see, I'm not Jesus."

Nathanial sauntered in, eyeing Elis disdainfully before returning to his lustful perusal of Sybille's body.

"You are all kinds of different, aren't you?"

"You have no idea." She led him over to the counter. Devin waited out the tension by thinking of the many ways this could all go horribly wrong.

The Blood King circled Juliana, his nose to her neck. "First mint, then cinnamon. You can't make up your mind, can you?"

"But you can make up yours. You already have." She reached out and stroked his arm. "*You want me*, Blood King.

He smiled, fangs on display. "How could any bloodthirster not."

If it was possible to be any tenser, Elis wasn't sure how. Nathanial was so close to biting her, so close to taking Sybille away from him. Shame flooded him as he realized he was jealous that this scumbag would get her, and he wouldn't.

"You're different, too, Blood King. Do you think I can't tell? That's why I've decided on you."

Nathanial raised an eyebrow. "You're already bleeding. Who did this to you?" He narrowed his eyes at Elis and scowled.

"Why are you assuming it was *me*?"

Juliana nodded. "Oh, he tried, but I prevented him. He's no Blood King."

Nathanial's eyes slid between the blood on Sybille's shirt and her bare neck. "Either way, he doesn't matter anymore. I've ordered my men to take care of him as soon as we're finished here."

She took his hand and drew it around her waist, holding the other palm in her own as though they were about to begin a waltz. "That makes my job all the easier."

Sybille continued her vigil, witnessing Juliana's every action, even admiring how easy it was for her to manipulate Nathanial.

The Blood King had not expected this, the paralyzing warmth that Juliana was spreading from Sybille's hand to his own.

"You want to break away, and yet you do not." Juliana sang these words, a lullaby for her resistant prey. "For a bloodthirster to feel warmth after so many years of cold—it's the most pleasurable kind of torture."

Nathanial's eyes grew until they'd become dark orbs, as though he was possessed by an alien rather than by the spirit of this madwoman. *So much the worse for him*, thought Sybille. She would have taken an old-fashioned alien bodysnatching over a Juliana possession any day.

Juliana sighed, part shock, part ecstasy. Sybille could understand why. Nathanial was not like any other bloodthirster. In his own way, he was even more extraordinary than Elis. Power coursed through him, cycling its way between his flesh and the tips of her fingers. It was shamefully intoxicating. Well, for Sybille it was. She sensed no shame from Juliana, who seemed to intuitively understand more about the Blood King than he himself did.

"Your life force is no longer of this world. And so, you can no longer be killed." She cocked her head from side to side, holding his hand steady. "That's an unanticipated development. Do you know you've cursed your innocent soul to be trapped for eternity? You are the monster of all beasts. I may not be able to kill you, but that doesn't mean I can't destroy you!"

And possibly destroy Sybille in the process... What was Juliana trying to do exactly? Sybille had hoped her unwanted body buddy was about to leave her in favor of Nathanial. Instead, she spread herself out, her energetic body filling every molecule of Sybille's physical one, while also stretching into Nathanial.

If Juliana's psychic expansion went on much longer, it would strangle the life out of Sybille. The calm that had first paralyzed Nathanial gave way to panic. He fought her, gripping her hand, her waist, and pulling away at the same time, his mind flaring as it attempted to resist Juliana's infiltration. Juliana pressed back, relentlessly attacking with the force of a hurricane.

The battle raged and Sybille was forced into the middle of it, an unwilling player in a war between evil and evil.

On top of her internal storms, the Low pushed at her from without, an invisible referee making all the calls against Sybille while the crowd of undead onlookers took in the show, waiting to be told that they could go from spectators to participants.

Now would be the time to give up. Now would be the time to eat a big old slice of custard pie. Or possibly take the entire pie and lower head to dish, consuming the whole of it until she descended into a sugar coma she would never wake from. The mere suggestion brought her back to her mother's kitchen. Margot was absent, but there the pie sat. She licked her lips as she inhaled the smell of caramelized sugar.

It was easy to forget that Elis and Devin and the others were still in the cabin with her. Hell, it was easy to forget there still was a cabin, a bloodthirster-infested forest on an angry land, and a larger world still beyond that. Sybille could no longer grasp anything aside from the turmoil playing out in her own mind. Yet, from far away a voice called her name, reminded her that a name was still something she had claim to and with it, an identity. She was still Sybille. She was apart from Juliana, from the Blood King.

"Sybille!"

Elis' voice was a child's whisper and a volcano exploding. It brushed against her, gentle as a feather, and shook her to her core. If she didn't crawl her way out of her increasingly tiny corner, Juliana would succeed in all her aims; she would use Sybille to take control of the Blood King, kill Elis, and feed what was left of Sybille to the awaiting bloodthirsters.

She would not allow this.

With the lurking undead kept at bay and Juliana distracted with her onslaught against the Blood King, now was Sybille's chance. Steeling herself, she let the pie tin crash to the floor. The kitchen dissolved.

Sybille stepped out from her corner.

A door opened—that's how Juliana thought of it. In her mind, which was really Sybille's mind with Juliana's willpower filling it, a door that had been closed and locked was unlocked and thrown wide open.

She shook in Sybille's body. The effort of possessing the hierophant while attempting to invade that wretched bloodthirster hadn't been strenuous until this moment. Once she'd broken through Sybille's weakened resolve, it had been easy to control her;, to become her. Having a taste of the bloodthirster merely served as an unexpected bonus.

He wasn't at all like what she'd thought he would be. When she first invited him inside the cabin, she thought she'd make him see that he was nothing more than a corpse rotting at the pace a garden snail crosses a continent. This was all he was, all any bloodthirster was, really: dead bodies given a reprieve from the grave probably by some demonic force long ago. Well, she would see that this particular bloodthirster's reprieve came to an end. Then she'd deal with Elis and any other thirster that dared come near.

That had been her strategy up until that cursed door opened in Sybille's mind. Juliana could have sworn she caught the slightest whiff of... muffins? Cake? Pie? Something freshly baked. Then Sybille walked through that door, punching and kicking as she came. Juliana gave a jolt.

No, *she* didn't. *Sybille* did. Sybille raised her arm—her *own damn arm*, and Juliana couldn't stop her, couldn't force the arm back down. She was unable to do much of anything.

"Get...out...of...me!" The words were labored, but it was Sybille speaking them. Horrified, Juliana tried to stop every single one of them. As Sybille fought to oust Juliana, the spirit found herself in a strange head-space Sybille seemed to have created for them. There Sybille thrashed at

Juliana until she had no choice but to retreat through the portal Sybille had so recently come out of.

She stopped in the center of a kitchen with black and white linoleum floors and a pink toaster matching the tiled backsplash behind the counter. "How quaint."

The remains of a pie lay smashed on the ground, golden custard oozing out of a bent tin. Juliana contemplated taking the time to clean up the mess, but she had more pressing things to attend to. She'd been baking cookies. She put on two red checkered mitts and opened the oven to retrieve a cookie sheet, taking in a big whiff as she did so.

Peanut butter chocolate chunk. Elis would be pleased.

Elis.

Juliana whipped around the room. Where was she? And why was she wearing pearls and a ruffled apron? She shuddered as realization dawned: she had finally been released from the Now World only to end up in Hell.

"This isn't Hell, though I suppose for you it comes close." Elis sat at the recently Elis-free table. "You're not in control now, Juliana. Sybille is back and you don't belong here. Neither do I."

Getting up from the table, he took a step towards her, a look of shameless desire reflected in his heavy-lidded eyes. Juliana could barely contain her surprise.

He took another step and now there was no doubt about the lust pouring off him; he was practically salivating. Finally, after all this time, he wanted to *be* with her again! "Elis, I—"

"Those look delicious! I'll just take one before I go." He snatched a cookie off the tray she still held, turned, then turned back again and grabbed several more. "Time for us both to go."

Elis took a bite and then he was gone. Juliana stood there with what remained of her cookies, uncomfortable in the realization that for once, he was right.

✿✿

"What in the entire hell just happened?" Elis shook his head. One minute, he'd been standing near Sybille's body, doing his best to prevent Juliana from making Sybille's vision come true. The next, his spirit was ripped from his body and sucked into Sybille's mind; specifically, into a space all too familiar to him. And there was his fifties housewife Juliana with her damned peanut butter cookies. Only this time, *he* was the one with the upper hand, not her. He'd helped kick Juliana out of Sybille and gotten fresh-baked dream cookies to boot. Now he was back, soul in body, and there was no more opportunity to dissect what had occurred.

The cabin was on fire. Not the sort with flames, but the kind of intensity that heavies the air, filling the room with a skin-burning fever. The Blood King stood in their midst, the mighty immortal of immortals, the undead undead. And Juliana, newly ousted from Sybille's head, had now turned all her focus onto him.

The results were terrifying. Nathanial let out a bellow, his thirster minions echoing him from beyond the cabin as though his agony was their own. Like a self-fulfilling prophesy, soon it *was* their own, and his as well. It brought Elis to his knees. Even Raelyn held her hands to her ears in a futile attempt to keep out the blinding pain.

By now, Sybille had recovered enough from Juliana's possession to crawl over to him. The humans in the room seemed immune to the anguish inflicted by the Blood King's battle cry. "Elis, you helped bring me back. Now you have to stay here too." She cradled his head in her lap. It wasn't until she wiped her hand on her sleeve that he realized he was crying.

Juliana and the Blood King continued their battle. Nathanial's scarlet-rimmed alien eyes were wild with terror as a fight for domination played out behind them.

In the moments when he could see through the torture, Elis spied Devin leaning his weight against the front door, but there was no longer any pounding upon it, the thirsters on the other side being preoccupied by the brain rattling banshee cry from their leader.

"I need you to stay, Elis." Sybille's voice rang out clearly over the chaos. It soothed him enough to let him do the opposite of what she wanted.

He blinked as a sandy beach and aquamarine waters came in and out of focus in front of him. His hand grasped an icy pitcher. "Do you want another margarita?"

"Do I...what?" Sybille slapped him hard. "Elis! Wake the fuck up!"

Elis turned in a circle. His cheek stung for some reason. And he could have sworn he'd been talking to someone. They seemed to be gone now, though.

No matter. Sometimes being utterly alone had its perks. More margaritas for him!

⚔

To Sybille, the Blood King's unearthly hollering was irritating but not nearly as debilitating as every other onslaught of supernatural madness she'd been subjected to that day. For Elis and the other thirsters, it was much more than mere annoyance.

She'd hoped to make use of Elis' mesmerizing abilities, thinking they might work on Juliana and the Blood King. Then he'd decided to go comatose and now he was totally worthless to her. She'd have to do this on her own.

With Elis incapacitated, Sybille could see only one more option remaining. Her plan wasn't exactly optimal, but then, she'd never let that stop her before. She had to try.

Rising from the ground, Sybille took a wide stance as she focused her mind. Juliana was gone from her, but the connection between the two of them had not been severed. If she could take advantage of that, if she could pull herself along the tether linking them, then…maybe.

Sybille reached out with her mind, let herself float as she did when she was searching for spirits in the ether. Only instead of going as far as the ether, she followed the tether until she reached the periphery of Juliana's spirit, currently struggling to take hold of the Blood King. Sybille swayed on her feet. Everything was frazzled here. Fractured. It was confusing to hover in that odd space between an old spirit and an immortal, but it was illuminating as well.

Juliana's hatred for the Blood King was a primal force, a thousand earthquakes hoping to swallow up this one creature. Sybille could only imagine what she would do when that wrath was refocused back upon her and Elis.

The spirit's energy was electric, her determination to undo the Blood King mighty. But Nathanial wasn't some run of the mill thirster either. He fought back. Sybille held steady, taking in the fight while trying her best to stay out of it. That situation couldn't last, however. It would be easy to get swept up in it and if that happened, Juliana or the Blood King, or some strange combination of the two of them, would swallow her whole.

Far away, she was half aware of Devin yelling at her, questioning what the hell was going on.

Sybille waved him off as the room became a whirlwind. She let it spin. Faster and faster it went. Deeper and deeper, Juliana dug into the Blood King. The more she dug, the more he rebelled. Sybille couldn't let him win. As dangerous as Juliana was to her and to Elis, the Blood King was a danger to the world. No one should have the power he held. *No one.*

The Blood King continued to wail. The thirsters in and around the cabin were by now senseless or well on their way to becoming so. Raelyn knelt at Devin's feet and whined piteously.

Still the room spun. Sybille held her place in the strange no man's land between spirit and thirster. The give and pull for control over Nathanial intensified along with his wails.

"Psychic, I know you're here," Juliana's spat the words out of Nathanial's lips in a break between his cries. "Help me end this and I will spare you."

Sybille stifled a laugh. Juliana didn't understand fully the situation she'd gotten herself into. Still, as incredible as it was, the two women were on the same side here. "Oh, great and noble Juliana, please spare me. I'll do anything…*anything*!"

Nathanial's lip quivered. "You don't have to be so sarcastic."

"How about this, then—I'll help you, and then you will be a good little evil spirit and piss the hell off!" With that, Sybille raised a hand and in true Nate the tablecloth-loving spirit fashion, she mimed herself pulling on her tether. "Make some room for me, Juliana."

Fully between Nathanial and Juliana now, Sybille redoubled her efforts, reaching all the way out into the ether this time, expanding herself infinitely in every direction. Now at the end of the tether that Juliana was still attached to, she grabbed onto the woman's spirit-self and swung. Juliana expanded with her, whipping around inside the Blood King's mind.

His screams intensified from banshee-level to cosmic force. The windows in the cabin shattered, glass shards raining down like deadly hail. Devin and Charlie fell to their knees beside Raelyn, clamping their palms over their ears. Had Sybille been fully in her own body, she would have collapsed under the weight of Nathanial's terror.

She continued to swing Juliana through the Blood King's synapses, destroying them one by one. Anyone observing from the outside would wonder at these two seething bodies. Sybille, arms outstretched and locked onto Nathanial's, gaze boring into him, rocked on steady legs as her body pulsed. There wasn't so much movement as there was the sense of an impending explosion, like pressure building up at a nuclear power plant. The tension was electric, and to Sybille, the inside of that power plant was as dynamic as a well-choreographed fight scene.

Juliana glowed. Sybille felt it like sand between her toes on a hot day. From the way the Blood King wailed, he felt it like the nuke was approaching a meltdown. This was what the spirit wanted. She might not like that she needed a human's help to achieve it, but burning the Blood King made Sybille's connection worth it to her.

Nathanial made one final push. Blood dripped down Sybille's nose as he attempted to rally what was left of his mighty strength. Every fresh wound, every old scar flared up as though she was being lashed with a whip. Even half removed from herself, she knew she couldn't endure this for much longer. Her body would succumb to the Blood King's attacks; her mind would cave to Juliana's will once more. No longer quite aware of where the boundaries of her own self ended and Juliana's began, Sybille continued to swing her psychic sledgehammer at Nathanial.

One more burst of agony came. It could have originated from Nathanial or Juliana or Sybille—in her exhaustion she couldn't tell. A moment later, the Blood King's wailing lessened and then, with one final heave, the cabin fell silent.

Sybille slowed her swing. Winding herself back into her own body, she swayed again and tipped to the side, only to have Devin catch her. "Sybille? What's ha—"

"Shh." She righted herself but kept a hand on Devin's arm for support. This wasn't the time to lose focus. Juliana was stunned, but only temporarily. When that moment passed, she would set upon Elis. Then Sybille would lose the tiny bit of control she had.

Wiping the blood from under her nose, Sybille blinked several times. Blur turned to clarity. The Blood King lay prone on the ground beneath her feet, his eyes staring dully at the wooden beams running along the cabin's ceiling. As Sybille took a surveillance of the various degrees of injury suffered by her friends, Juliana's spirit began to stir. Now was Sybille's chance.

In her mind, she found a familiar door, placed her hand on its knob, and twisted; sunlight and the scent of pastry dough poured out as it creaked open. Quickly as she could, Sybille reeled in her tether, being careful not to let the line go slack.

A prize catch waited for her on the end of it.

CHAPTER THIRTY

A TORNADO MIGHT AS WELL HAVE TOUCHED DOWN INSIDE THE CABIN. CHAIRS lay overturned, broken legs reaching out at odd angles like porcupine quills stuck to the nose of an overcurious dog; every plate in the kitchenette now resided on the floor, splintered pieces of earthenware mixing with shattered glass from the cabin's windows. Zareen, who had remained unconscious throughout the ordeal, lolled in a corner with Charlie attending to her. Raelyn rocked back and forth at Devin's feet, and Elis remained unconscious, his body curved in on itself, his breathing shallow.

It was hard to make sense of it all. Devin struggled to keep up as Sybille gave him a brief recap. So much of what she referred to as a "showdown" had taken place inside of the hidden worlds she dealt in and to which he had no access. He gathered this much: Sybille had teamed up with that crazed spirit woman, Juliana, and together, they killed the Blood King.

"No, not *killed*." Sybille kicked Nathanial's head. He looked dead enough to Devin, but then, so had Raelyn back when he'd dosed her with Strike. "He's temporarily incapacitated. It's all we can hope for until we find a way to undo the invincibility potion that, um…well, that you seem to have brought to the table, Devin. Until we figure that out, we need to keep him locked away somewhere secure so that he can't reclaim his position as Blood King again."

"I may be able to help with that." Raelyn pulled herself back onto her feet and slowly glided over to stand beside Sybille. She gave Nathanial's head a kick of her own. The bloodthirsters outside remained silent, most of them in no better shape than Elis. Devin had a feeling this situation would not hold long.

"How can you possibly help, Raelyn?" He rubbed his elbow where he'd slammed it against the door while trying to keep the thirsters at bay.

"The Blood King keeps several secured cells in his basement, meant to hold the strongest of thirsters. I'll lock him up there. He'll stay put until you devise your solution."

Sybille winced as she shook her head. "Why should we trust you? Won't you just release him as soon as he heals?"

A snort coming from the corner of the room sent everyone's focus in the direction of Charlie. "Don't you get it, dummies? Why would she release him? *She's in charge* now."

Sucking in air through a clenched jaw, Devin looked at his sister with dawning horror. "What are you saying?"

Raelyn put a hand on his shoulder. "I'm trying to decide…stick with Blood King for the sake of consistency, or should I ask to be called Blood Queen instead? Or maybe scratch that all together and just go with Phoenix. That seems appropriate. What do you think, Dev?"

Devin couldn't bring himself to contemplate a Low run by his sister. Instead he brushed past her, turning his attention towards Sybille's attentions, which were no longer aimed at him or Raelyn or even at the unmoving lump formerly known as the Blood King. Sybille knelt beside Elis and gently lifted his head into her lap, smoothing his hair to his forehead. She leaned over and whispered something into his ear, crying out in relief as his eyes fluttered open. She pressed her lips to his forehead.

Devin turned away, right into the bemused face of his sister. "Sucks to be you, brother."

Did it? Right now, maybe. At the same time, as shitty as some of his choices had been in his life, most of them he had made because his aim was true. That much he knew; that much he trusted about himself now. Becoming part of Sybille's team, even if she never looked at him the way she was looking at Elis right now, even if it led to heartache, even if it killed him some day—it would still be the best choice he'd ever made. It wasn't the only difficult, for-the-greater-good type decision he'd made, either.

"I always wanted to be the big brother who protected you, Raelyn. I can't tell you how guilty I was because I failed to do that. I can't undo anything that happened. I killed you to free you because I love you. I always will. Even if you're the Blood Phoenix or whatever the hell it is you want to call yourself."

Raelyn's smug expression faltered. It was as close to a sentimental gesture as Devin knew he'd get from her. "I meant it when I said I need Charlie out of the Low. Take her, Dev. She'll have a chance with you that she won't have if she stays with me."

He nodded. "Of course, I'm taking her. But I've gotta know...who's her father?"

With that, the smirk was back. "All you have to know is that *my* decision regarding Charlie's future is the one that matters." Her eyes narrowed. "Her father is none of your concern."

Charlie tugged on his sleeve. "We should really leave before the monsters wake, Uncle Devin."

⚜

Sybille and Raelyn, with Charlie in tow, carried a semi-conscious Zareen to her car while Devin and Elis, still groggy but otherwise okay, struggled to lug Nathanial's massive form out to Raelyn's SUV. They stepped on more than a few thirsters lying here and there on the pathway leading from cabin to vehicle. Thankfully, the beasts weren't biting at the moment. The most energetic of them raised her arm in protest, then flopped it down over her face as she attempted a halfhearted growl.

The plan was for Sybille to accompany Raelyn back to the mansion so she could oversee Nathanial's imprisonment. Even though she'd have no control as to what Raelyn did with him after she and the others left the Low, Sybille still felt obligated to at least see that he made it behind bars before his brain put itself back together.

The others would meet her at the mansion—Devin and Charlie in his truck, and Elis driving Zareen. They'd regroup and then drive until the Low was a speck of dust on the road behind them.

After unceremoniously dumping Nathanial into Raelyn's white

Cadillac, another vehicle came bounding slowly up the driveway, kicking up dirt as it made its way towards them.

Beside her, Elis' haunches raised as he got ready to face a new enemy. A sky-blue van in need of a paint job pulled up beside them. Elis' face scrunched up. "Is that...the Mystery Machine?"

"Close." Sybille stepped towards it. "It's my mom's ride." She opened the passenger side door to reveal her uncle and across from him, Margot behind the wheel. A familiar hooded figure leaned forward from the back seat and waved to her. Bore.

"Seriously? You show up now. What are you doing here?" Struggling to control her annoyance, she nodded to Bore. "Hello, Patron. What a pleasant surprise. Super great timing!"

"Good Lady Sybille, it is an honor to be in thy presence again."

They exited the van, Bore eyeing the beasts strewn on the lawn, Uncle Peter rushing off to attend to his daughter, and Margot rounding the front of the van to confront her own. "Don't think that I like it any more than you. I just couldn't sleep a wink thinking how your handsome thirster friend might be trying to turn you."

Elis walked up to stand at Sybille's side. "I've been a good thirster. Sybille, on the other hand, was quite the ass-kicking hellion last night."

"Oh?" Margot raised an eyebrow, which was slightly askew. Could it be that her mother was so worried about her that she'd rushed her eye makeup regiment?

The thought made her chuckle.

"This is not an appropriate time to be laughing, especially in front of the Patron." She lowered her voice. "He's agreed to pay us in exchange for a tour of the Low. Anyways, I don't understand. What's so funny, Sybie?"

Sybille put an arm around her shoulder. "I destroyed the undestroyable."

"That sounds hard. I'm glad I missed that part. So, what happened to Zareen's spirit? Juliana, was it? There's something off about her. That's why I had to come. Peter thought maybe she was telling the truth, but I had a feeling..."

"Juliana." Elis staggered backwards. He gripped his torso with one hand and his head with the other. "I'd forgotten."

Sybille laughed again. "You'd forgotten? You'd forgotten that your vengeful ghost of an ex-wife tried to stab me with a knife to make you suffer before she killed you too?"

Margot gasped. "See, I was right. Peter," she called over to him. "I was right. Juliana was bad news!"

Struggling to makes sense of everything, Elis' turned in circles, convinced Juliana might pop up from behind a tree or from inside a beached canoe. "The Blood King—you have no idea what his *death cries* were like. It was as though I'd been in a completely silent room for a hundred years and then suddenly had a high school marching band bust in playing the Star-Spangled Banner."

He turned around again, still trying to locate where Juliana might be fluttering about.

"It's okay, Elis. I've taken care of her. She can't hurt you. Or me."

"Where is she then?"

Sybille tapped her head. When she'd reeled Juliana in, the spirit had been too caught up in the thrill of destroying Nathanial to realize what Sybille had planned for her until it was too late. She shoved Juliana through a door in her mind, closed and locked it, then chucked the key. It wasn't the end of her, but like Nathanial, she would at least be contained until Sybille could figure out her next move. Storing a four-hundred-year-old spirit in her mind didn't come without its risks, of course, but for the time being, Juliana wouldn't be rattling any chains.

"Let's just say she's going to be donning pearls and baking cookies for a good long while."

Margot insisted Sybille tell them everything that happened in minute detail, but business had to be attended to first. She gave her mom and Bore the Cliff Notes version of Nathanial's takedown and explained how his mansion had a prison that would contain him, should he recover. "I need to bring Nathanial back to his house. Sorry you came all this way for nothing, especially you, Patron."

"Maybe not for nothing." Peter joined them just as Raelyn came around from where she'd been speaking with Charlie. He nodded to the thirster. "I take it you're in charge now, Raelyn?"

A collective gasp filled the air. Devin, who had been listening in while leaning against his truck, was over in a flash. "You know my sister?"

Peter shrugged. "I understand your surprise. You deserve to know the whole story, Devin. All in due time. Right now, I think it's best if I'm the one from our group to take Nathanial back to the mansion's dungeons. I'll ride along with Raelyn. Bore, if you're feeling adventurous, you can join me. Margot, follow us there in the van and then wait for us outside. The rest of you should clear out of the Low right now. Do you agree to this plan, Raelyn?"

The newly self-anointed Queen of the Low nodded. She led Peter and Bore, who looked like a genie had just granted his wish, to her SUV before anyone had the chance to pick their jaws up off of the ground. Margot mumbled something incomprehensible, shaking her head at her brother's retreating from, then climbed back into her van and sped off behind Raelyn, swerving to run over a thirster or two as she left.

Devin kicked at the wheel of his truck. "Peter. I can't believe him! All this time…"

Sybille was just as dumbfounded. "We'll get the truth out of him, Devin."

"Yeah? How, exactly? He's been lying to us for years. Is that going to stop all of a sudden?"

"I'll find out what's going on, Devin." Elis stepped forward. "I'll mesmerize the fuck out of that bastard." He gripped his temples again. "As soon as my head stops throbbing."

"Just because you're getting what you want…" He nodded in Sybille's direction. "Don't act like you want to help, like you're my *friend* all of a sudden. Because the feeling's not mutual."

Elis bristled and Sybille stepped in between them. "Devin does have a point, Elis. Are you going to stick around after we get back home or ride off into the sunset, margarita in hand?" She lowered her voice so that Charlie, who was stoically watching her mother drive away, wouldn't hear. "We don't know what to expect once we bring Charlie out of the Low. We could use your help, thirster."

"You'll always have it." He reached over, sliding his hand over hers. She wrapped her fingers around his and squeezed.

"I hate to break up your little *we'll always have Paris* moment, but our several hundred demon lawn ornaments are starting to stir." Devin kicked at the one nearest him and was rewarded with a hiss.

Taking a step away from Elis, Sybille surveyed the property. The ground resembled a Whack-A-Mole game, thirster heads popping up here and there. It wouldn't be long before they were active again. With horror, she realized that the events of the last few hours had made her forget about the Low's relentless attack. Now that she was consciously aware of it again, it was back in full force. And now too, the thirsters' desire for her was awakening from its hibernation. Her skin crawled as though a jar full of centipedes had been released onto the base of her spine.

"All right, everyone. Let's get out of here."

A few minutes later, she was speeding as fast as the Low's bumpy roads would allow, Elis beside her with Zareen, still not completely back to herself, asleep behind her. The day lamps from Devin's truck flashed in her rearview mirror. They had agreed to stop once they'd crossed the Low's border, but until then, they kept moving forward, down the mist-covered roads, their frazzled minds attempting to shake the Low's hold. Sybille remained grounded by counting her wounds, both seen and unseen: burns running along her back, a long, shallow gash on her left temple, a mind haunted. Injured or not, they were all leaving the Low alive. *All of them.* This fact should have been enough to settle her nerves, but instead, she was consumed with a sense of foreboding. Her imaginary centipedes continued to do their dance.

Miles sped by; the Low's border inched closer. The oppressive weight on her chest lifted but her sense of dread refused to abate. She steadied her hands on the wheel and stole a glance at Elis, only to discover him staring at her.

He nodded slightly and then spoke in a whisper. "You feel it too, don't you?"

Without replying, she turned her attention back to the road. They were nearly there. Everything would be okay once they crossed out of the Low. In the distance, a moss-covered wooden sign reading "Thank you for visiting Low Hollow" grew larger. They passed it and Elis let out a sigh of relief.

"I don't know why I did that. I don't actually feel relieved at all."

"Me neither." Sybille bit her lip. "What's that?"

They leaned forward and squinted at something in the middle of the road one hundred yards ahead. As they approached, Sybille realized it wasn't a *something* but rather a *someone*.

Elis squirmed next to her. "Who the hell...?"

Sybille drew to a stop. A moment later Devin pulled his truck up behind her.

A young woman stood calmly before Sybille's car, short lavender hair tucked behind her ears.

"Oh, *you have got to be kidding me*." Sybille put the car in park, cut the engine and opened the door.

"What are you doing?" Elis pulled on her sleeve. "Do not engage! Didn't you see her eyes?"

Sybille had—brilliant purple orbs, an exact match to her hair. "I have to speak to her, Elis. She wouldn't be here without a reason. And she won't let us pass until she's had her say."

Elis let go of her arm. "But who the fuck is she?"

"I don't know *who* she is exactly, but I know *what* she is."

"Which is?"

Ignoring him, Sybille got out of the car. By now, Zareen had stirred enough to take note of the woman in front of them. Her words were slurred yet still weighted enough to convey her shock. "Holy shit, Sybille!"

"My sentiments exactly."

Soon, all three of them were out of the car.

Sybille took a deep breath and stepped towards the woman. "My name is Sybille. If you need any assistance, I can--"

"I need nothing from you, hierophant." Her voice was raspy, her words spoken with a strange lilt Sybille couldn't quite place. She stuck her palm out at Sybille, who froze where she stood. An unsettling image of a rabbit caught in a snare popped into her head.

"Then why are you here?"

"Sybille, what's going on?" Devin came up beside her, pausing when he saw the lavender woman. "Is she a spirit? Oh wow, can I see spirits now? Do they all have purple hair?"

Sybille tried to push him back, but her arms, her legs, her body all refused to follow her instructions. It was like being possessed, only the possession was coming from without rather than from within. "No Devin, she's—"

The woman cut her off again. "Here he is now." She sang her words as though she was cooing to a baby. "Did you think you could hide from me?"

Devin looked around in confusion. "Who're you talking to?"

She glided towards him. It took all of Sybille's will to force a protective arm in front of Devin, who continued to glance around like a confused dog unable to determine which owner would give him the most treats. Elis moved to charge, but Sybille caught his eye and motioned him to stand down. She turned her attention back towards the strange woman. "What do you want with him?"

The woman laughed. "What does it matter? You have no claim to him, do you?" She took Sybille's arm and gently pushed her away.

A mew escaped her mouth as her brain caught up with the reality of what was happening. Everything made sense now. Most people had a touch of psychic power, however small, but Devin was a complete void. Yet somehow, his blood was able to make bloodthirsters immortal. Why?

"It can't be."

Devin shifted on his feet. "What can't be? Sybille, I'm not liking this."

The woman took hold of his hands, then pressed herself against him, her lips inches from his own. "Are you sure about that?"

"Well…I mean, you *might* persuade me to change my mind, but…"

She let go of one of his hands and put a finger to his lips. "I'm going to have fun with you."

Sybille's breath came in short, uneven gulps. Dammit! She was as helpless as when she'd been discussing the liberal use of butter in her fake mother's dream kitchen.

Devin glanced at her, then turned his attention back to the woman currently nibbling on his earlobe. "Is this really happening? I can't decide now if I like it or not."

She pulled away from his face. "You like it. I can tell. But I'll warn you now: it won't be all fun and games. We have work to do."

"Work? No. Maybe another time. Right now, I've had a shit couple of days. I have to get home, and—"

"Yes!" The woman's eyes sparkled. "You have to get home. You do understand."

"I kind of think I don't."

Sybille attempted to move towards the purple woman again. Maybe if she distracted her long enough, Devin could make a run for it.

A second after having this thought, she was on the ground, pinned down by an invisible train the woman had chugged her way. Elis rushed over to her, but even his strength did nothing to help Sybille pry herself away from the asphalt.

The woman kept one palm extended towards Sybille and slipped the other hand easily around Devin's waist. Devin cocked his head from side to side. "I should be more upset about what you just did to Sybille. But I think you're right. I do like this."

He spoke slowly, as though he'd just dosed himself with Crave. Sybille closed her eyes, attempting to stop the tears from flowing.

Elis stroked her forehead. "I'll take care of this." He began to stand.

"No!" Sybille grabbed his elbow. "She'll hurt you if you show your fangs. Besides, you can't stop what's about to happen."

"What's about to happen?" Devin's surprised expression hovered in Sybille's view just over the woman's head. Her heart clenched.

"Uncle Devin?" Charlie stepped out of the truck and made her way forward. The lavender woman twirled her eyes, curled her lips away from her teeth and growled. Charlie shied away.

"The cursed one stays." She pulled Devin to her. "But you...you're coming with me. Say bye-bye to your nice friends, Damhán."

"Who?"

She kissed Devin's cheek, flicked her palm away from Sybille and snapped her fingers. There was no smoke. No sparks flew. No magic words spoken. She was simply gone and Devin was gone with her.

Released from the woman's hold, Sybille shrugged off Elis' grasp and stood up on her own to stare at the empty road where Devin had just been. Zareen held Charlie, who cried into her chest.

Elis looked around, confused. "What just happened?"

Sybille took a moment to respond, hoping to keep herself composed enough to at least make it through one complete sentence. "What happened is that we just found out Devin is *not* who we thought he was."

She turned away from the Devin-less road, the pain of his absence much starker than she was prepared to handle. Zareen spoke quietly to Elis; their conversation may as well have taken place a million miles away.

She caught enough though to know that Zareen had spared her from having to explain to him what was going on. One word stood out from their conversation, spoken from Zareen's lips and repeated like a never-ending echo in Sybille's head. One word that summed up everything that had happened over the last twenty minutes and would continue to define, quite possibly, the rest of her life. One word to explain why one of the most important people in her life was now gone from it entirely. The word reverberated, vibrated, shuddered, dropped her to her knees and let the tears, finally, run free.

Elis turned from Zareen to Sybille and mouthed that word as if it were a question, asking her to confirm unbelievable things. Sybille nodded and mouthed it back to him, one final echo in her bruised and battered mind:

Fae.

THE END

Thank you for reading! Did you enjoy?

Please Add Your Review! And don't miss more paranormal novels like, TIDES OF TIME. Turn the page for a sneak peek!

SNEAK PEEK OF TIDES OF TIME

Magic and family drama sucked Cami in the same as riptides. Sometimes, she could spot them coming on the horizon. Other mornings, like today, they swept her away without warning. Such was life in a legacy witch lineage with all its rules and expectations.

She pushed through the staff door of the emergency animal hospital and blinked against the blinding Southern California sun after another all-night shift. She scanned her surroundings as she'd done everywhere for the last year, balancing her backpack on her hip so she could fumble through it. Had she forgotten her sunglasses? She jumped at the approaching squeal of tires, her scattered nerves fraying. Her older sister's Mini Cooper skidded to a halt less than three feet away from where she stood.

She scrubbed her hand over her face. Why was Delia here? Shouldn't she be at work? Her courthouse was an hour away in Los Angeles traffic. So why was she here shoving open the passenger door?

"What the heck, Deals?"

Delia met her gaze. "Mina's missing."

Just like that—*riptide*.

Cami jumped into the car and dumped her bag on the floorboard.

"More like she's temporarily lost." Swinging her sleek blonde ponytail over her shoulder, Delia slammed the car in reverse and shot out of the parking lot. "She slipped unsupervised."

Cami sucked in a breath. Their youngest sister's power was slipping through time. Mina's body would move in the location as it was today, but her mind traveled to see a different time through another person in the same geographic space. Scenery changes after the psychic impression made for perilous slips. "Where? When?"

"She toured a historical mansion last night courtesy of a USC alum." Delia spat the last words.

"Focus." They didn't have time for sibling or college rivalries. "Mina's slip?"

"Right." Delia shifted gears and raced down side streets toward the ocean. "She followed a woman named Sunny Sol out of the mansion. I ran a search on the name. It came back to an actress from the 1920s and '30s. Mina trailed Sol along the bluffs down to the beach."

"The bluffs?" Panic shot through Cami, and her own powers thrummed in response to the strong emotion. Mina had chased an actress from old Hollywood along steep cliffs? Mudslides and falling rocks could've easily changed the landscape over the decades. Mina wouldn't have been able to distinguish the past surroundings from her present ones.

"Don't get me started." Delia switched lanes. She barely squeezed between a bus and a truck.

Cami grabbed the handle above her head. "We can't find Mina if you get us killed with your crazy driving." Her older half-sister might be the ultimate protector, but Delia drove as though her little race car had its own force field.

"Mina sent a 911 text fifteen minutes ago. Luckily, I was already in Santa Monica interviewing a witness for a trial next week." Delia slid a look her way. "I knew your ringer would be off so I called her back."

Cami spent every hour either at the animal hospital, cramming for board certification, in the ocean, or sleeping. She'd graduated with honors from the top veterinary medicine program in the country last year. Her psychic affinity for communicating with animals helped, but she still had to put in the work. Her vet residency didn't leave much free time. As a deputy district attorney, Delia understood long hours.

"I figured I could catch you before you left work." Delia streaked through a yellow light. "Mina's phone died before she told me where she was. She forgot to charge it."

Typical. Mina could be flighty handling the basics of life.

Delia swung a hard left onto the downhill ramp for the Pacific Coast Highway, locally known as the PCH. "You'll have to use your call to find her."

No. Cami's chest tightened. She didn't tap into her elemental magic, and there was no way she could tell her sisters why. She—the quintessential "good girl" Donovan sister—had broken the first rule of magic. There'd be no coming back if others discovered why she'd really walked away from her element.

"I wouldn't ask if it wasn't the only way without spending hours driving up and down the coast hoping to find her." Delia's stone-faced glare gave nothing away, but her voice had softened. "You and I don't know spell craft. There's only one person who could whip up a locator spell in an instant, and I didn't think you'd want me to call her."

"Ama." Cami sighed. She couldn't call Ama. Her mother, a powerful spellcaster, would ask too many questions if she discovered Mina had chased a historical psychic vision alone. Mina didn't need a one-way ticket to magical mommy guilt trips. It was bad enough Delia knew. "We're not telling Ama."

She fingered the pendant at her neck, similar to the one all four sisters wore. Ama had spelled the charms to warn them of danger. Hopefully, Mina had hers on.

"She called from the shore. I could hear waves and seagulls." Delia swerved into the turning lane and pulled into a beachfront parking lot. She stopped the car. "I know you and your element had some kind of a falling out a year ago."

Each of the four sisters had a call to an element. Cami's was water. She could manipulate it, communicate with it, cause damage with it.

It hadn't been a simple breakup with her element. She had nearly killed a man with her connection to water. So much for *harm none* with magic. While she'd gone to the beach daily since then and surrounded herself with its comfort, she hadn't let herself give in to her power. Not when she'd abused and then refused it.

But her sister needed her. She swallowed back the fear of what might come if she tapped into that big source again.

She unbuckled the seatbelt and tugged her stained scrubs off, stripping down to a threadbare graphic T-shirt and undies. She wadded the work clothes into her backpack, slid a pair of shorts on, and switched Crocs for flip flops.

Delia opened her door.

Cami stopped her. "Why don't you keep your couture, 'dry clean only' self in the car?" She didn't want anyone witnessing her return to her element, because what if it all went wrong?

Delia paused with her hand on the door. "Want some privacy?"

She bobbed her head, checked her necklace, and climbed out. The ocean breeze snagged her short curls. "Give me five minutes."

"Hey, Cams?"

She ducked into the open car window.

"If you can't do this, it's okay." Delia unlocked her phone screen. "I'll keep trying in case Mina finds a way to charge her phone."

Cami took a deep breath. "I've got it." If only her voice hadn't wavered.

Stepping onto the sand, she slipped off her shoes and strode toward the water's edge. She wouldn't risk this but for her sisters.

While she longed for her elemental magic to soothe and guide her, the very same source could rebuke her for misusing her power. She feared its condemnation. It'd be too much, but Mina needed her help. She leaned down, sweeping her fingers into foam on the wet sand.

Fighting doubt and worry, she reached for her magic and sent a tentative call to her element. The ocean responded in warm welcome without judgment, and she forced back the urge to tap fully into her power.

Oh, how she'd missed this.

She wanted to walk into the waves and savor each precious lap against her skin, to let the water bathe away the fear and darkness she'd carried. The need to link to that tidal power pulled her in, promising absolution she didn't deserve. She had to focus on Mina before she lost herself to the water's beckoning homecoming.

She pushed past the water's thrum of longing and expectation until her power conjured images of Mina waiting at the water's edge further north. Cami breathed a sigh of relief and gratitude along the connection.

"Thank you," she whispered and said a reluctant goodbye. With a single glance over her shoulder, she hurried back to the car and jumped inside. "Found her. Head north."

Delia tore out of the lot and zipped across three lanes of traffic. She smacked the steering wheel with her palms when they got stuck at another red light at the busiest intersection on the PCH in Pacific Palisades.

Gas stations, grocery stores, and a restaurant jammed together in the precious real estate across the street from the shore. Cami craned her neck to check the signs as they passed through the intersection and accelerated. Corraza's Restaurant.

"If Mina has slipped, she'll be starving." Each sister's magic had a price. Mina's had always been hunger. "We can head back here if they're open."

"I'll check once we find her."

They passed beneath a pedestrian bridge next to a steep set of stairs cut into the bluff.

"Here," Cami said. "She's close by, near the water's edge."

Delia flipped a U-turn in the parking area of a large Spanish-style building with arched entrances and windows below a hexagon-shaped center. "Go. I'll catch up with you."

Cami jumped out of the car and sprinted for the water. Her power called to her, directing her. She hopped the concrete barrier and raced across the sand, searching for her sister. Perched on a rock jetty, Mina stared over the waves.

Cami called out, relieved when her sister turned with clear eyes, not the dazed obsidian dilation of magic.

Mina ran a shaky hand through her hair. "You came for me."

"Always." Cami stooped to pick up her sister's hooded sweatshirt and sandals tossed nearby. She studied the strain in Mina's eyes, the dark smudges beneath. "Were you out here all night trailing Sunny Sol?"

Mina took her hoodie and gave a weak smile. "Hazards of slipping. I should've known better than to be curious."

"When I think of what could've happened to you." Cami slid her eyes closed.

"I couldn't resist, and then I got pulled in too deep."

She knew all about the overload when magic overwhelmed logic.

Mina's lips twisted. "Do you ever want to be normal? No elemental powers? No psychic ability?"

Cami wanted a lot of things: to stop looking over her shoulder; to have a good man adore her without going crazy stalker abusive on her; to have her hard work correct the bad choices she'd made so she wouldn't doubt every new one; to not have to worry about their family's magic.

She nudged Mina. "Come on. Let's go save Delia from ruining whatever designer shoes she's wearing. We spotted a place to eat a mile back. Maybe they've got pancakes."

Minutes later, Cami half-dragged her younger sister through the glass doors into Corraza's Restaurant to find a table while Delia parked the car. The swift change from bright sunlight to the darker interior had Cami blinking behind sunglasses she'd borrowed from Delia.

If only the dimmed lighting and dark glasses could excuse her gawking at the man behind the front podium. All muscles and tanned skin, he looked up from his notes, and his gaze locked on her face.

The exhaustion of back-to-back shifts must have caught up to her. Or the cost of her magic decided to crash into her as it did for Delia, who'd black out from using too much.

Cami bit back a groan. She'd drawn so hard on her psychic ability to connect with animals last night and then her elemental magic this morning, she should've expected her powers would demand replenishment. Her magic craved fulfillment from a hot guy. *This* hot guy. She'd probably leaked the desire all over him. She swallowed, shoving down the need as best she could with the powers calling for collection of a debt owed.

With one hand bracing her sister, Cami tugged her sunglasses into her tangle of curls and blew out a breath. Feeding Mina was top priority. No more sexy daydreams about a handsome guy.

The fleeting second she'd given in to the fluttering in her belly had been the best part of her week. Time to return to the reality of her witchy family.

Don't stop now. Keep reading with your copy of TIDES OF TIME available now. And sign up for the City Owl Press newsletter to receive notice of all book releases!

Want even more paranormal fun? Try TIDES OF TIME by City Owl
Author, Luna Joya, and find more from Amber K. Bryant at
www.amberkbryant.com

A witchy good girl hiding secrets from her family...

Cami yearns for a regular, ho hum, average life. Or at least as normal as
she can get in a family of witches. But she can't tell her sisters about her
violent ex. Or that she broke the first rule of magic to "harm none." Yet,
when her youngest sister asks for help unraveling the death of a 1930's star
abused by loved ones, Cami can't refuse.

A reformed bad boy who doesn't know his family's hidden secrets...

Sam lives for his restaurant and the intrigue of digging into Hollywood
history. He avoids the entanglements of relationships since even his own
parents didn't want him. But when the enchanting Cami needs his help to
crack an unsolved mystery, he can't resist. The closer they come to finding
the killer, the more they crave each other. But someone is determined to
stop them.

Can they solve the mystery before history repeats itself?

Please sign up for the City Owl Press newsletter for chances to win special
subscriber-only contests and giveaways as well as receiving information on
upcoming releases and special excerpts.

All reviews are **welcome** and **appreciated**. Please consider leaving one on
your favorite social media and book buying sites.

For books in the world of romance and speculative fiction that embody

Innovation, Creativity, and Affordability, check out City Owl Press at www.cityowlpress.com.

ACKNOWLEDGMENTS

Tales of *vampiresque* beasts have been woven into our lives for thousands of years. Our fascination with these dark beings—who pay for immortality with their own humanity—has failed to fade. Urban fantasy is folklore reimagined; as someone who writes/reads this genre, I owe a great debt to several millennia of storytellers, most with names lost to time, for developing the rich context I drew upon for this book.

Thank you to my brilliant editor, Tee Tate, for seeing this story for what it could be. Your encouragement came at all the right moments! To the entire City Owl Press team, this story could not have been in better hands. A special thanks to Tina Moss for managing the project with such professionalism, and for holding my hand whenever I needed it. Thank you to my fellow City Owl authors—I am honored to be included in your ranks.

To my writing friends: I would have called it a day long ago if it wasn't for the sense of community you gave to me. To Debra Goelz and Darly Jameson, I'm not sure thanks will ever be enough. I owe you both puppies and mermaid sparkles and all the good things in the world. To Jessica B. Fry, Sarah Benson, Vic James, Lindsey Lippencott and the rest of the Wattpadres, thank you for bringing me into your fold and making me feel like I belong. To Kristine Inchausti, you are the greatest writing bestie and contest buddy a woman could ever hope for. Thank you to all my Wattpad writing friends—Rita Kovach, Leigh W. Stuart, Tamoja Oja, Kristin Jacques, Gaby Cabezut, Keri-Lee Kroeger, Calla Roark, Jolene Straus, Red Harvey, Rebecca Sky and everyone else who I've connected with through that platform. A special shout out to Lynn Santiago for hosting the contest that sparked the genesis for *Blood King*.

To my friends and co-workers, old and new, thank you for the companionship, advice, and laughs at different stages of my life: Patrick Gulke, Kim Auterio, Lisa Taglialavore, Sue Elsey, Jill Nealey-Moore, Tina Piper, Heather Purcell, Paula Smith, Barb McClard, Beth Carroll, Jessica LeClair, and Amie Abendroth. To my parents, Randy and Nickie Bryant, thank you for showing up to each activity I took part in, and for reading everything I write—except when I tell you not too! Thank you to my sister Jennie McCann and her kids Adam, Anna, and Austin for being the creative and awesome people you are. Thank you to the Gammon-Kunz side of the family for always making me feel like one of you.

Most importantly, thank you to my husband, Drew Kunz, and son, Silas. Life is a lonely path unless you make a concerted effort to walk it with others. Get your stakes and magic crystals ready: we still have a long journey ahead!

ABOUT THE AUTHOR

Amber K. Bryant is an award-winning speculative fiction and romance writer living deep within Sasquatch territory in Washington State. Her stories have gained over ten million reads on Wattpad, where she has built a world-wide fanbase. She collaborated on a short story with R. L. Stine and won several contests judged by Margaret Atwood. When she isn't writing, she works as a librarian and spends time with her husband and son enjoying the beauty of the Pacific Northwest. She has yet to spot Bigfoot but has faith it will happen one day. *Blood King* is her debut novel.

| Photography by Drew Kunz

www.amberkbryant.com

facebook.com/amberkbryantauthor

twitter.com/amberkbryant

instagram.com/bryantamberk

ABOUT THE PUBLISHER

City Owl Press is a cutting edge indie publishing company, bringing the
world of romance and speculative fiction to discerning readers.

www.cityowlpress.com

61138387R00137

Made in the USA
Middletown, DE
17 August 2019